To
Greg

Dating A Cougar

Book One of the NEVER TOO LATE Series

By

Donna McDonald

With love –
your Cougar
xo

Acknowledgements

I would like to thank RA Bettez for taking the time to read this book several times and provide feedback. Your effort at helping me with the content was second only to propping me up emotionally when I *really, really, really* needed moral support to keep writing.

I would like to thank my fiancée, Bruce McDonald, for being my real-life Marine inspiration. You taught me there are two things to say to our soldiers after their service, and I now say them to you with utmost gratitude. "Thank you for your service to our country" and "Welcome Home". You are every hero to me. *Semper fi.*

Dedications

I would also like to thank every reader thirty-five or younger who reads this story with an open mind about what it means to be older and in love. I wrote this book for you so down the road when you are living where I am, you will have least have heard this from one other perfectly average woman. Love and sex are great at any age.

Prologue

All Alexa Ranger wanted in the whole world was a hot bath and an early night's sleep. Days like today where she ended up arguing with her entire staff made her seriously question why at fifty she still wanted to be the creative force behind her lingerie designs. She should be soothing herself with jazz music and bubbles. Instead, she was heading to a cocktail party still dressed in her work clothes, even though last minute socializing was not her idea of fun anymore. But then who was she kidding? Nothing was fun anymore. Her moods shifted from contented to maudlin in the blink of an eye. She hadn't been able to wine, dine, or pleasure the restlessness away in a very long time.

Angry with herself for agreeing to something she didn't want to do, Alexa frowned as she pulled into the parking lot of Seth Carter's condo, her mind finally slowing down enough to think about checking her appearance. She parked and flipped down a mirrored visor that had seen a lot of use.

Pulling a lip gloss from her purse, she quickly and expertly dashed it across the generous lines of her mouth.

Mascara and eyes still looked okay at least. No need to add more, she decided.

Her mineral powder seemed to still be keeping down the shine on her face. Thank goodness for great foundation.

Alexa pondered her reflection, finally deciding against

brushing her hair and making it flatter. Instead, she finger combed it until she had achieved what she considered to be an attractively disheveled look falling somewhere between slutty-just-out-of-bed and alluring come-mess-me-up-further. At least the lush hair she invested in maintaining would partially save her this evening from looking like frump mom in jeans and a shirt with a coffee stain decorating one breast.

Maybe she dreaded this evening because the crowd inside was just Seth's business acquaintances. They weren't even friends of Jenna's, but in the end it hadn't mattered who they were. Alexa had caved because her twenty-seven-year-old daughter rarely asked for anything from her these days.

"Stop by and meet Seth's cousin Casey," Jenna had encouraged.

"Two minutes—that's all," Alexa had promised in return.

It wouldn't kill her to make the effort to meet Seth's only remaining family, Alexa had reasoned. Plus, she could no longer think of excuses to put off stopping by.

Unfortunately, her motherhood righteousness didn't even last the whole trip down the sidewalk. She rolled her eyes at the loud throbbing music as she neared the front door.

Great, Alexa thought, feeling the vibrations in her teeth. She was tempted—very tempted—to turn right around and call Jenna from the parking lot.

Before the idea of avoiding the torture could take stronger root, Alexa made herself push the doorbell. The person standing nearest to the door immediately opened it for her.

Alexa smiled in thanks and moved inside slowly, scanning for Jenna or Seth. Not seeing either, and not remembering where anything was from her one previous visit, she moved through the mash of bodies in the living area toward what appeared to be the kitchen.

Casey's first thought when he saw Alexa Ranger heading toward the kitchen and him was how much she looked like

Jenna at first glance. His gaze lingered to study her as she wound her way through the people leaning against the sides of the hallway.

Males she passed, either discreetly or not so discreetly, followed her progress down the hall. Women stopped talking, to frown as she moved by, especially when they noticed the men they were talking to being distracted by the attractive older woman.

Trained by the military to be a keen observer, Casey smiled at both the wariness of the females and the predatory glint in the gazes of the males. Jenna's mother had to be at least a decade older, possibly two in some cases, than most of the people Seth had invited.

Not that he was immune to her allure either, Casey thought, despite the fact she was at least a decade older than he was as well. It was damn impressive to watch the woman move her tall, curvy body through the crowd.

Along with every other male she passed by, Casey couldn't help noticing aging ex-model Alexa Ranger was even better looking in person than online or in the papers. Jenna had definitely come from a beautiful master mold.

Once in the kitchen, Alexa sighed with what Casey could see was genuine relief to be in the clear of the people crush.

"Hi," she said to him breathlessly. "I don't suppose you've seen Jenna Ranger or Seth Carter, have you?"

"They're around somewhere, but it's probably safer and less trouble in this crowd to let them find you," Casey told her with a casual smile. "I'm your bartender this evening. Can I get you a drink while you wait?"

"Got a bottled water?" Alexa asked, smiling back.

"We've got filtered on the rocks or carbonated with just a hint of lime," Casey said, teasing. She was much more appealing than he'd imagined she would be from Jenna's descriptions of her.

"Filtered—straight up, no rocks," Alexa said, joking in return. "I need the hard stuff. It's been one of those days."

Casey nodded and filled a glass with cold filtered water from the refrigerator door. Behind him, he heard her laugh at the unglamorous source of her drink. She was smiling and obviously amused when he handed the full glass across the counter to her. He watched her take a couple sips before she spoke to him again.

"Thanks," Alexa said finally. "I'm Alexa Ranger by the way—Jenna's mother."

"You know I figured that out already. She looks a lot like you. I'm Seth's cousin, Casey," he said, introducing himself.

Casey put one hand on the counter to brace himself and support his bad leg as he reached the other hand over it for Alexa to shake. He smiled when Alexa set down her water glass and leaned her long body partially over the wide counter as well to make it easier for him to reach her.

"Casey? Well, hello. You're actually the reason I stopped by. Well, it's nice to meet you, fin—finally," Alexa said, stumbling a little over the words.

When Casey slid his palm across Alexa Ranger's, he was surprised at the electrical current that shot through him. He almost laughed when Alexa's startled gaze locked itself to his.

Looks like she felt that zing, too, he thought.

How long had it been? Two years, Casey decided. Two years since he'd felt *anything* for a woman, much less an attraction that made his blood rush. Alexa's pupils dilated, and Casey felt a tremble in the slender fingers wrapped around his palm.

He was as keenly aware of her reaction as he was of his own, but Casey could think of nothing sensible to say in reply to her introduction. Mostly because he was too distracted by what was happening to the lower half of him under the counter. If it continued, he was going to have to adjust himself as soon as he dropped her hand. Not that he would mind. He wasn't the kind of man who embarrassed easily, but Alexa might be a little shocked at the reaction she'd caused.

He tightened his hold on her hand just a little and watched her eyes darken to the color of storm clouds. Her breathing grew a little erratic, but she never looked away. As they looked at each other, suddenly an image of kissing Alexa Ranger flashed through Casey's mind.

The sigh he'd been holding in came out like a breathless groan of anticipation.

Casey never would have dreamed in a million years Alexa would respond to that kind of mating signal from him, but she drew in a sharp breath and blushed. His erection hardened even further, confirming the intense attraction.

When Alexa lowered her gaze to their still joined hands, it took every ounce of his self-control not run his thumb over her knuckles just to see what she would say or do.

She caught her bottom lip in her teeth, sucked it in thoughtfully, and swallowed hard when she released it. Casey heard her clear her throat, and watched her open her mouth to speak. She met his gaze again, and—said nothing. Her reaction made him want to laugh.

By now, Casey was guessing thirty seconds had passed with nothing more than a tight handgrip between them. She still wasn't tugging her hand away, and he wasn't moving to end the contact either. He still held tightly enough to keep her body stretched across the counter.

Casey thought Alexa looked a little afraid he was going to yank her over it the rest of the way, which actually seemed a pretty natural next step to him, he admitted.

He opened his mouth, intending to tell her what was happening to him, to ask what was happening to her. He decided one of them needed to say *something*, at least acknowledge the situation.

"Oh, good. You found each other," Jenna declared loudly, entering the kitchen. Her gaze went immediately to his and Alexa's clasped hands, and she smiled.

Casey let go at last, shocked further by his reluctance to do so. He heard the echo of Jenna's words in his head as he considered how close he had been to making a serious pass at her mother.

Yeah, we found each other all right, he thought.

Casey watched Alexa take a large step back from the counter. Her face was a fascinating shade of embarrassed pink. He knew with the tiniest bit of honesty that he could probably cause it to darken several more shades.

Jenna put a hand to her mother's face. "Mama, are you okay? Your face is so flushed."

"I'm fine, Jenna," Alexa protested, pulling Jenna's hand from her forehead.

Alexa looked at Casey, and then turned her attention to Jenna and shook her head.

"I'm fine," Alexa repeated. "Just a rough day. I need to make it an early night."

"Okay. Let's find Seth, and then you can go," Jenna said, looping her arm through her mother's. "Thanks for coming by to meet Casey."

"Of course. It was nice to meet you—Casey," Alexa said, pronouncing his name very carefully.

Casey could tell Alexa forced her gaze to meet his once more even though awareness of their attraction colored her face still.

"It was good to meet you too," Casey said, smiling in approval of her nerve. "I'm sure we'll be seeing each other."

Alexa nodded absently, which told Casey she was already trying to rationalize away what passed between them. Too bad, he thought. He wasn't going to forget it so quickly.

Thanks to Alexa, Casey now knew for sure the trauma of the last two years hadn't made him impotent. And he wanted to know how Alexa Ranger had simply touched his hand and turned him to stone.

Picking up the glass of water Alexa had left behind, Casey put his lips where her lips had touched the glass, right over the lipstick marks he licked with his tongue. He drained the contents and lectured his body about this intimacy being all it was ever going to get of Jenna's mother. His body's response to the command was to ignore that decision completely.

Laughing at the irony of his intense arousal to an inappropriate woman, Casey sighed and adjusted himself beneath the counter.

Chapter 1

"Why so glum, gorgeous?" Sydney asked, unwrapping his sandwich with great anticipation. "Trust me. I made sure you got double avocado." Something was up. Normally, Alexa would have been three bites ahead of him by now.

"I don't know. Do you think fifty is old, Sydney?"

Alexa Ranger watched her thirty-five-year-old assistant and good friend take a giant bite of his club sandwich and swing his gaze to hers in shock at the same time. Then she watched him pound his chest to keep from choking as he attempted to swallow the bite around a coughing fit.

At six two with a trim waist and shoulders like a football player, the brown-haired, brown-eyed Sydney could easily be the most handsome man Alexa had ever known. He designed and wore his own line of clothes and looked like a male model himself.

When Sydney didn't answer right away with one of his usual smart-ass quips, Alexa concluded he was really surprised by the question. Surprise was okay. If he looked at her with pity, she would probably throw her sandwich at him.

"It's all about the quality of the preservation," Sydney said at last, joking to give himself time to think.

In the ten years he had known and worked for Alexa, Sydney had never known the woman to be truly insecure about anything, especially her age. Not that Alexa hadn't let herself go a little bit in the last couple of years. A lack of male companionship had taken a negative toll on her. She hadn't shown any real interest in anyone specific in some time, or in making a fashion statement. Most days the woman wore jeans and a shirt, which in Sydney's mind was barely better than a uniform.

Still—*insecure*? What could cause such a foreign emotion? Alexa was not the type of person to worry about much of anything for long. Alexa was brash, boastful, demanding, and many, many other things, but the woman was not insecure.

Pulling himself from his contemplation, Sydney noticed Alexa was intently waiting for his reply to her question. Sydney made himself focus on the possibility of being fifty. Naturally, his stunning life partner came immediately to mind.

"Do I think fifty is old?" Sydney said, repeating her question. "Well, Paul is fifty-two. I certainly don't consider him old. The man just gets sexier with each passing year."

Despite being starved, Sydney took a smaller bite of his sandwich this time just in case Alexa shocked him again.

"It's different for men," Alexa said with a wave of her hand, hating the self-pity in her voice and the dark cloud of female worry over her head. "Men get better with age, and Paul is proof. Women—well, women just get old, Sydney. Even women like me."

"Okay, this is too weird," Sydney said, putting down his sandwich. "That was definitely self-pity I heard in your voice. What's wrong with you today, Alexa? Years of good maintenance are paying off big-time for you, honey. You look great."

Alexa shrugged her shoulders. She enjoyed her looks. In fact, she built her business on her looks. The problem was that looking younger at fifty didn't make her feel as good as it had in her thirties or forties. Now, regardless of how she looked on the outside, inside she *felt* fifty.

"Oh, just forget I said anything. I don't mean to whine—

you know I hate whining." Sighing over her depressing thoughts, Alexa took another bite of her sandwich.

Sydney hurriedly finished his last bite and leaned back in the chair. "When was the last time you had a date?" Sydney asked, inspiration striking. "I mean a real date where you dressed up and went out somewhere nice."

"Don't remember," Alexa said around a bite. "It's been a while I guess. Nine months, maybe? It's harder at my age to find someone interesting."

Which was mostly true, she thought, if you didn't count the attraction she'd felt shaking hands with Casey Carter last month. The retired Marine was appealing, but definitely too young, and definitely too related to her daughter's boyfriend. Her life was talk show worthy enough as it was—she certainly didn't need to add to it.

"I can't believe turning fifty is making me this crazy. Most women have their mid-life crisis at thirty or forty," Alexa protested.

Sydney laughed. "Needing sex is not a crisis, honey. It's a highly solvable problem," he told Alexa, studying the shifting expressions on her face with a frown.

"Who says I need sex?" Alexa asked, rolling her eyes at the statement.

Okay, so maybe it had been nine months ago with a friend, and who knew how long ago with a man she genuinely desired. Maybe she even secretly worried on some level about never wanting sex again, because not dating had been a relief instead of a sacrifice.

Determined not to sink into an even deeper funk dwelling on her voluntary celibacy, Alexa took a big bite of her awesome sandwich and chewed.

Sydney looked at her and smirked. "Do you have a booty call man you haven't told me about?"

"No," Alexa said sadly. "Not anymore. I gave him up too. He started talking about setting up a regular time for us every week. I stopped seeing him about nine months ago."

"Bad call. Abstaining does not suit you, Alexa. You are a vibrant woman. You need sex," Sydney argued. "I could hook you up with one of my straight friends. I have several who think you're hot."

"Good lord, you're offering me a pity date?" Alexa laughed, shocked under her amusement. "Am I that bad off?" Sydney nodded. "Your insecurity is showing, honey, which is so not like you. I think you need someone in your life who can make you feel young."

"Thanks, but no thanks. I don't even let Regina and Lauren fix me up with dates. I prefer to just meet a guy and follow a little feeling that says he's worth getting to know."

"Well, I hear you there. Certainly sounds like the best motivation, but when was the last time you had a feeling about a guy?" Sydney asked with a grin.

"Last month actually," Alexa confided, revealing the truth to Sydney, who would never betray her, mostly because he valued his life too much. "It happened with Seth's older cousin, but Jenna would simply kill me if I put any moves on him."

"So don't tell her," Sydney said, laughing. "Swear the man to secrecy."

The idea of asking the former Marine to indulge in a secret love affair with her struck Alexa as more funny than possible. What would Casey Carter want with an older woman like her when he could have a younger, more attractive one?

And if she did get that far, what would she do with Casey when they weren't in bed? There might be different problems dating younger men, Alexa concluded, but all dating had the same damn depressing outcome for her.

Not to mention there would likely be hell to pay if Jenna found out.

"Right," she smiled, drawing the word out. "You expect me to date Seth's macho cousin, and convince him never to mention it to Seth or Jenna? That's a bold play, even with my dating history."

Sydney stood and gathered their lunch trash. "Since when is Alexa Ranger afraid of being bold?"

Alexa shook back her reddish-brown mane of brunette

hair, her eyes glittering in amusement as she laughed. If only she could find a straight man who understood her as well as Sydney. He knew just which buttons to press.

"What would I do without you, Sydney? You're absolutely right," she said, nodding, not wanting to argue further about his plan.

"Of course I am. Now go be bold," Sydney replied sternly. "And make notes so you remember the details. You know how forgetful people are at your age."

Alexa swore at him, laughed, but ultimately blew Sydney a kiss as he headed back to his desk. Even if Casey wasn't a possibility, now that Sydney had all but dared her to date someone younger, the idea was churning inside her. However, a decision this important needed more than the sanction of a gay friend. It required the advice of female experts, Alexa decided.

Fortunately, she was already meeting her two favorite experts for dinner that evening.

The food at Lucinda's was always good. If it hadn't been, Alexa would have rousted the manager for a heart-to-heart. Not just because she was part owner, but also because she truly loved meeting there for dinner. Part of what she liked was that the management trained the staff well on deflecting unwanted attention from its more famous customers. Anyone with a press badge or camera had to check their electronics at the door.

Both she and Regina felt safe there, and Alexa wanted to keep it that way.

"So when was the last time you felt a genuine interest in getting to know a man," Alexa asked the two women seated at her table.

They had demolished three plates of appetizers in less than twenty minutes with no complaining about calories. It was a point of honor between them never to feel guilty about food. Regina—aka Dr. Regina Logan—was polishing off the last of the veggie pizza.

"I love pizza. It's such happy food. And all those carbs

make for a good snooze after. Did you ask a question, Alexa? Sorry, I was in the middle of a pizza orgasm," Regina explained.

Alexa laughed when Lauren McCarthy—one of *The McCarthys* of Falls Church, Virginia—rolled her eyes at Regina's response. Lauren had the sexual sensibilities of a twenty-year-old and the sexual urges of a forty-year-old. It was not a happy combination in a woman who worried daily about what people thought of her.

Stranger still, Lauren risked her prized reputation weekly by hanging out with Regina and Alexa, definitely two of the most sexually notorious women in Falls Church.

While she waited for her friends to think about the question, Alexa thought about the differences between the women she trusted with her deepest secrets. Regina and her work as a sex therapist drew the interest of the press regularly. Fortunately, Alexa's notoriety had dwindled when she'd stopped dating so much.

Only Lauren avoided the press, rarely even making the society pages. They teasingly called her *Saint McCarthy* because the woman never did anything even remotely scandalous. The worst thing Alexa had ever known Lauren to do was buy a vibrator after her divorce, but what single woman didn't own at least one of those?

Alexa looked at Regina, smiling as she watched the most outrageous woman she knew lick cheese off her fingers.

"Come on you two. I need your opinion. When was the last time you felt a genuine interest in getting to know a man?" she repeated.

Regina frowned as she wiped her hands on a napkin. "Wow. I just realized I'm stalling because I don't have an easy answer to your question. That's so depressing. I guess it's been almost a year for me."

"Like you want to get to simply know him, or you want to—you know, get to know him in the biblical sense?" Lauren asked.

Alexa shook her head at Lauren, who squirmed whenever any of them talked about sex. Only Lauren could make forty-

16

two look as innocent as twenty, Alexa thought, amused. Even her daughter Jenna seemed more knowledgeable.

"Biblical sense," Alexa answered around a grin.

Lauren sighed, "I guess I'd have to say about two years ago and for yet another womanizing man. The one before him was six years ago when I first got divorced. I developed an urge to date my lawyer."

Regina arched an eyebrow. "Your lawyer? Honey, that was gratitude, not a sexual urge. Haven't you ever wanted a man so much you just went for it?"

"Absolutely not," Lauren answered honestly and sincerely. "Technology is a much better solution and more satisfying."

"No, it's not," Alexa said gently, but with great conviction. "There's nothing like falling into a satisfied sleep after you've had a man inside you two or three times. There's no substitute for that kind of man-to-woman connection."

"True. And I agree. So—have you been connecting to someone lately, Alexa?" Regina asked, smiling at the thought of her gorgeous friend getting lucky.

Alexa laughed and sighed, "No. I'm just a little attracted to someone, that's all. It's been a while for me, too. It's complicated because the man is a lot younger than me."

"Younger can be good. How much younger?" Regina asked, inspecting the appetizer plates for any lingering bites.

"I don't know," Alexa said frowning. "Why?"

"Less than eight years makes you a Puma. Over eight years makes you a Cougar," Regina said wisely, as Lauren nodded in agreement. "That kind of hookup is happening a lot these days, and women are benefitting greatly. I wish I had an eye for younger men. I could have a lot more dates. Unfortunately, I get irritated with their conversation long before the mating urge can take hold."

"So who's the younger guy you like?" Lauren asked, truly interested in the answer.

Both Lauren and Regina looked at Alexa, who just stared back silently, blinking. Alexa's reluctance to share his identity had both of them giggling.

"Hmmm . . . this is interesting, Lauren. Alexa doesn't want us to know. Is the boy-toy in question at least of legal age?" Regina asked Alexa, teasing.

"Of course. He's around thirty-eight I think," Alexa finally confessed.

"You're a Cougar then, but honestly—thirty-eight is not that young," Regina exclaimed, rolling her eyes. "When you said young, I was picturing a twenty-something who checked himself out in the mirror every two seconds."

Lauren laughed at Regina's description because it fit her own mental image. "I was thinking the same. Anyone over thirty-five is fair game, Alexa. Though I'm a bit like Regina, I like men closer to my own age. Younger men seem to be too anxious and needy."

"Amen, sister," Regina said, holding up a hand and high-fiving with Lauren, making her giggle.

"So neither of you would pursue this if you were me simply because of his age," Alexa repeated, wanting to make sure she understood.

Regina and Lauren looked at each other. Surprisingly, it was Lauren who piped up with "depends on the amount of attraction."

Regina smiled widely and nodded in agreement.

Alexa closed her eyes and crossed her arms. "This is not helping," she complained.

Regina removed the white linen napkin from her lap and folded it into a neat triangle before placing it on the now empty plate in front of her.

"Do not try to fool the sex therapist, Alexa," she said ominously, making Lauren giggle again. "You've dated slightly younger men before. What's the real problem with this guy?"

"The only younger man I ever dated was only two years younger than me. The term younger barely applies in that case. But you're right, the real problem is he's Seth Carter's cousin Casey. He's the older one that raised him, so it's not like he's Seth's age or anything," Alexa confessed at last.

Conversation paused while Regina and Lauren absorbed

the news.

"Jenna would probably kill you," Lauren finally said, wincing at how dramatic that announcement sounded, even though it was also true.

"Yes, exactly," Alexa agreed. "I'm not sure any man is worth risking my life. My daughter is my worst critic when it comes to dating."

Regina squinted hard as she considered the frown on Alexa's face and the disappointment reflected in Alexa's gaze.

"I agree it's a tough twist, but I wouldn't let it be the deciding factor. Jenna and Seth might not work out anyway. If you don't take this chance, then everybody loses. Sometimes it's okay to be selfish, Alexa. This may be one of those times," Regina told her.

Alexa nodded, but none of what they said made her want to call Casey up and ask him out.

The idea of a fifty-year-old woman dating a thirty-eight-year-old man just smacked of desperation to her. If the press found out, she would make the headlines again—*Aging Model Dates Young Marine*. She wasn't ready to deal with the public or private fallout that might happen. She had come to like being less notorious.

"Do you think fifty is old?" Alexa asked them sadly, knowing her age was the biggest reason she wasn't even considering Casey as a potential.

"You're kidding, right?" Lauren proclaimed, shocked at Alexa's sad tone.

Alexa sighed. Talking to Regina and Lauren was turning out to be worse than talking to Sydney. No one seemed to understand her concerns.

Regina swore and got up from her seat to gather her things. "I have to go catch a plane, so I'll be quick with my two cents on the subject. No, fifty is not old, and you make it look better than thirty anyway. Lauren and I are using you as our role model. You know damn well that at forty-seven, fifty's just around a corner for me. Go have sex and shake this mood, Alexa. You need the oxytocin high from intercourse to fight the hormonally depressive funk you're in right now."

"Hormonally depressive funk? Is that a precise medical opinion, Dr. Logan?" Alexa asked sarcastically.

Regina just gave her a look that asked if Alexa needed a little more proof, or *a lot* more proof. She would happily give either to her friend.

"Fine. I'll take care of it," Alexa said sarcastically. "You're probably right, anyway. Sydney said the same thing."

"No, I'm *probably* right about the weather changing, and that the plane ride will be bumpy to Boston," Regina told her. "I am *always* right about sex."

As they split the bill and debated the tip, Alexa thought about how best to follow Regina's advice. Instantly, Casey Carter's image popped into her mind and her heartbeat picked up.

No, she told herself, consigning her longing for getting to know him better in the realm of fantasy instead of reality.

Instead, Alexa made herself think about the ever-available Todd Lansing who was a *friend-with-benefits* as Jenna would say. A couple years ago her comfortable relationship with Todd had been enough because it kept her from bed-hopping while she casually dated other men. Now, the thought of using Todd for gratuitous sex held no appeal, much less desire.

It was just bad luck that the only man who sexually interested her at all was not a good possibility. Which was just as well, Alexa concluded. She didn't need another empty sexual relationship without the remotest possibility of happily-ever-after attached.

Chapter 2

The moment Casey Carter walked through the door of Eddy's Bar and Grill, his attention zeroed in on Alexa Ranger sitting at a polished dark wooden table with two other women. Since meeting her a month or so ago, his body had developed a radar for her presence that refused to be ignored no matter how much his brain argued about it.

Looking around, he saw Seth was not waiting for him as promised—no big surprise there. Luckily he was having a good day and hadn't needed to use the cane, so he chose a seat in a dark area of the bar near the door. It was as far away as possible from Alexa's table, but still with a view of her.

Slipping off his sunglasses, he pulled the Marines' logo ball cap lower over his eyes, not wanting to draw attention to himself while he studied her. Casey guessed Alexa had to be at least forty-five years old despite the fact that she looked much younger.

The intensity of his attraction to the older woman was a mystery, but the reality was that when Alexa was within view, he couldn't stop himself from meticulously planning what he would sexually do to her and with her if he ever got the chance. And he had that reaction even the very first time he'd met her.

Over the last month, Casey had not only been avoiding

the necessity of dealing with his attraction to Jenna's mother but also avoiding even minor social contact. Jenna and Seth had finally given up trying to include him in their activities. Not that it looked like Alexa was having the same problem. Looking at his watch, Casey saw thirty minutes had passed now without her even once glancing his way. Evidently, Alexa did not have the same physical radar for him, though he still believed she had been attracted to him too. Maybe she was just better at denial. Maybe she was seeing someone else. Who knew?

As Casey studied Alexa, he considered it a point in her favor that she didn't constantly scan the bar for men like one of her companions was doing, or look around in disgust like the other one. No, Alexa just kept on talking, her focus completely on the conversation.

His phone buzzing with an incoming text message finally snagged his attention away from Alexa.

Can't make it after all. Last minute problem keeping me here. TTYL.

Casey texted back a reply.

WTF? Drinking your beer and mine then. Your fault if I don't make it home.

Seth's obsession with work matched any Casey had ever had with the Marines. Only eight years older than Seth, Casey felt a couple decades ahead in understanding about what was important in life. There had been some rough times for him during the last few years, but he hadn't let a hip replacement or a wife dying of cancer take him down for good.

Casey watched Alexa shift her attention when the door to the bar opened. Even at a distance, Casey could read the depth of Alexa's concern in her unsmiling lips pressed into a firm line.

He shifted in his chair, willing his body to relax when all it wanted was to get up and go to her—comfort her. It was the craziest reaction he'd ever had with a woman he barely knew, certainly a lot more crazy than simple attraction.

Casey's attention finally shifted to the person Alexa had watched come through the door, as that person passed by his table. There was a blur of blue and a whiff of some expensive scent that made him think of silky sheets, pulled blinds, and ceiling fans. From the tall heels all the way up the seamed stockings to the more interesting curves outlined by a skintight dress, the woman was a dream come true for the lucky guy she had dressed to please.

Wow, Casey thought, *that is a take-me-now-I'm-yours dress*. Though it had been a while since Casey had seen one, he still recognized them. And thank God for that—or rather thank Alexa Ranger for reminding his body of things it had almost forgotten.

Dragging his attention away from the woman, Casey noticed pretty much every man in the bar was watching her with great interest. She was heading directly to Alexa's table.

When the bartender yelled the woman's name, Casey swore silently. What the hell? The woman was Alexa's daughter—Seth's girlfriend.

So where was Seth?

Seth hadn't mentioned anything about Jenna in his text. What had detained Seth at home if it wasn't Jenna?

Casey drummed his fingers on the table.

Some clichés were truer than others, especially where military men were concerned. All Casey's instincts were telling him—no, yelling at him—that this situation was not good. So Casey put his sunglasses back on, picked up his beer, and discreetly moved to the other end of the crowded bar nearer Alexa's table where he could do some further reconnaissance.

Or in other words, where he could eavesdrop on their conversation.

Alexa's mother radar went on full alert when Jenna walked into the bar. Seeing Jenna in seductive woman gear was a thrill, but the look in her daughter's eyes spoiled the perfect picture. She sighed with resignation when Jenna frowned at all the males avidly watching her swinging curves move across the room.

Oh hell, Alexa thought. *What had Seth done to Jenna now?*

Jenna stopped at the table and put her hands on hips, mirroring a physical gesture Alexa recognized as one of her own. Her heart contracted with love.

"Is there an age limit to join this hen party?" Jenna demanded, her gaze meeting her mother's.

"Yes. Lauren barely makes the cut, but at twenty-seven you're good," Alexa teased.

"Wonderful—because I really need a drink right now," Jenna said.

Alexa offered her still nearly full glass of red wine to her daughter who took it while still standing and drank greedily.

"Well, don't you look yummy tonight? If I were a lesbian, I would make a pass," Regina said in her best sultry voice, giving Jenna an admiring perusal.

"Thanks," Jenna bent forward to brush her lips across Regina's forehead, "I'm glad the dress is getting an appreciative response from somebody."

Alexa's eyebrows rose into her hairline at the comment, but Jenna looked away before she could ask the obvious question.

Lauren looked at Regina. "*Lesbian? You?* I can't even imagine you giving up men," she said snidely.

"I don't know. How much harder could being a lesbian be?" Regina asked dryly, pushing her auburn-red waves back from her face. "When I suggested male enhancement drugs to the last man I hoped to be intimate with, he told me I needed to grow up. I told him he needed to get it up, patted him on the hand, and left."

Lauren looked at Regina in complete and utter shock, because that was appalling behavior, even for Regina.

"You didn't really suggest your date take male enhancement drugs, did you?" protested Lauren, blushing at the thought. "You probably hurt his ego. If you'd just slipped it in the man's drink at dinner, he'd have thought you inspired lust."

"Lauren, I would never trick a man into taking male enhancement drugs. Besides, drugging someone is a felony. Don't you ever talk about sex with the men you date?" asked

Regina. "Communication is key, you know."

"I have no need to discuss sex with my male companions. My dates are strictly platonic, and I like it that way." Lauren insisted, saluting Regina with her mineral water. "You are the only person I ever discuss sex with, Dr. Logan."

Regina rolled her eyes and took a long drink of her pomegranate martini. "I feel sorry for you then."

Alexa breathed a sigh of relief when Jenna belly laughed at the argument between Regina and Lauren, and smiled the first real smile since she'd come into the bar.

Looking at her vital, lovely daughter, Alexa couldn't help wondering for the umpteenth time what Jenna found so appealing about Seth Carter. The man was good looking, but not very physical. Jenna constantly worried about his lack of desire and complained about it frequently. It eluded Alexa how any hot-blooded woman could tolerate being sexually ignored. It made her mad as hell to think of her daughter doing it. After meeting Seth's cousin Casey, Alexa was baffled more than ever about Seth. Casey's sexuality had plastered her over the kitchen counter with just a handshake.

Sighing at the irony of her concerns, Alexa figured she was the only mother in history who ever worried about a man *not* putting the right moves on her daughter. But she wanted Jenna to have a real relationship, and well—she would like to have grandchildren someday.

"Sweetheart," drawled Alexa, "if your ego needs stroking, all you have do is turn around. There are at least eight pairs of eyes glued to your lovely rear right now."

Jenna sighed, walked around the table, and leaned over the stunning brunette who had borne her for a lingering hug.

"Thank you, Mama. If you were standing up, you know every man would be looking at you instead of me," Jenna said.

Alexa crushed Jenna to her in a fierce embrace. "Not today. That shade of blue is amazing on you and matches your eyes perfectly, which is only secondary to what it does to enhance your—"

The sound of glasses dropping interrupted Alexa. It was

followed by someone big hitting the floor with a loud thud and swearing.

The other women at the table giggled, and then laughed outright as Jenna straightened red-faced from the hug.

"I guess I shouldn't have bent over so much," she admitted, face flushed with embarrassment.

A booming voice yelled, "Jenna Lee Ranger, no more bending over the table. I can't afford any more losses here, cutie pie."

Several people in the bar laughed. The women at the table laughed louder than anyone. Jenna's blush spread upwards to the roots of her hair. She pulled out a chair to sit, but could barely manage to wiggle into it because the dress was so tight.

"Sorry, Eddy," Jenna yelled over her shoulder. "I'm sitting down now."

Alexa patted her shoulder in support, while she worked to stifle her own laughter. It was not nice to laugh at your child—your *only* child.

"Well, *that* was mortifying. What makes an intelligent woman think a dress like this is a good idea?" Jenna whispered, complaining to the women.

She sighed, laid her head back in the chair, and slid down as unglamorously as possible into the seat.

"I can't sit comfortably. These three-inch heels are killing me. The dress is so tight I can barely breathe. I'm an idiot for wearing this stupid outfit."

Alexa thought Jenna looked more like a pouting twelve-year-old than an accomplished woman of twenty-seven. When her daughter had walked into the bar dressed up, Alexa had internally raised two fists in the air and screamed "Yeah!" Being an architect in a profession mostly populated with men, Jenna rarely bothered with her feminine side.

Men, Alexa fumed. Only a few were even worth the expenditure of hormones.

"I bet you were thinking Seth Carter would want to chew that dress off you with his teeth," Regina offered, eyeing the dress with envy.

Jenna opened her mouth to reply, but Lauren interrupted and patted her hand.

"At your age Jenna, hormones cause a temporary form of female insanity. Men briefly look good for a few years, but the urge passes eventually."

"Stop that!" Regina scolded Lauren, smacking her hand off Jenna's. "You'll scare her. Just because you swore off sex years ago doesn't mean you get to warp Jenna."

"Ouch! Your watch scratched me, Regina. And I did not swear off sex. I swore off men. It's a different thing altogether. You of all people should know that," Lauren protested.

Regina turned to Jenna and said seriously. "Sex with men does not have to ever go away. Or at least it doesn't have to if you want to keep on living and not become a dried-up prune at age forty-two."

Alexa looked at her friends in both amazement and wonder. There couldn't be two more different women or two more differing views on men. Jenna certainly had unusual role models with the three of them.

She focused her piercing sapphire gaze intently on her daughter's slumping form. "Well, I bet you were thinking the dress would once and for all get Seth Carter's attention off his cell phone and focused instead on you. Just like you thought the red dress, the pink shorts, and the black lace bra I gave you would do the trick."

When Jenna didn't reply, Alexa gave her daughter a long, knowing stare.

"Sweetheart, you are one hundred percent sure Seth's not gay, aren't you?"

Jenna's chin lifted at the question and she pulled herself completely upright in the chair.

"I'm sure, and—*no*," she answered her mother, embarrassed. "Seth's not gay. I don't know what the problem is, but it's not being gay."

Alexa knew quite well the good and bad of men. She loved men, but in her experience, most men were better in bed than out of it.

Jenna looked away from the women staring at her intently, and then finally brought her gaze back. "I just wanted to surprise Seth. When he answered the door, the phone rang. He took the call, turned his back to me, and left me standing in the doorway."

"Left you standing the doorway? *In that dress?*" Shocked, Regina could only shake her head and think that Seth Carter needed his testosterone checked if a phone call was that damn distracting.

"Was it bad timing, maybe?" Lauren suggested, choosing to believe there had be an answer other than Seth didn't want Jenna as much as Jenna wanted him.

"It's always bad timing with Seth," Jenna told Lauren, sighing and unable to keep the sadness from her voice.

Jenna looked at her mother. "Earlier this week Seth kissed me good night, and I know—damn it, *I know* he was interested in that moment. I mean I'm not *completely* stupid about men."

"*Jenna,*" Alexa scolded. "You're not stupid at all. Any man in this bar would happily take you to bed. This is obviously about Seth and not about you. Don't even go there."

Jenny looked at her with huge eyes, and Alexa winced.

She sighed and reached for Jenna's hand. "It was an observation honey, not a suggestion to take a strange man to bed."

Of all the people who thought poorly of her dating habits, her own daughter was the worst critic. But it was a fact that Alexa would never, ever have let a man she dated make her feel as bad as Jenna felt right now because of Seth's lack of response.

"Let me rephrase my comments," Alexa said, having had a lot of practice soothing her daughter's ego. "I admire your sincere affection and longing for Seth. He's damn lucky you came to see us instead of picking up the first great-looking guy you saw. If Seth Carter is worth the emotional investment, he's yet to prove it to you. Most men would never have turned a sexy woman away. If you don't believe me, ask Lauren and Regina."

Jenna looked at Lauren who squirmed, then sighed. "Your mother is right. Most men would never have turned you away, not in a killer dress and those heels. The message you're sending is loud and clear." Jenna swung her gaze to Regina. "So am I being a doormat? Am I letting Seth make me feel bad for no reason?" Regina hesitated, but as usual opted for honesty over diplomacy. "Yes. It's probably because you love him."

"This is just great," Jenna pronounced sarcastically, leaning down and banging her forehead on the table. "I am definitely an idiot then."

Alexa and Lauren looked across Jenna's bent head to Regina. Regina tugged at her Rolex and pulled herself reluctantly into Dr. Logan mode.

"Jenna, listen. Seth may have reasons for rejecting your advances," she softened her tone, "reasons that make sense only to him. You should consider dating other men. It might at least help you decide if Seth is worth the risk of more rejection."

Jenna's forehead was still pressed to the table, so Regina leaned over and touched Jenna's hand to make sure she was hearing.

"If you keep repeating this specific rejection pattern with this particular man, you put yourself at risk of believing the problem is yours alone. Seth may be passive-aggressive about it, but he is rejecting you, not the other way around. You wouldn't even be here if he had reacted the way you had a right to expect."

Jenna raised her head and sighed in defeat. Alexa saw the decision in her eyes before she spoke, and she hurt for her daughter.

"No matter how much I care about Seth, I refuse to spend my time wanting a man who's never going to want me back the same way."

Jenna reached out, linked her hand with Alexa's and squeezed hard.

"One Ranger woman already did that. I'm not repeating the same mistake," she said tightly.

Alexa brought Jenna's hand to her lips and kissed it in support. She was grateful there was at least some understanding between them. She was also grateful she'd always opted to tell Jenna the truth, even about her father.

"Okay—to hell with feeling sorry for myself. I'm so done with that tonight," Jenna said firmly.

She stood and lifted her chin as she smoothed the dress down.

"I love you all," Jenna told them, her gaze scanning the table. "Thanks for letting me vent. I need to go home, change clothes, and try to forget about tonight. I'll call you tomorrow, Mama. Is Daddy coming this weekend?"

"I left the invitation open. I'll call you when I hear for sure."

Alexa watched her daughter walk out, not acknowledging the men who looked longingly in her direction.

"Men," Alexa spat the word like an oath. "Life is so much less complicated when you don't want one."

"I'll drink to that," Lauren said, lifting her mineral water.

"Well, I'm not drinking to such foolishness," Regina informed them. "And since when have you given up on men, Alexa? At fifty, I consider you the ultimate optimist for trying so many for so long to find the right one."

"Very funny, Dr. Logan," Alexa said. "For your information, I haven't seriously dated a man in a couple of years."

She paused for dramatic effect, sipping her now meager glass of red wine, thanks to Jenna. "But that doesn't mean I've given up sex." Alexa winked at Lauren, who grinned back.

Regina saluted Alexa with the rest of her drink, and polished it off. "Thank God for that at least. It's *use it or lose it* after menopause starts, honey."

Behind them, Casey sat in silence trying to absorb all he had heard. First, a big one for him was Alexa was fifty instead of forty-five, which made the age gap between them even wider than he had thought. He would have to think about whether or not it bothered him. Certainly, knowledge of their exact age difference didn't stop him from wondering if Alexa would heed her friend's advice to *use it or lose it.* Since the idea of Alexa using it with another man bothered the hell out of him, Casey supposed his reaction likely answered his question.

And *why* was the red-haired woman talking so much about sex anyway? They called her Dr. Logan. Casey made a mental note to look her up online. She was the one scanning the room for men earlier. The other woman, a polished blonde, seemed to not like men at all.

The entire conversation made Casey wonder just what kind of woman Alexa Ranger was. Not that Casey was a prude or anything, he just preferred a woman with at least some modesty.

Okay, so maybe he was used to having more experience than the women he'd been involved with sexually. He had been his wife's second lover and last one. The thought still pleased him. That didn't make him sexist, did it?

He didn't even want to contemplate how many lovers Alexa had had looking like she did. It was one more thing he would have to think about before getting involved with her—*IF* he decided to do so.

Still, the worst bit of news to ponder was that something might be seriously wrong with Seth. Did he really send Jenna away tonight? *Holy shit if he did,* Casey thought, swearing silently as he refused to believe it.

Casey would bet his entire military pension Seth was not gay. The boy had not slept around indiscriminately as a teenager, but Casey had bought him box after box of condoms when there had been a woman in his life.

Seth was not gay—incredibly stupid, definitely—but not gay.

Eavesdropping had seemed like a good idea to Casey when he'd moved around the bar. Now the only part of the conversation Casey was glad he'd heard was Alexa Ranger wasn't currently dating anyone.

Chapter 3

Just a few more months was all he needed, Seth thought. The import and export business Seth started two years ago was taking off at last. Soon he would have to hire an assistant to help him keep up with it. After that, he could finally slow down and enjoy what he had accomplished.

He could also pursue his relationship with Jenna Ranger without constantly being interrupted by work problems. Seth tapped his phone and ordered flowers to be sent to her home along with an apology.

Tomorrow he'd call in person and apologize again. Seth was becoming well practiced at saying "I'm sorry. I'm a jerk. I'm crazy about you, so you have to forgive me."

Normally, Jenna didn't hold a grudge, though Seth expected this time it might take longer. Before, she had at least complained about being ignored. This time Jenna had just left without saying anything.

Silence was never good.

After finishing his apology note, Seth pressed send on his phone just before Casey came through the door. The look on Casey's face instantly propelled Seth back to being a teenager again.

Casey glared at Seth. "What is your problem? Are you gay?" he demanded.

The question was so unexpected Seth dropped down on

the couch and laughed. "Are you drunk on two beers? I'd be mad, but I can't believe you'd ask such a stupid question. Have you seen Jenna? You know, the incredibly hot woman I'm dating?"

"Yes, I saw Jenna. In fact, I saw a lot of Jenna, and so did thirty other horny guys in Eddy's Bar when she bent over a table to hug her mother," Casey informed him.

Seth opened his mouth, but nothing came out. He closed it again and put his hands over his eyes. The thought of other men seeing Jenna dressed up that way made him nauseous.

"Did you really send Jenna away tonight?" Casey asked, his brain still not able to wrap itself around the thought. "*In that dress?*"

"No. I did not send Jenna away," Seth protested. "I got a phone call from Japan I'd been waiting for all evening. Jenna must have left while I was talking. When I finished the call, she was just—*gone.*" Seth ran a nervous hand through his hair. "It's okay. I sent flowers and an apology note. Tomorrow I'll call her. This will be okay. It's happened before."

Casey swore viciously and glared at Seth. "Yeah, I heard all about how it wasn't the first time when Jenna was complaining about it to her mother and friends."

When Seth only blinked in reply, Casey threw up his hands.

"Do you have any idea how much trouble Jenna went through to try and seduce you?"

Seth closed his eyes, mostly to block out Casey's glare. "*I know.* I messed up—*badly.* I sent flowers," he said quietly. "This will be okay."

"I don't think flowers are going to make up for Jenna sleeping alone tonight when she so obviously had other plans. You better hope she's as much in love with you as you are with her. Otherwise, she's going to be looking for a man without a cell phone," Casey said, taking off his coat and hat.

"You know, I'm trying like hell to put my expensive Harvard education to good use by getting my business going. Now all the work is finally paying off," Seth insisted. "I just need a couple more months, and then I can have a different kind of life."

"I hope you get lucky then," Casey said, "because you sure as hell aren't being very smart about Jenna. If you don't have time for her, cut the woman loose."

Seth watched as Casey walked off mumbling about dresses and stupidity, leaving him digging in a side table for the pills he took to settle his stomach.

He refused to think tonight was the disaster his cousin seemed to think it was. He was in love with Jenna, had been in love with her since the first time he saw her. There was no choice except to believe things would work out. If not easily, he'd just see to it they did anyway.

Through his business, Seth had discovered he was very good at making things work out.

A couple weeks later, Casey stood outside the building where he knew Alexa Ranger worked. He had accused Seth of being dumb about Jenna, when he was being just as dumb about his attraction to her mother. When a woman was on a man's mind as much as Alexa was on his, it was time to do something about it.

Or at least, it was time to explore it and see if it was worth doing something about or not.

The doorman of the building opened the door and nodded respectfully as Casey walked into the lobby. Casey could literally feel the man's curiosity and concern about the limp.

"Morning, sir," the doorman said with a smile, holding the door for Casey. "Let me get the door for you."

"Thanks," Casey said, noting the man's concerned gaze dropping to the cane.

"I'm good—just a military injury," Casey said with a shrug, before smiling and walking on. "Cane beats a chair any day."

"Indeed it does, sir," the doorman answered with a respectful nod. "Thank you for your service to our country."

"You're welcome," Casey replied, nodding respectfully in

return.

At the elevator, he scanned the building occupants' list looking for Alexa's business. Casey called the elevator and moments later was standing in the middle of the most chaos he had ever seen. A giant sliding door off the receiving area was opened, revealing what looked like might have been an impressive art gallery, but was instead filled with several nearly naked women standing around in nothing but underwear.

After almost two years with no woman in his life, the sight of so many scantily clad ones had Casey momentarily frozen where he stood. A multitude of pleasing female faces looked up at him briefly. One or two smiled and finger waved, causing Casey to grin, but eventually they went back to their tasks, which seem to include all of them talking at once.

Casey shook his head. There was a time not too long ago when his presence would have earned more than just a brief glance. One of them might have broken away to come speak to him, at least until Susan chased her away.

Maybe the cane was slowing him down a bit, he thought. Until recently, he hadn't given much thought to what women he met might think about his injury, or him. Now he suddenly found himself wondering how Alexa would react.

"Can I help you?" a distinctly masculine voice asked from behind him.

Casey turned a little too quickly and stumbled sideways into the tall, incredibly handsome man belonging to the voice.

"Damn," Casey said. "Sorry about that."

"Easy," the man said with a small laugh, righting Casey and making sure he was stable before letting go. "I didn't mean to startle you. Let's not do more damage to your military injury."

Casey looked surprised at the accurate guess, but the man merely smiled.

"Did the doorman call you or is it tattooed on me somewhere? I thought they removed the label before I left,"

Casey said, joking to cover his embarrassment.

"The haircut—it's a direct giveaway. Plus you carry yourself like a solider. And judging by the haircut," the man said, his gaze inspecting Casey's head with a serious perusal, "I would guess you served in the Marines."

"And you would be correct," Casey admitted, surprised again.

The man just smiled and shrugged. "I've dated a few."

Dated a few? Of course, Casey thought, instantly grinning. It made all the sense in the world to him that only a gay guy could work sanely around all those scantily clad women every day.

"Forgive me, I'm being rude," the man said, reaching his hand out to Casey, "Sydney Banes—Alexa Ranger's assistant. What can I do for you today?"

"Casey Carter," he said in return, shaking automatically. "I'm here to see Alexa, hopefully."

Casey paused. He hadn't practiced well enough what to say, so he simply decided to lie. "Actually, she's not expecting me. I was in the neighborhood and thought I might surprise her with a visit."

Sydney narrowed his eyes as he noticed the slight flush accompanying the smooth lie. Granted, it had been a couple of years since a man had been a problem around the office, but Sydney still recognized the signs of interest. The hopeful expression and the dreamy look were unmistakable.

Though Sydney had never known Alexa to date a military man, there was always a first time. What interested him more than work background was Casey Carter being much younger than her usual fiftyish stuffed-shirt yuppies. Sydney was guessing the man's age to be somewhere between thirty-five and forty.

Maybe Alexa was taking his advice after all.

Whatever the case, Sydney's gut instinct was to let Carter in to see her and he rarely acted against them.

"I apologize for the chaos, Mr. Carter. We're prepping for a buyer show this weekend. Alexa is hiding from it in her office. Let's walk back and see if she has a few minutes,"

Sydney said, motioning to a long hallway with his hand.

Alexa stood at the biggest window in her office, staring out into the street while counting her many blessings. She had a business she loved, some really great friends, and a wonderful—even if odd—family. Now if only Jenna could find a way to be happy, her life would pretty much be complete. *But what about you?* a voice inside her taunted. *What about sex? Love? You deserve those too.*

Sure she did, she decided, but then so did everyone. Alexa was old enough to know for a fact that life didn't always work out the way you wanted. At least she was content, which was more than many people could say at her age, scolding her inner voice for stirring up trouble where there was none.

Sydney called her name as he knocked and opened the door. "Alexa? I brought someone by to see you. He said he wanted it to be a surprise."

Alexa watched Casey Carter come through the door behind Sydney. She noticed the cane and how good he looked at the same time. The entire package was sexy as hell.

"Casey?" Alexa was almost shocked speechless. *"This is a surprise."*

Casey walked into the office slowly, looking around in awe at the expensive furniture and the beautiful woman in the middle of it. Oh hell—maybe he should have called first.

"Sorry to barge in on a business day. I was just in the neighborhood and wanted to talk to you about something if you have some time," he said.

Alexa motioned with her hand to one of two brightly patterned chairs in front of her desk. "Sure. I can take a few minutes. Sit—please. Sydney, will you tell Angela I'll be a little late? She can start the meeting without me."

Sydney nodded and closed the door with a decisive click as he left.

Casey sat, relieved to rest his leg and hip. He would have to take a taxi back. Walking six blocks had not been a good idea today. In his determination to come see Alexa, he had all but forgotten some days were a lot better than others.

"I don't mean to keep you from working," he told Alexa sincerely. "I just didn't know how else to get in touch with you."

Alexa waved his apology away and walked from the window to sit at her desk. "I love a surprise now and again."

Turning her chair in Casey's direction, Alexa locked her gaze with his and smiled fully.

"What can I do for you?"

Casey's mind easily drew a picture, even when he could do nothing more than stare. Alexa Ranger was undoubtedly the most beautiful woman he'd ever met. From her curious, but only friendly stare, she also seemed to want to pretend she hadn't felt the instant lust flare between them last month. Today her smile held nothing remotely hinting of their shared moment. No signs of blushing were happening either.

Well damn, Casey thought, chagrined to think he might have made more of it than it had been.

"I like your office," he said, stalling while he considered how to explain coming to see her. "The doorman is very nice."

"Eric? Yes, Eric has been here a long time," Alexa replied dryly, wondering why Casey was chatting about the doorman. She watched Casey caressing the end of his cane while he searched for what he wanted to say next.

She liked his hands. They were big and looked strong. *They are strong. You remember his grip—so stop pretending you're not interested.*

Giving in to the voice at last, Alexa let herself imagine how wonderful Casey's hands might feel on her. A harmless fantasy, she assured herself, refusing to feel guiltier as her mind conjured up all kinds of delightful scenarios.

"So do you lease your space?" Casey asked.

"Actually, my company owns the building. We lease out the first and fourth floors. I was already settled on the second floor when the sale went through. I was too lazy to reorganize," Alexa said with a laugh.

Casey mentally searched for another safe topic of conversation while he pondered the wisdom of telling Alexa why he'd really stopped by her office. Despite his attraction to her, she was a lot more intimidating in her office than she had been in Seth's condo. Her rock-steady composure actually made him wonder if he'd imagined her response to him.

"How's Jenna doing since the break-up?" Casey asked. "I think Seth's hoping she'll eventually forgive his stupidity. Of course, he still needs to learn how to appreciate a sexy, intelligent woman who's crazy about him."

"True enough. Maybe you could give him lessons," Alexa teased, the provocative statement sliding smoothly off her tongue like it had been waiting years to be said to this man. She held Casey's gaze, pleased with the interest in his eyes, not so pleased with the confused expression on the rest of his face.

Bad girl, Alexa, she told herself. *Don't make things worse by flirting with him.*

"Lessons? What kind of lessons?" Casey asked, frowning and wondering if daily exposure to Alexa would grant him immunity to her teasing smile and the sexy dare in her gaze.

When he noticed the corners of her mouth tilted in a smirk, Casey decided he'd like nothing better than to kiss the amusement right off her beautiful face. Maybe then he'd stop being so intimidated. It also might make her think twice about torturing him.

Alexa gave Casey points for not swearing or yelling at her yet because he looked quite capable of both. She laughed softly when Casey just kept frowning.

"You heard me right, Carter," Alexa demanded in her most commanding business tone, trying not to laugh and failing miserably. "Do you know how to treat a sexy, intelligent woman or not?"

Her outright laughter broke whatever spell her smile was casting over Casey's brain. Once free of it, he glared at Alexa, embarrassed and turned-on at the same time. Casey wished like hell he could pass a little of his personal discomfort back to her. Irritation made his voice rougher than he would have liked as the unvarnished truth just came pouring out of him.

"I sure as hell wouldn't have sent a woman in a seduction dress away from my door to take a damn phone call, if that's what you're asking," Casey said roughly, through partially gritted teeth.

The next laughter rose from her gut. Alexa was delighted with the genuine disgust in his tone.

"Well, I'm really glad to hear you say that. I would have hated for my instincts about you to have been wrong," Alexa said sincerely.

She leaned back in her chair and studied Casey's face. He was about as embarrassed as she had ever seen a man be, but still managing to hold his ground with her. Most men fled from her teasing when they got offended. Alexa found she liked Casey's emotional courage. She liked it a lot, actually. So she decided to just tell him the truth.

"Sorry for teasing you. I get a little wicked sometimes." Alexa said in apology. "Okay—let me tell you about my daughter, Casey. I always insisted Jenna keep searching for the one person who would best meet all her needs. Sex. Love. Caring. All of it. Do you know what I mean?"

Casey nodded yes. Of course. Wasn't that what everyone wanted from a relationship?

"Then along comes Seth into her life. I think Jenna may be a little in love with him, but his rejections have hurt her pride. Right now, I'm forbidden to speak his name around her."

Alexa turned her head, frowned into the space beyond her desk.

"Jenna told me she broke up with Seth through a text message. She told me it was poetic justice since the man was so obsessed with his phone," Alexa explained, still in partial disbelief that Jenna would choose such a wimpy method.

"I can't argue with the phone obsession part," Casey said quietly, "but Seth does have reasons for being so focused on his work."

"Yes, I'm sure he does. Don't get me wrong, I don't think

Seth is a bad guy at all. I probably share that work-obsessed quality with him. Still, Jenna didn't come home even for her birthday last week because she doesn't currently want to be in the same town as Seth. My daughter can be very resistant when she has her mind set against something. She gets that trait from her father."

Casey studied Alexa who had dropped her gaze from his again.

"Everyone is resistant sometimes. I'm sure even you are," he said, mouth quirking as he watched her study her manicured nails as if she had never seen them before.

"No, I am very flexible and forgiving about most things," Alexa said easily. "I roll with the punches life throws and jump back up for more. My experiences have required me to react that way. Jenna is a product of her own life."

Alexa felt the heat come into her eyes to match the anger she felt in the rest of her.

"I didn't raise my daughter to be ignored by anyone," she told Casey. "If I had been Jenna, I would have snatched the phone from Seth's hand and thrown the damn thing across the room."

"What would you do now?" Casey asked.

"Now? Same thing probably, but at my age I can't imagine thinking any man was worth that kind of drama. Besides," Alexa said with a dismissing wave of her hand, "the kind of men I like would toss the phone themselves. I don't think younger men work that way."

Casey laughed, appreciating her honesty. He was immensely glad Alexa had stopped flirting to really talk with him.

"Seth was just being stupid about priorities. I'm pretty sure he's learned from the experience," Casey assured her.

When Alexa smiled at him fully, the corners of her eyes crinkled, causing her laugh lines to take center stage in her amazing face. His body tightened immediately, wiping away any remaining doubts about whether her age bothered him. It for sure didn't stop him from wanting her. Casey figured his reaction made him exactly her kind of guy whether she knew it or not.

"Okay. I've run out of small talk. I didn't really stop by to talk about Seth and Jenna. I came to see you. Have dinner with me tonight," Casey ordered, pleased at the shock Alexa wasn't able to hide. He smiled, letting his wicked thoughts run free at last. "I can't believe you didn't see the invitation coming. I've spent the entire time here trying to ask you out."

Alexa raised her eyebrows. "Ask me out? Why? Don't you think I'm a little too old for you? I certainly do."

But as soon as the words were said, Alexa looked away. She couldn't help herself. After the thoughts she'd been allowing to obsess her lately, the last thing her ego needed was to see confirmation of her aging.

"Too old? What's too old?" Casey asked, laughing. "Hell, I'm too old for some things. But I'm definitely not too young for you."

"A smart woman never gets tired of hearing a sincere compliment," Alexa replied with a soft smile. "However, I simply can't imagine dating someone your age. Jenna said you weren't even forty yet."

Casey imagined tracing her smile lines with his tongue, making her laugh just for him, and then he thought of a very pleasurable way of showing her just how sexy she was. He started to tell her what he was thinking, but then saw Alexa's gaze was reluctant to hold his still. Her vulnerability was just as alluring as the way she looked.

It suddenly didn't bother him that the young lingerie models hadn't found him very interesting, because the older one across the desk from him obviously did. Knowing he could draw Alexa's attention was far more flattering.

"So I'm thirty-eight and you're fifty. Big deal. Beautiful women like you are ageless anyway. I'm sure you don't need my reassurance about how attractive you are," Casey told her, enjoying the relieved smile Alexa gave him.

"Who knew you were such a flatterer?" Alexa declared with a laugh, caught off guard enough to start flirting again.

"Look, I appreciate that we're playing nice with each other, but it's taking all my nerve to keep asking out a woman who looks as good as you do," Casey said honestly. "Can you just put me out of my misery and say yes to dinner?"

"And now even more flattery. Just what do you want, Mr. Carter? And when can I give it to you, Mr. Carter?" Alexa asked, fighting a growing urge to giggle at Casey pressing his advantage.

"If you've got a little more time this afternoon, I can make you a list of what I want," Casey said with a true smile.

Alexa laughed and searched his teasing gaze, more than a little intrigued by the genuine interest she found there. He probably does want to make me a list, she decided, feeling the urge to giggle again at the knowledge. The man was certainly fun to flirt with. Was this what she had been missing?

Before she could figure it out, her gaze fell from his face to her watch, making her sigh. She was running much later than she had planned.

"Sorry—I just realized the time. I'm afraid your list will have to wait. Right now, I really need to go to a meeting. I'm glad you came by, Casey Carter. It was a lot of fun talking with you."

Alexa stood and started to walk around the desk.

"Wait—*stay*. You haven't answered me yet," Casey ordered sharply, not yet moving from the chair.

"What do you mean?" Alexa looked puzzled, and then frowned. Did Casey Carter just order her *to stay?* She was torn between laughing in his face and telling him off.

"I'm actually a passable cook," Casey said, grinning at her frown. "Come to dinner tonight and see."

She looked panicked at his demand, Casey decided, his smile widening. His determination to talk her into it grew as she hesitated.

"It's just dinner and you have to eat. What could it hurt?" Casey challenged. "Seth will even be there to chaperone."

Alexa knew she'd been out of the loop for a while, but the gaze holding hers was definitely saying dinner wasn't all he had in mind. Fantasy and flirting were fine, but she wasn't ready yet to really think of Casey being interested in her sexually.

Going would be a bad idea, but not going would make more of it than there was. Going might be the easiest way to prove to both of them there was nothing between them worth pursuing other than a friendship. And maybe he was a passable cook—she had to eat.

"Okay, I'll come to dinner, but I doubt we need a chaperone," Alexa conceded. Casey's answering laugh did not reassure her that she was making a wise decision.

Not able to put it off any longer, Casey stood and stretched his legs, walking a bit stiffly to her door. Alexa followed slowly behind him.

"Great. See you tonight about seven. Do you like pasta?" he asked.

Alexa nodded earning her another wide smile. She walked beside Casey down the hall, his spicy masculine aftershave pleasantly tingling her senses and making her aware of him. When she found herself wondering if Casey's scent was a reflection of his personality, it was fairly obvious why she'd given in so easily. She wanted to know more about Casey Carter even if she didn't think there was any future in it. He was the most interesting man she'd met in a long time.

And it was just dinner, she reminded herself. They could visit, talk, and move their attraction into friendship. *You mean friends-with-benefits*, her inner voice corrected.

"No. I don't think I'll be sleeping with this one," Alexa said aloud, once the main office door closed behind Casey. "That would be a very bad idea."

She was glad Sydney wasn't at his desk. Her nosy assistant was too damn observant and would ask too many questions for which Alexa didn't have any answers yet.

Chapter 4

"You asked Jenna's mother to dinner? *Why?*" Seth looked at Casey as if he had lost his mind. "I could have gotten you a real date if I'd known you wanted one."

Casey looked at Seth and shook his head sadly from side to side.

"See, this is why Jenna is no longer in your life. You need your testosterone checked. Have you ever looked at Alexa Ranger? She's the kind of woman men fight wars over."

"*Fight wars over?*" Seth wrinkled his face as he tried to understand the statement. "Oh—that's a military euphemism for sex. I get it. Wait—you're planning to date Jenna's mother for sex? *Why?* Couldn't you find someone younger?"

Seth dipped his finger in the bowl of chocolate frosting. "I mean I agree Alexa looks great and all, but she's probably forty-five at least."

Casey smacked Seth's hand with the icing spoon. "Actually, she's fifty."

Seth made a face and rolled his eyes. "*Fifty?*"

Casey pointed the spoon at him. "I want to get to know her. I have my own reasons. You should be thanking me for this golden opportunity to talk to the woman. She might actually put in a good word with Jenna for you."

Seth looked hopeful for a moment, and then the phone rang. He raced off to answer it, leaving Casey to ponder the insanity of his plan to include Seth in his first dinner with Alexa.

When the doorbell rang fifteen minutes later, he heard Seth answer. Moments after, Alexa walked into the kitchen carrying a bottle of red wine. She looked like a taller, slightly older, and much more interesting version of Jenna in her loose white shirt and jeans. In fact, Alexa looked just like she did the first time Casey had seen her, and was every bit as appealing.

"Hi," she said. "I came straight from work, but I brought wine."

Casey stopped chopping the vegetables for the salad. He wiped his hands on his apron and walked over to take the wine. Alexa was almost as tall as he was and looked into his eyes as she handed him the bottle.

She smelled like peaches and ginger. When Casey got a good whiff of her, every muscle in his body went on instant alert. His reaction to her was going to be obvious sooner or later. There was only one way to find out how she was going to feel about the fact she turned him on.

"What are you wearing? I'm usually allergic to perfume," Casey admitted, holding her gaze. "I really like it—maybe a little too much."

Alexa smiled at him, her laugh lines crinkling. "It's my favorite of the three organic scents I'm looking to start selling soon. Lauren calls this one *Revelation*."

"Apt name," Casey answered dryly. "I think I'm having one myself."

A knot of need twisted inside him, instinctual and insistent on being met. He started to step into Alexa, fully intending to put his mouth on hers.

Recognizing the intent in Casey's gaze, Alexa pushed the wine more firmly into his hands and laughed at the look of shock on his face as he backed up a little.

"Thanks for the compliment," Alexa said, reaching out and tugging on a pocket of his apron. "It's good to know you're not allergic to me."

She wasn't ready to kiss him, but she didn't want to

totally reject him either. The man had her heart beating hard in her ears by just staring at her. She wanted the safe emotional distance between them, but she wasn't a total hypocrite.

Alexa saw Seth walk into the kitchen just in time to witness the end of their exchange. Casey gave him a deadly look. *Well, there's the Marine,* Alexa thought, fighting her urge to grin and barely winning.

She found herself intrigued by the menacing glint in Casey's eyes and clenched jaw. Seth seemed oblivious to both the intimacy of their conversation, and the angry glare Casey was sending him about being interrupted. While it was easy to understand why Casey was so irritated, Alexa was still glad for the reprieve Seth had provided.

"What made you think you were allergic to Alexa's perfume?" Seth asked. "Maybe you need to get an allergy test. I get a newsfeed from a health site and they say allergies can be deadly."

Alexa grinned when Seth picked up a carrot and crunched. Casey, on the other hand, looked at Seth with near disgust. She wanted to laugh out loud, but thought it was too impolite. She settled for sending Casey a knowing look.

When Casey saw the amusement in Alexa's gaze, it instantly deflated some of his anger. And he made a mental note never to underestimate her awareness.

"You know, Seth, there are other sources of information than the Internet. You should try paying attention to the people around you for starters," Casey said, returning to his task of viciously chopping the stack of vegetables he had been working on earlier.

"What did I say wrong now?" Seth asked, confused at Casey's anger, looking between Casey and Alexa.

Alexa shrugged, her blue eyes twinkling with amusement. No way was she getting in the middle of two verbally sparring males.

Casey's mouth lifted in a snarl as he continued to chop the vegetables. "Why don't you show Alexa the patio and get her a glass of wine? I thought we'd eat outside tonight."

Casey turned his back as they left the kitchen. The kid was pathetic, Casey decided. Seth was just hopelessly distracted by the wrong things.

Throughout dinner, Casey tried unsuccessfully to get Seth to engage Alexa in some genuine conversation. All Seth could talk about was the latest business trends. Never once did he ask about Jenna or how she was doing.

No wonder Jenna had dumped him.

Casey frowned, seeing proof that Seth was as disconnected from reality as he feared. Though Seth did redeem himself slightly with Casey later by offering to do the dishes.

When Seth had removed the last of the dishes and left for good, Alexa reached over and patted Casey on the hand.

"Come on, Marine. The mission was not a total waste," Alexa told him.

"Mission?" Casey was surprised at first, and then resigned when he saw Alexa was grinning. "That obvious, huh?"

"The only thing obvious to me is how very proud of Seth you are. And well you should be—top of his class at Harvard? That's pretty impressive."

Alexa was relieved when Casey sighed and got more comfortable in his chair. She smiled at him in approval.

"Dinner was great, by the way. You really can cook," she told Casey, lifting her wine glass.

It was very clear how much Casey loved Seth and wanted him to be happy, as any parent would want their child to be. And a parental figure was obviously how Casey saw his role in Seth's life.

Setting down her wine, Alexa smiled at Casey, trying to communicate a level of understanding she hoped he would find one day. Maybe the big Five-O birthday had brought some wisdom after all.

"Have you ever considered Seth is just being the person Seth needs to be right now? He's driven to succeed. Some would say that kind of ambition is a positive trait," Alexa said.

"Not Jenna," Casey said bitterly. "And not me—I know how short life is."

"Well, my daughter is just as focused. She's entering the prime of her life. Right now Jenna's hormones are driving her every bit as hard as Seth's ambition is driving him." Alexa shrugged. There was little to be done about her daughter bending to mother nature. Her twenties and thirties had been just as challenging.

Casey sighed. "Would you believe Seth is actually the fun-loving one in our family?"

"No. I will never believe such a thing. You are a lot more fun," Alexa said easily.

"It's the truth," Casey's protested, even at Alexa's choked laugh.

She leaned her elbow on the table and put her chin in her hand, "So tell me about your life, Casey Carter. I have a policy never to conspire with men I don't know."

Looking at her, Casey wondered if Alexa had any idea how appealing she was leaning forward to listen, all her attention focused on him. He drank a bit of wine and shifted his leg into a more comfortable position.

"For years, I was every bit as focused on the military as Seth is right now on his business. Both Seth's parents died in a car accident when he was twelve. Susan and I were living in Japan at the time. My parents had been killed in a boating accident a few years before his. Seth and I ended up being the only family either of us had left. So Seth came to live with us."

Casey paused his story, remembering for a moment how it had begun. "Susan and I didn't have children of our own. For a long time, we didn't know what to do with Seth or how to deal with him. Somehow we managed. Susan was great. We probably didn't do much real parenting, but we gave him love and support as best we could. He turned out okay in most ways—female stupidity not withstanding."

When Casey paused a second time, Alexa could see good memories of his wife and Seth softening his face. She felt an admiration for Casey and envy for the woman who had shared his life. She couldn't help wondering what it was like to be loved so much.

"You and your wife did a great job, Casey. Seth is a good man, just self-absorbed, as many men tend to be at his age," Alexa said, validating his success even as she kindly dismissed his concerns. "What happened to your wife? Divorce?"

"Death. Cancer," Casey answered flatly. "When we got Susan's diagnosis, they gave her less than two years. I had severely injured my leg while on embassy duty. I was medically discharged right after we found out. Susan lasted less than six months. Cancer's a vicious disease. Worst combat I ever engaged in, and worst fight I ever lost."

"I'm really sorry," Alexa told him, all laughter gone. She couldn't even imagine watching someone she loved die.

"Me too," Casey admitted, genuinely realizing how sorry and that he hadn't said those words before to anyone quite as honestly.

He missed his wife, missed the military, and in fact missed the entire life he gave up. He knew he was still coming to terms with losing all of it in such a short period of time. For some reason Casey couldn't yet explain, receiving genuine sympathy from the woman across the table was helping tremendously in easing the resentment that always seemed to ruin happier moments.

There was a comfortable silence between them while they sipped their wine.

"So how about you?" Casey finally asked.

Alexa sighed and laughed at the question.

Casey decided prodding was in order. "Come on now. I've spilled my guts. What's the story for Alexa Ranger? I need to know if you are friend or foe in my campaign."

Alexa leaned back and stretched her legs out under the patio table. Had she ever been this comfortable just talking to a man? Had she ever been this interested in one? Surprised but content to trust her instincts, Alexa found she wanted to tell Casey her story, which really was far more worrisome than merely wanting him sexually.

It meant she liked him. She couldn't remember the last

time she'd genuinely liked a man other than Paul or Sydney. "You want to hear about my business or the other stuff?" Alexa asked at last.

"We'll save the business for another time," Casey told her. Alexa nodded, feeling a little buzz at thinking Casey really did seem interested in hearing her story. "Well, the personal and business stories are kind of linked anyway. I was a model at seventeen and did well at it. I gave up modeling a few years into it when I got pregnant at twenty-three with Jenna." Alexa noticed Casey's gaze stayed on her as she talked.

"Her father and I married shortly after I discovered the pregnancy. He left me for someone else a couple months before Jenna was born. We officially divorced before Jenna was a year old. Sounds bad, but really it was for the best. We've been good parents together, but are much better friends than we ever were lovers," Alexa assured him.

Casey nodded. "Jenna is great, too. You and her father did good work."

"Thanks. After Jenna was born, I took some of my modeling money and opened a lingerie store. I brought Jenna to work with me everyday when she was younger. It was a very good life for a single mother."

"Did you ever marry again?" Casey asked.

"No." Alexa looked at Casey while she wondered how honest she dared be. The older she got, the less she wanted to play the "good woman" role for a man. She sighed heavily before continuing what she considered to be the crux of her life's story.

"Throughout my twenties and my thirties, I kept looking for one man who would love me madly and who I would want in my life all the time. In my thirties, I developed quite a reputation for my search because I dated so much."

Alexa sighed and shook back her hair.

"During my most active dating period, I was an up-and-coming businesswoman often in the public's eye. When Jenna hit her teenage years, she and I had some problems because of my dating. I was not always discreet and saw no reason why I should be. A friend sent me to see Dr. Regina Logan."

"I think I saw her on TV once. Isn't she a . . ." Casey hesitated as he remembered the two women he'd seen her with in the bar. It suddenly dawned on him Dr. Logan had been one of them.

"Sex therapist? Yes. That's what she does for a living." Alexa lifted her chin and met his gaze dead on. "Regina told me I was using men to make me feel better about myself. I spat swear words at her, yelled at her, and we've been friends ever since. She was right of course. I don't think Regina is wrong very often about anything or anyone."

Alexa drained the last of her wine for courage, not looking to see if Casey was shocked or not. She decided to just spill it all to him.

"By the time I hit my forties, I was dating less. In the last few years, I haven't cared about dating at all. With the exception of my ex-husband, whose company I still like, most men my age are boring to be around. I have more fun with my friends," she concluded.

"Don't you miss the sex?" Casey was shocked at the boldness of his own question, and relieved when Alexa only laughed. "Sorry. I meant to say—don't you miss the companionship."

"No, you didn't—and *yes* as the answer to your question. Sometimes I miss the companionship," Alexa admitted, laughing, using his euphemism. "How about you?"

"*Hell yes,*" Casey stated firmly, crossing his arms over his chest. "Susan died two years ago. I'm still trying to figure out what to do with myself. Walking is a challenge some days. My retirement is meager in this economy and I don't have a new job yet. Up until just recently, it seemed like kind of a minor thing to worry about a lack of—*companionship.*"

"I hear you," Alexa told him, smiling in sympathy. "Sometimes it's just all about timing, isn't it? That becomes more obvious to me with every passing year."

Casey believed Alexa Ranger really did hear him, and that she somehow understood the hurt of his life, accepted how he dealt with it, and thought well of him. His short conversation with her made him feel a hell of a lot better than the weeks of therapy he'd endured through the veteran's center.

The bottom line was that Alexa Ranger looked at him with more approval than Casey had received from a woman in a very long time.

Alexa smiled warmly at Casey. "You seem to be a good man, Casey Carter. There are a lot of women out there looking for a good man. I have a feeling companionship is just right around the corner for you."

"What about you? Are you still looking?" Casey asked, the question just coming out of his mouth on its own.

Instead of answering, Alexa laughed softly and got up to leave.

Casey started to stand as well, but was afraid he'd be too slow. In a panic to detain her, he reached out and grabbed her wrist, practically pulling her across the patio table. It was another reminder of when they first met. He could see in her expression his action had reminded her, too.

This time he wasn't letting her go without letting her know how it affected him.

Alexa tried to pull away, but Casey wouldn't let her. She felt his firm grip on her wrist pretty much everywhere. She sighed and swore softly. She didn't know whether to thank Casey for making her feel excitement again or run like hell from him because he was too young to be making a move on her.

She tugged her wrist trying to break free.

"No. Don't run away this time," Casey said, moving to stand in front of her. "Are you still looking? I would really like to know, Alexa."

"Find a younger woman, Casey Carter. Have a happy life. I wish my daughter was interested in you instead of your cousin," Alexa said.

Casey smiled wickedly at her words and tightened his hold on her wrist.

"That's bullshit. I was married to a sexy, strong-willed woman for a long time. I can tell you want me. Can't you tell the feeling is mutual?" he demanded.

"Look, check your ego, okay? I didn't say you weren't great. I'm just telling you in the nicest way I can—*I'm too old for you*," Alexa said sternly.

He kept his grip on her as he stood, and then Casey tugged her toward him until his nose was only inches from hers.

"If you're too old for me, then why do I want to kiss you so badly right now it hurts to leave these few inches between us?"

Alexa hissed, annoyed with herself for underestimating Casey, or at least for underestimating their attraction. It didn't mean it was a smart thing to indulge it, but she had seriously messed up not acknowledging it.

"Fine. I am attracted to you, but I'm not interested in pursuing it, so I'll answer your question. No, I'm not looking any longer. Okay? I gave up looking long before you came along. And I was never looking for a man as young as you. I don't date younger men."

"I'm not buying the age difference bullshit either," Casey said easily, letting go of her wrist. "Whatever the real reason is you're ignoring the attraction between us, you can tell me. I know I'm not exactly in a position at the moment to be super competitive with the type of men you usually date."

"Oh, bloody hell," Alexa said, exasperated with Casey's mood shifts, which were worse than her own. One minute he was humble. The next he was bossy. And then the next he was the nicest man she'd ever met. It was simply driving her crazy trying to keep up.

Alexa rubbed her wrist, trying to minimize the feel of his grip.

"Do not use your physical limitation as an emotional weapon with me. There are two really good reasons I'm not climbing all over you. The first is you're related to Seth, and I do not need that kind of drama. The second is I'm twelve years older than you, and I *prefer* men my own age. None of my reasons have anything to do with your injury or your cane."

She closed the distance between them, brushed her hot,

angry mouth across his just once, before quickly stepping an arm's length away.

Big mistake, she conceded, as her lips vibrated in response. Kissing him was an even bigger one than not acknowledging his feelings. Casey's mouth had been hot and hungry too, and he hadn't even kissed her back. Part of her wanted to step back into him. The other part wanted to run because she truly did not need the drama he represented. All of her was melting for the first time in years.

"Damn it, Casey. I don't see anything about us working, and I'd rather not start something that will cause problems. Jenna would have a cow. And Seth—well, never mind. You know what I'm trying to say."

Casey nodded to let her know he was hearing her, and then licked his lips while she watched. He tasted the wine and her. The fact she didn't look away from the action made him wonder just how brave Alexa would be with a lot of other things. It moved him instantly from being just interested to being determined to find out.

"I hear what you're saying. The family thing is complicated, but I still want you. I wanted you the first time I met you. I haven't been sexually attracted to anyone in a long time. In fact, I never met a woman before you who could make me hard as a stone by just breathing."

Alexa burst out laughing and brought her hands to her hips.

"Then you haven't been looking. There are many good women—beautiful, younger, sexually desirable women—just waiting for a great guy like you to show up and pay attention. Oh hell, this is none of my business. Look, thanks for dinner, Casey. Time for me to say good-night."

Casey watched Alexa walk away, admiring the swing and sway of her hips in the jeans she wore. It was a private show just for him.

He wasn't stupid. Alexa wanted him back. It wasn't his ego either. It was in her damn hungry kiss. It was also in her gaze on him. It was in her laugh and her smile and the low, musical laugh he could all but still hear.

Casey readily admitted both Alexa's stated reasons were solid, though the age thing bothered him less and less as he got to know her. Sure, he supposed it could become a problem long term, but then so could many other things. What relationship was free of challenges?

And who knew if they would get that far anyway.

For now, he thought it was just good to genuinely want a woman again, and even better to know the woman wanted him in return.

The rest was just a matter of logistics.

Fortunately, he was just as good as Seth was at figuring out how to get what he wanted.

Chapter 5

"So before we get to the business part of our agenda, how was dinner last night? Did you do anything *bold* you want to share?" Sydney asked, watching as Alexa moved restlessly in her chair. "I see you squirming, so don't try to lie to me."

"I am so looking forward to replacing you with someone who doesn't know me so well," Alexa said, avoiding the question but not the knowing look in Sydney's eyes. The one that said he knew she was hiding something good.

"You'll miss me, Alexa. And I will miss you. You know I could stay part-time at both places almost indefinitely," Sydney said, laughing at her pained expression.

"Absolutely not," Alexa said firmly, putting on her dreaded reading glasses and peering over the top of them at him. "You are a men's clothing designer masquerading as my assistant. It's time to spread your wings, little bird, and fly. Oh, and make me richer while you're at it or buy me out. I don't care. I'm sure Paul has a list of investments that are must-haves before I get too old to work."

"I want to stay another year, Alexa—no, seriously. I've talked to Paul about it. The clothing shop is humming along without me. I would just be in their way if I were there more. So there's no reason for me not to be *here* a bit longer. Besides, it might take a while for us to find the perfect replacement."

"You know, I'm not half as picky about your replacement as you are," Alexa informed him. "But okay, I want to see some paperwork showing a one-year phase-out plan for you soon. I'm going to gift you some stock when you leave to make sure you remain tied to my apron strings."

"I am tied to you by love, Alexa," Sydney said quietly. "You gave me Paul. He's the best gift I ever received."

"That was a win-win because I got to keep both of you in the bargain," Alexa reminded him. "Our family connection is not going to change when the SydneyB label goes international. We'll just be a richer family."

Sydney nodded. No matter what his bank account said, or how many times he went home to the best looking partner in the world, Sydney still ended up shaking his head in disbelief at his good fortune in knowing the woman across the desk from him.

Alexa Ranger was mentor, second mother, friend, and a dozen other role models of how to move through the world. He didn't want to leave her daily care to anyone else just yet. She was just going to have to live with him sticking around a bit longer.

Alexa nodded with her chin to the PDA Sydney carried. "If you're done grilling me, what's the first item on the list?"

"Karen says it's time to plan the Milan trip because it takes months to reserve everything. Who are we sending?" Sydney asked.

"Not me," Alexa said, not willing to spend another trip alone in the beautiful Italian city. "Why don't you go and take Paul? Busman's holiday for a month."

"Seriously?" Sydney's face lit with joy. "Wonderful. I accept."

"Can Ellen sit the front desk while you're out?" Alexa asked about the person who usually filled in when Sydney had to be away during the day.

"No, I have someone else I want to try. His name is Allen Stedman. He's young, strong, well-rounded, and extremely heterosexual. I think you'll like him."

"For pity's sake, Sydney. I'm not planning to date the

man," Alexa said around a laugh. "I just want a good guard dog."

"Trust me, Allen will do fine at guarding you," Sydney told her. "Take a look at him though before you decide about the dating part. He's in the same league as your Marine, in case your tingle chasing there meets a dead end."

"Gee. Thanks for looking out for me," Alexa said, laughing again.

She didn't see herself losing interest in Casey Carter quickly even though the tingle chasing, as Sydney called it, had already hit a brick wall. He was too young and too related to Seth—end of story. She was sure Casey's attraction to her would fade once he started dating again.

They worked their way through the rest of the Sydney's list before he mentioned a meeting that afternoon with her marketing group. Her friend Lauren's new organic scents were in demo mode and they were planning a full launch of three scents by Valentine's Day next year.

Alexa was already personally addicted to *Revelation*, the ginger and peach scent Casey also really liked—a lot apparently. Her mind drifted off as she remembered his confession in the kitchen and the single step he took toward her that had her heart pounding in anticipation of a kiss for the first time in years.

She came back to reality and saw Sydney waving his hands in the air and laughing.

"Alexa? Where did you go, honey? Have you stopped taking your memory supplements again? You know you need those at your age," he teased.

Alexa held up a middle finger, which made Sydney laugh harder. "Can't a woman have a fantasy in peace?"

"Only if said woman shares the fantasy with her assistant," Sydney replied with a grin.

Relenting, Alexa told him about the exchange she had with Casey over *Revelation*, including the kiss she had held off with the wine bottle.

"That's not a fantasy," Sydney said laughing, delighted for Alexa. "That's just you avoiding the inevitable."

Alexa laughed. "Sex with Casey Carter is not inevitable," she protested. "My instincts go on full alert around him. Part of me wants to drag him off somewhere, but the other part is warning me to be careful about him."

"Well, where did careful ever get anyone?" Sydney asked. "I can't think of a single amazing thing that's ever happened to anyone I know because they chose to be careful."

"Good point," Alexa said, her mind drifting off again. The only careful she would have to be with Casey was because of his injury. She'd been giving that some thought lately as well—just in case she ever crossed the line from fantasy to reality.

Her attention came back once again to the sound of Sydney's laughter as he stood to leave.

"I think we're done today, Alexa. I'll leave you to your fantasies. I'll buzz you to make sure you make the marketing meeting."

"Thanks, Sydney."

After Sydney left, Alexa pulled the reading glasses off her face and dropped them on her desk. It had been a while since she let a man become a distraction for her. Since Casey was pretty much all she could think about, she was afraid it was already too late.

Sydney walked to his desk and almost laughed at who was sitting in the waiting area. After what Alexa had just shared, he wasn't surprised to find Casey Carter stretched out in a chair, flipping through a fashion magazine. The man had obviously not gotten enough last evening.

"Hi, Sydney. Is Alexa in?" Casey asked, putting down the magazine.

"Yes. Why? Are you just *dropping by* again?" Sydney asked in return, shrewdly taking in Casey's low laugh and grin.

"Something like that," Casey said. "Hell. Truth is I'm interested in her, Sydney."

"Please," Sydney said, tilting his head and laughing. "That was obvious yesterday."

"Not to her. Alexa thinks she's too old for me. I think I'm not in the best shape physically to take a woman like her on, but I want to anyway. So what do you think?" Casey said.

"Why would my opinion count?" Sydney asked in return, sitting down in his desk chair, surprised enough by the question to not answer flippantly.

"I'm not sure your opinion will count," Casey said around a grin. "But Jenna mentioned you were more family than assistant. Since I can't ask Jenna about her mother, for reasons I'm sure you can understand, you're next in the line of people whose opinion I need to care about."

Sydney looked at Casey Carter, trying to see the real person. Between the military and the hard knocks, Casey was self-contained and gave little away. It was the hungry eyes he used on Alexa yesterday that betrayed his interest.

Sydney understood that kind of longing. And since Sydney really didn't have a choice other than to take Casey's words at face value, he decided to put the man's integrity on the table as a discussion point.

"I knew you were lying in order to see her yesterday, but I thought it was too cute at the time to stop you. I've been deflecting unwanted attention from Alexa Ranger for a decade now," he said, looking directly into Casey's eyes and receiving a nod of understanding.

"Do you think my attention to Alexa is unwanted?" Casey asked, more nervous about the answer than he realized he would be.

"I haven't decided yet. Maybe I could pass Alexa a note in one of our meetings to see if she likes you," Sydney said, drumming his fingers on his desk, pretending to contemplate the problem.

Sydney already knew Alexa was interested in Carter, but the jury was still out about whether or not Carter would be good for her.

Casey laughed and ran a hand through his hair. "Please don't ask her about me. I couldn't take the rejection right now. Alexa's answer would be that she's too old for me. She's not, but it's not going to be easy to convince her otherwise."

Sydney laughed, delighted Casey was every bit as insecure as Alexa was about the attraction between them. Still, Casey had come to the office and was doing the pursuing. It meant the man was at least worth a shot in Sydney's book.

But open support of Carter would only bring out Alexa's stubborn side. No intervention, Sydney decided. They needed to fight this initial stuff out themselves.

"I'll tell you what I'm going to do today, Carter. I'm going to head to the restroom and pretend I didn't see you. If asked later, I'm going to swear you just got by me. Go to her office and ask her if she's been thinking of you. I've never known Alexa to be less than honest to anyone but her mother, who still disapproves of her," Sydney told him.

Grinning, Casey stood. "How long before she has a meeting or other commitment?"

"A couple of hours. Think it's going to take that long?" Sydney asked, biting his tongue to keep from laughing again.

"Depends on how it goes," Casey said, heading down the hall, leaning heavily on his cane as he walked.

Alexa was staring out her office window again when she heard the knock. The sound was wood on wood instead of knuckles. She was halfway across the room when it occurred to her the knock was from a wooden object—possibly a cane.

Pulling open the door, she noticed Casey had the cane up getting ready to knock again.

"Hi," Casey said, walking around her, not waiting for an invitation to come in because he was afraid he might not get one. "We need to talk."

He noticed Alexa was dressed in jeans again today with a shirt the color of a summer sky. It fit her curves well, he thought.

Alexa closed the door behind him, and then put her hands on her hips.

"How did you get past Sydney?" she demanded.

"I'm a lethal weapon with this cane. Sydney's tied to the desk chair out front. Don't worry, I gagged him so he wouldn't be able to call for help, but I left a few magazines on the floor. He can turn the pages with his toes, once he gets his shoes and socks off," he told her. "He should be adequately entertained for a couple of hours."

Alexa walked to her desk and buzzed the front desk. When there was no answer, she narrowed her eyes at Casey. "He's not there."

"I like my story better," Casey said, grinning at how quickly she had checked.

"Why do we need to talk?" Alexa asked.

Casey stared at her for long moments, and then walked to the chair to sit. He opted for direct honesty.

"I've spent every moment since last evening wanting to kiss you. Since you don't want to let me, we have to talk until you get around to agreeing to some sort of compromise about it. I'm not leaving until we do," Casey said with a shrug.

Alexa sat and stared at Casey, wondering where the nervous man was who came to see her yesterday.

"Talk? You came here in the middle of a business day to talk to me about what exactly? Casey, we hardly know each other," she protested.

"Wow. That's really good, I almost feel guilty for coming. Your tone is frosty as hell," Casey acknowledged. He hooked his cane on the chair arm because it did look like it was going to take awhile. "My wife used to tell me I was a rare man because I understood women needed to talk until they were comfortable with a situation. I never minded talking to her about what bothered her, even when I didn't understand completely. In the end, it was always better for both of us to talk it out."

Alexa pushed her hair behind her shoulders, linked her fingers together on the desk, and gave him a sparkly blue stare. "Casey, I really don't have time for word games or a lengthy discussion that will lead nowhere. I have a meeting in—"

"—two hours," he finished for her. "I checked Sydney's PDA. He left it on the desk." He felt no guilt whatsoever in lying to protect Sydney.

"That's—"

"—underhanded and probably illegal, I know. I'm a determined man, Alexa. You're all I've thought about since you touched your lips to mine. Haven't you been thinking about it, too?"

The last thing Alexa intended to do was confess how much thinking she'd done about kissing him. "Anyone ever tell you that you're pushy and rude?"

Casey merely smiled at her rant, which cut it off completely. Alexa finally saw that he was working hard to rile her up. He wanted her upset and off balance for some reason, probably to prove he could make her that way. Well, it wasn't going to happen.

"Casey, go home. The urges you have about me will pass. I'm sorry about last evening. I shouldn't have kissed you, even the little brush against your lips that was barely a kiss. It was a mistake. I don't intend to make any more mistakes with you," Alexa assured him.

"If you can tell me honestly I haven't been on your mind, then I'll leave and say nothing else about this," Casey told her. "But I have it on good authority you don't lie to anyone except your mother."

"Who have you been talking to about me? Jenna would never share that kind of information. I don't even think she knows," she protested.

Casey leaned forward and studied her intently. "I like you, Alexa. I like you a lot, and I want to kiss you."

"Do you think if you kiss me it will change my mind about being too old for you?" Alexa asked, incredulous at his gall, but thrilled to hear him say her name while demanding to kiss her.

At the same time, she wondered how Casey carried his oversized male ego around in just a regular sized body like his. He was so nervous yesterday, now today he was demanding and arrogant. The men in his family definitely had issues.

"What are you afraid of, Alexa? It's just a kiss. I'm sure you've kissed lots of men in your life. Kiss me and find out what we have between us. I know you want to know as much as I do," Casey said.

Alexa let go a string of swearing that surprised Casey because he heard the f-word being used a couple times, and found it only revved his engine harder to watch her get that angry. He watched, fascinated, as Alexa stomped around the desk to hold out a hand to him.

"Fine. Up against the wall then, Carter. If your legs give out, I'll need help holding you up."

Casey almost laughed at her orders and her fear of him falling, but decided he'd pushed her as far as he could. He let Alexa take his full weight as she helped him stand. It was a nice way to find out she was strong and had a firm grip.

They walked to an open wall in her office and Alexa leaned back against it without a smile or eye twinkle in sight. Her eyes were dark blue sapphires, cold and uninterested.

Casey held up a finger to her, signaling to wait while he walked to the door, threw the lock, and then walked back to her. He used the time both to shore up his own courage and to keep from getting mad at her for fighting the attraction between them so much.

"If this is my one chance to convince you, I don't want any interruptions," he told her as he walked back.

Casey stepped close to Alexa and brought his hands to her arms, rubbing them for comfort while she pressed herself back into the wall. She was tight and tense under his hands, but he felt a tremor too, which told him she was more affected than she wanted him to know.

He leaned into her and whispered. "You make me nervous as hell, but it isn't going to stop me. I need to kiss you."

When she opened her mouth to respond, Casey took advantage of it and closed his lips over hers. Instead of moving though, he just held himself still, absorbing the various quakes starting in both of them. Then he moved his lips across hers gently, and inserted one of his legs between hers, leaning his knee intimately against hers.

When a bigger tremor shook them both, Casey had to pull

his lips away to keep from devouring her. He leaned back a little to look in her eyes.

"Kissing you is even better than I imagined, Alexa. Are you feeling anything yet? Be honest."

She started to answer his question, but he just repeated the process of cutting her off again with his mouth. This time there was nothing gentle in what he did. His mouth was hungry as his tongue slipped inside to graze her teeth before moving on to tangle with hers.

Hands previously fisted at her sides came up to Casey's waist. Casey groaned in pleasure as Alexa clutched two handfuls of shirt there.

His hands slid down her arms and around her back, and then dipped down to lift her hips against his. He let his weight fall into her then, pressing her hard against the wall. She arched, matching her hips to his.

When he tore his mouth away from hers, he swore and pulled her hips tighter against the erection he wanted her to acknowledge—hell, crave.

"Kiss me back, Alexa," he demanded against her mouth, his lips touching hers as he talked. "I can tell you want to. Stop fighting what is between us."

Alexa swore harshly, but pulled him closer. Casey felt her slide a long, jeans-clad leg up one of his to lock it around his waist. And then he felt one of her hands move up behind his neck. When she touched her mouth to his, the contact was electric. She moaned into his mouth and Casey shook so hard he had to let go and brace both hands on the wall to keep from taking both of them to the floor.

Diving in deeper wasn't a conscious decision. Neither was rocking his erection against the cradle of her thighs and center of her heat. Both were just something happening that seemed as important as breathing to him.

"Casey." She breathed his name against his mouth as she broke for air, and then desperately returned for more.

While Casey held them up, Alexa pulled his tongue into her mouth and sucked so hard he thought he might erupt. He wanted to pull back and look at her, to see her desire for him, but he couldn't yet bear putting the necessary distance between their bodies.

Casey felt Alexa freeing his shirt from his jeans and seconds later her hands found their way between their bodies to Casey's chest. She let go of his mouth and wound herself around his neck again. Then she let go of his neck and moved her hands down to his waistband of his jeans again. He was thrilled she was on the edge and trying to get to him.

When he heard the snap of his jeans give way, Casey stilled his hips at last. He honestly hadn't meant to take things so far, hadn't been sure Alexa would admit to wanting him back.

Her hand slipped past his waistband and he felt his zipper sliding down.

Casey stopped gloating and panicked instead.

"Stop. Wait," he begged roughly, all but yelling the words as he pressed his hips against her hand.

"Alexa. Please, honey. We have to stop or I'm going to take you. I'm so far gone—please not here, not this way. Not the first time. Okay? Oh God, tell me it's okay."

Casey was incoherent in his pleading and he knew it. Two years with nothing and he had picked the hottest woman he'd ever met to kiss for the first time. Sanity and pride were both gone. Begging was all that was left for him.

He felt Alexa remove her hands from his pants and couldn't stop his disappointed sigh. Moments passed while Alexa seemed to be debating what to do, but Casey eventually felt her leg slide down the back of his leg, and her arms move away from him. He had to close his eyes against the loneliness that swept through him. The loss of her heat and her passion was physically painful.

"No. Don't let me go completely yet. I need—just hug me, okay?" Casey let out the breath he was holding when Alexa's arms came back around him.

Casey felt her straighten as she hugged him back. It felt wonderful to wrap her tightly in his arms, and he hugged her until he felt Alexa struggle against his hold and try to pull back. When she would have pushed him away from her,

Casey pressed against her, refusing to budge.

"No. Don't look at me yet. Just hold me. If I see desire in your eyes, my noble intentions won't be worth a shit," he growled.

He stroked a hand down her spine, liking the way she arched against his entire body just because of a single stroke.

"I know we're mostly strangers still. I know neither Jenna nor Seth would be happy with us wanting each other. But this is not about other people. I lost the last woman I felt like this about. Don't ask me to walk away from you just because you have a problem with the age difference between us or because I have the wrong last name."

Casey waited, but she said nothing for a long time. "Alexa?"

"Is it finally my turn to talk now?" she asked sarcastically, her voice raspy and thick with arousal. "You keep interrupting me. I just want to be sure."

Casey reached down and pinched her backside, hugging her tighter when she yelped. "Don't be mean. I didn't intend to take things this far. It just happened."

Alexa didn't know whether to punch him or kiss him senseless again. He meant for something to happen. It wasn't her fault it turned out to be more than he'd bargained for.

"You can be an arrogant brute, Casey Carter," she said, eliciting a deep laugh from him.

"Yeah, I'm a guy. I think it comes with the Y chromosome," he explained. "I can be a lot of other things too, Alexa. Want to find out? I would sure as hell love to show you."

Casey did move away from her then. He wanted to see her face when she answered the question.

Her heart was still hammering in her chest. Alexa opened her mouth to answer, fully intending to send him away from her, but never got the chance. Her desk monitor buzzed and Sydney came on.

"Uh—Alexa, the office door was locked when I checked a minute ago, and now Jenna is on her way back. Are you okay?"

"Oh, hell." Alexa stepped away from the heat of Casey's body, looked at his shirt hanging out and the erection straining against the front of his unzipped jeans.

Her fault, she conceded, running a shaky hand through her hair.

"I don't suppose you would want to hide in my office restroom for a while?" Alexa asked flatly.

If he said no, she'd likely shove him in there anyway.

Casey put hands on hips and smiled at her. No blame for the kiss, no censure for stopping though it frustrated both of them. She even had her anger in check as she asked him to hide from Jenna. Her poise under pressure was damned admirable. He had used up all of his composure kissing her and stopping. Now he was an emotional wreck.

Casey felt the nervous laughter building in him, but he kept it soft.

"Sure. I'll hide in the bathroom. Will you go out with me afterwards?" he asked her, wanting to laugh at her look of disbelief.

"First you seduce me and stop. Now you're trying to blackmail me for a date?" Alexa asked around a reluctant smile, fighting to choke back a full out laugh at his audacity.

"I'll use any means that works to spend more time with you," Casey said, purposely shifting his erection to a more comfortable location as he zipped his jeans, grinning as Alexa watched with great interest.

"How about I just take you home with me?" she challenged. "I'm done pretending I don't want to rip your clothes off and work out some of this tension you've caused."

Casey froze, tucking in his shirt. She was serious, and he wanted to, but—no, not a good idea yet.

"Damn tempting lady, but too soon. If I go home with you, we'll end up in bed for a week. But I do like the way you're thinking. Let's go out instead. Wings and beer somewhere we can talk," Casey said.

"Talk? More talk? You know, men your age aren't supposed to want to talk, Casey. They're supposed to want to f—"

Alexa froze at the sound of a knock and a soft voice calling "Mama" through the door.

Casey smiled and pointed at the restroom. Happy with Alexa and her reaction to kissing him, he walked inside, locked the door, and settled on the toilet lid to listen.

Chapter 6

"Why did you have the door locked? Were you working out?" Jenna asked.

"Working out?" Alexa asked, noting Jenna was looking at her hair. She reached up and felt her hair all mussed. "No. I wasn't working out, just trying to handle a problem that came up this afternoon. I guess I was looking in my hair for a solution."

She ran still quivering fingers through the strands Casey had ruffled, trying to smooth them back into place. She could still feel his hands on her.

Jenna took a seat in front of the desk. Her eyes immediately lit on Casey's cane. She picked it up, looked at the cane with recognition, and then at Alexa.

Alexa swore in shock, not the shock Jenna probably thought, but because in the heat of the moment both she and Casey had forgotten about his cane.

"Well, how did I not see that hanging on the chair? That's Casey Carter's cane," Alexa said to Jenna, opting for the truth.

"Casey was here? In your office?" Jenna asked. "Why?"

Alexa sighed.

"Casey came to see me yesterday to ask me to put in a good word with you about Seth. I can't believe he forgot his cane. I guess I'll have to get Sydney to return it to him," she lied.

"Casey came about Seth? Did Seth put him up to that?" Jenna asked, swallowing hard at her embarrassment.

Alexa shook her head. "No. That didn't seem to be the case to me. Casey was very nervous the whole time he was here and my impression was Seth didn't know about it. I told him you wouldn't be affected by my opinion because you'd heard the same song and dance apology for months from Seth."

"I can see why Casey would want to help Seth, but it's just—it's over between us. I'm clear about that now," Jenna said, studying her hands.

Alexa looked at her daughter's bent head. Jenna was probably working on making it true, but didn't seem to be over the man yet. Her actions told a different story.

"I wasn't planning to keep Casey's visit from you, honey. I was going to tell you eventually but probably would have waited for a bit if you hadn't found the cane. Frankly, it's a relief to see you marginally happy for once," Alexa said.

"Well, I'm not exactly happy, but definitely less miserable than I was spending every day trying to figure out what was wrong between me and Seth. There's nothing worse than wanting someone who doesn't feel the same way about you. How did you ever stand it with Daddy?" Jenna asked.

"It hurt and I didn't handle it well. Letting it go for real and moving on is a better answer. Promise me if someone genuinely interests you, you'll give it a chance at least. Don't let the thing with Seth keep you from dating or finding love," Alexa told her.

Jenna lifted her chin and nodded. She hadn't always thought her mother did the right things, but her intentions were right. Her mother had never settled for marrying a man she hadn't completely loved.

"Let's make a deal then. I won't stop looking if you don't. You deserve to find love too, Mama. When was the last time you took a chance?" Jenna asked.

Alexa laughed softly, thinking of the man currently hiding in her office restroom that she'd almost undressed just minutes ago. "I'll spare you the details for now, but let's just say I've been taking more chances lately."

"Good. I know I used to give you a hard time about dating lots of guys, but I truly don't want you to be alone. I can't remember the last time I even saw you with a man at all," Jenna commented.

Alexa got up and walked to her daughter to give her another hug. "It means a lot to me you feel that way, honey. I hope you find happiness, too."

Jenna stood and laughed bitterly. "Well, don't be worrying about me. I just wanted to say hi since I'd been gone so long. I just need to use your restroom, and then I'll head to the office."

"Honey, mine's broken," Alexa lied smoothly, a second time. "Use the one down the hall, okay?"

"Sure. I love you. Call you for dinner soon, okay?" Jenna said, hugging her.

"That would be great. I love you too," Alexa replied, hugging her in return.

When Jenna had gone, Alexa closed her office door and locked it again. Then she went to the restroom and knocked softly on the door.

Casey unlocked it and stepped out into the office. He smiled at the sparkle in Alexa's eyes.

"I can't believe I lied to my daughter for you," Alexa said to him. She saw Casey was completely dressed again and frowned, chastising herself for even noticing.

"You didn't lie. Not really," Casey denied. "The only outright lie I heard was that the restroom was broken."

"Did you hear everything we said?" Alexa asked, perturbed.

"Enough to want to know the story about Jenna's father and why he didn't want you back," Casey said honestly, deciding prying was not a bad way to get information, even though it was rude as hell.

"His disinterest wasn't about me, but her father did leave me for someone else. It hurt at the time and I handled it poorly," she said. "That's most of the story."

Casey snorted. "When you kissed me and put your hands on me, I was ready to drag you to the floor. I can't imagine any man not wanting you, much less leaving you for another woman."

Alexa sighed, not really wanting to tell Casey the whole truth, but not seeing a way around it. Protecting the people involved from additional judgment was a long time habit. When Paul left, he continued to be discreet so even the press hadn't known the whole truth.

Well, if Casey said anything ugly, she'd just boot him out of her life.

"Jenna's father didn't leave me for another woman. He left me for a man," Alexa said reluctantly.

Casey just stared at her in absolute shock, trying to understand how a man could trade a gorgeous woman like Alexa for a man. It was beyond his understanding, though he knew it happened.

Alexa noticed Casey's shock, but no judgment, so she decided to tell him a bit more.

"Her father's relationship with me—our marriage—was his last attempt at living the way his family wanted him to live. The problem was I loved him even though he couldn't feel the same about me. It took me years and a lot of men to give up the fantasy that Jenna's father might one day change his mind. You could say I succumbed to the fantasy of trying to convert a homosexual partner into a straight one. It didn't work."

Casey walked to her and put his hands on her shoulders.

"I'm sorry, Alexa," he said, meaning it. "I don't understand it, but I'm sorry you loved someone who didn't feel the same about you. It would have hurt like hell if Susan hadn't loved me back."

Alexa shrugged under his hands. "It was a long time ago, and it doesn't hurt anymore."

But she didn't resist when Casey gathered her into his arms for a comforting hug that held a great deal of sympathy and understanding. It was just as potent as his earlier embrace full of lust and longing. As Casey let her go, he kissed her temple, rendering her speechless with the friendliness of the gesture.

The man was far more complex than you'd ever guess looking at him. Crude one minute, sensitive the next—that was Casey Carter. Again Alexa felt like she couldn't keep up.

"Come on," Casey told her, turning her toward the door. "Since tonight was my idea, wings and beer are on me. You can buy next time."

Alexa laughed. "Sure you don't just want to go home with me? We could rock each other's world for a while and forget the hard knocks of our past."

"Again, the offer is really tempting, and I want you—*a lot*," Casey said, retrieving his cane. "But I can wait a little longer for you to at least like me at little in return. When the time comes for us to be together, I'm planning to wear you out. You're going to walk funny for a week afterwards."

Alexa rolled her eyes at the crude expression. "Really? *Walk funny for week?* How charming. You think that's appealing to me?"

Casey laughed, enjoying her consternation over his crude language.

"Want to go another round up against the wall and see if I'm right?" he asked.

"Not with your other threats hanging over my head. I might be tempted to hurt you, and not in a good way. Are you going to think less of me if I have a glass of red wine instead of beer with my wings?" Alexa asked him.

"Probably not," Casey said easily, again noting how serious she was in her reply to him. "Depends on how many wings you eat."

"I may surprise you," Alexa told him. "I have a big appetite."

"Lucky me," Casey said smiling broadly.

They walked out of Alexa's office and down the hall arguing about which restaurant in town made the best hot wings. When they reached Sydney's desk, Casey was glad to see Sydney had no problem showing shock at the sight of them together.

"Casey snuck in to see me. I had to hide him in the restroom while Jenna was here," Alexa told Sydney. "That's why the door was locked."

"He snuck in to see you?" Sydney asked, pretending to be surprised about Casey's appearance when he was more surprised at the easy way Alexa was talking to the man.

And Sydney was even more curious about the flush on Alexa's face and the twinkle in her eye.

"I'll have to be more careful about the length of my bathroom breaks in the future," Sydney said dryly.

"It's okay," Alexa said, smiling. "I'd have tossed him out myself if needed. We had some things to discuss. We're going out to eat now. Can you attend the marketing meeting for me?"

"Sure. Going out to eat?" Sydney asked, eyebrows lifting as he looked at Casey, who was trying hard not to grin. Casey just shook his head from side-to-side a little, the universal sign for *don't ask any more questions.*

"I lost a bet," Alexa told Sydney. "So I have to go eat hot wings. See you tomorrow."

"Sure," Sydney said, as they turned their backs and headed toward the door. "Uh, Casey? You might want to tuck your shirt into the back of your pants before you leave."

Casey's hand flew to the back of his jeans, but he felt nothing out of place. He had been ninety percent sure he'd tucked everything back in earlier. It was the ten percent of unsure layered with make-out guilt that had his gaze swinging to Sydney, who just laughed.

"Yeah. Well, good thing I didn't put any money against you, Carter. I hate to lose a bet," Sydney said, turning back to his work as if he had better things to do with his time.

Casey made a mental note never to try to get one over on Sydney Banes. The man was sharp enough to work for any intelligence agency.

He was chastised a little as he stood by Alexa in the hallway waiting for the elevator.

"Was I just grilled about what happened between us? And did I fail when I actually checked my pants?" Casey asked when they were in the elevator alone.

Alexa sighed and smiled at Casey, thinking he was more charming when he was nervous than in caveman mode.

"Sydney's a little protective of me. Don't be surprised if you're investigated in the next week. He investigates his own clients before he lets them buy clothes at his shop. I can't convince him to take anyone at face value," Alexa said.

"My clearance is good. He won't find anything on me the Naval Investigative Service didn't find. I'm more worried what he would do if he knew for sure I made a pass at you," Casey said, making her laugh.

"Let's not worry about that yet," Alexa said in reply, not wanting Casey to know that Sydney would be thrilled. "I'm the one in trouble, not you. I'm going to get cross-examined tomorrow morning."

Casey leaned on his cane and studied the elevator ceiling, then swung his gaze to Alexa, looking as serious as he could manage. "I know at least eleven ways to kill a man, Alexa. Some even look like accidents. How much do you like Sydney?"

Alexa crossed her arms and raised one eyebrow, pretending to consider the offer. "Wow. You'd do that for me? I'm flattered."

She uncrossed one arm, and pretended to study her manicure as she sighed. "Unfortunately, I invested in Sydney's business. So he owes me money and I'd like to see him live long enough to pay me back—with interest."

Casey shrugged as if he was more than a little disappointed with the information. "If you change your mind tomorrow, just give me a call. I have the afternoon free."

Alexa giggled and Casey grinned. He started to move toward her, intending to kiss the smile off her face, but the elevator stopped in the basement garage.

"I guess I should have asked if you brought a car here," Alexa said. Casey scrambled her circuits, and she wasn't thinking clearly enough to be polite.

"Took a taxi," Casey told her.

Alexa looked at him, her gaze heading south to his legs

and the cane. "Can you climb a little without hurting?"

Casey tilted his head and studied her, wondering what Alexa was getting at with the question. She held out an arm, pressing a button on the key fob in her hand. A giant green pick-up truck on the first row of the garage blinked its lights.

"You drive a pick-up truck?" Casey asked, his shocked gaze traveling back and forth between the woman and the vehicle.

Alexa drew her lips together in a pout. "Well, today I am. I have other vehicles, but I—I like the truck sometimes. Getting blackmailed and having to chauffeur a date weren't in my plans for the day."

"The truck is great. I love Fords. I guess I expected—"

"—a girlie car?" Alexa suggested.

"How bad is it going to count against me if I say yes?" Casey asked, trying not to laugh.

Alexa shook her head in sad disbelief. Despite his age, Casey Carter was as stereotypical in his views of women and vehicles as every other man she'd ever known.

"Men," Alexa said with a growl, striding purposefully to the truck and leaving Casey to follow slowly behind her.

After Casey climbed into the cab with her, Alexa turned to him with eyes bluer than he'd ever dreamed of seeing. Sometimes her beauty was mesmerizing. He could have just looked at her all night.

"So here's the deal, I don't drive as well as Regina does, but I'm proficient and I love cars. When you see my garage, you'll understand." Alexa fastened her seatbelt and tucked her purse between the seats.

Casey continued to look around the truck, surprise still in his expression when his gaze landed on Alexa again, who was watching him closely.

"I guess if you can wait, then I can wait too," she said finally, turning the key in the ignition.

"Wait for what?" Casey asked, wondering why he wasn't tracking what she said with more sense. It was the truck and her, okay, and her driving a truck as if she'd been driving one forever. It didn't compute with what he knew of her.

"I guess if you can wait for me to like you back, I can wait for you to see the real me. Men look at my face and think they know all there is to know about me. We'll see if you still like me as much when you know what kind of woman I really am," Alexa warned him, seriousness coating every word.

"Sounds like a threat," Casey replied, studying her as she pulled the truck out into traffic.

"Maybe it is," Alexa offered. "I usually feel the urge to protect myself. With you, I want to rub your nose into the secrets of my life and let you get a good smell. I don't know why. You seem to bring out the worst in me."

Casey laughed, pleased to hear her admit he affected her, even if she did view it as a negative.

"Sounds like fun," Casey said, his brown eyes dancing with humor.

Alexa thought about the two cars and two SUVs still tucked nicely in their garages back home. Casey didn't know her, not really, hadn't even scratched the outer layer of the woman she'd made of herself. He had no idea. But he would, she decided, before they hit the sheets. She would see to it.

Then they both would see if that cocky *walk funny for a week* threat held anything solid. Men more macho than Casey had gone limp with her when they realized she was more successful then they could ever dream about being.

When Alexa left her thoughts and glanced at Casey, he was on his cell sending a text.

"Don't tell Seth about our—*date*," she pleaded, stumbling over the term. "Let's wait a little bit before we make this public. You may find you don't like me after all and we'd have stirred everyone up for nothing."

"Seth already knows I'm interested in you," Casey said. "But I'll be discreet if you want. I'll tell him I'm doing some errands and will be home late. He's usually too busy to miss me, but I check in with him anyway. It just seems like the polite thing to do."

"You're a good man, Casey Carter," Alexa said, sighing. "It's a shame you don't know anything about good hot wings. Since I'm driving, I'm picking the restaurant tonight. If you don't like the wings there, I'll even pick up the tab for dinner."

"I won't lie to spare your feelings, Alexa. I decided that when I was hiding in the restroom this afternoon. I want you to trust what I say. So if the wings stink, I'm going to tell you," Casey warned.

Alexa snorted and drove them to where she knew the best hot wings in town waited.

What she omitted saying was the restaurant belonged to her, or at least mostly belonged to her. Thanks to Paul, she had investments in many businesses in Falls Church.

She decided to save that little tidbit of information for dessert.

Chapter 7

Even though Alexa, Regina, and Lauren had been having dinner on Thursdays at Lucinda's for at least six years, Alexa still let the hostess walk her to their usual table. It was just proper Virginia etiquette, even if you were part owner of the restaurant.

Regina was already waiting, but Alexa knew the always-punctual Lauren wasn't far behind them.

"Better order two drinks at once," Alexa said to Regina, who was talking intimately with the waiter. "I've got a long story to tell."

"Will I need a drink, too?" demanded Lauren.

She had walked to the table from the direction of the restroom, sporting crisp denim jeans, a teal tank top, and carrying her gym bag. Alexa smiled at Lauren's casual attire, which she saved for wearing around them. Formal and proper at all times was her family's mantra about appearance, which Alexa had learned meant drab and ugly clothes for Lauren.

Today Lauren looked relaxed and more attractive than usual. Alexa thought it was a shame she still hung out the "not interested" sign. It had been many years since her divorce.

"I'll have a mineral water and glass of white wine," Lauren told the waiter. His eyes moved from Regina's face only to become glued to the impressive cleavage peeking from Lauren's top.

Alexa couldn't stifle her laugh. The waiter never even looked at Lauren's face. It took a while, but he finally pulled his eyes away from Lauren's cleavage to Alexa.

"A glass of the house red and ice water," Alexa told him, gracing him with a dazzling smile that momentarily froze his pen. Lauren wasn't the only one oozing sex appeal today. Hot wings and good male company after a long dry spell were working some magic on her. The make-out session against her office wall hadn't hurt either.

Regina laughed and shook her head sadly when the waiter finally walked away. "I guess he doesn't like redheads," she said sadly.

Then Regina looked at both Lauren and Alexa with equal parts fire and amusement. "You'd think by now I should know not to flirt with the two of you around."

"For pity's sake Regina, he's a *child*," Lauren protested. Regina's candid comments still embarrassed her, no matter how much she tried not to let them.

"For your information, Ron is twenty-five and an Economics major at Stratford. He is also practice, my dear Saint McCarthy," Regina said with a grin. "And the subconscious reason you're wearing a top advertising your womanly wares."

Alexa watched her friends engaging in the typical debate over what Regina considered friendly flirting and Lauren considered lewdness. Today their sparring didn't amuse her as much as usual. Instead, she found herself wondering where her opinions lay in the matter.

She was still obsessing about what Casey could do to her in bed that would make her walk funny afterwards, which was definitely a worry Lauren would have. But since so many wonderful, wicked things came immediately to mind, and Alexa had already begun putting her own spin on them the more she fantasized, she guessed she was more like Regina.

Pulling her wandering mind away from her thoughts of Casey, Alexa realized both her friends were looking at her in stunned silence.

"That must have been some good daydream," Lauren said to Alexa, sighing with envy. "Your face flushed and your eyes dilated. Are you feeling okay?"

Regina laughed huskily, saying nothing, eyes lit with wicked humor. Alexa wasn't surprised when Regina's sexy laugh finally snagged all of Ron's attention as he set drinks in front of them. He smiled and winked at Regina before he left the table, barely nodding to her and Lauren.

And wicked Regina gave him another sexy laugh in return.

"Score one for the redhead after all," Alexa conceded, lifting her wine to salute Regina. "Zero for the flashy brunette and the silver blond with the perky boobs."

Alexa's teasing had Lauren flushing scarlet, but laughing right along with them because it was funny—and true.

"Hey," Lauren complained, "I work hard to keep the girls perky."

Regina reached over and patted Lauren's hand. "And it works, darling. My girls haven't been perky in years. Now Alexa could give you some competition if she still strutted her stuff like she used to."

Lauren, recognizing a segue when she heard one, leaned her head on her hand to study Alexa's smile with new interest. She waited for Regina to start harassing Alexa. It was her favorite sporting event.

"So tell us, Alexa," Regina began, searching carefully for words that wouldn't send Lauren running to the restroom, "have you been seeing your boy-toy lately?"

"Actually, Casey came to see me at the office twice this week," Alexa said, looking away from their interested gazes.

"And . . .?" Lauren prompted, when Alexa drifted off looking lost in memories again.

With thoughts of Casey short-circuiting her brain, Alexa had to work hard to focus on the conversation.

"The first time he visited we talked about Jenna and Seth breaking up, but then he ended up asking me to dinner—or rather tricking me into it. I actually had a good time talking to him, but then I made the mistake of kissing him goodbye. Well, it wasn't a real kiss, just a lip brush, and I only did it because he made me feel sorry for him. I told him I was too old for him. Casey said he was—that he hadn't—that I—."

Alexa stopped trying to talk and simply swore. Not being able to put it in words even for her dearest friends was not a good sign. Seeing Regina and Lauren hanging on her every word, their drinks forgotten, Alexa sighed.

"Anyway, Casey came back to my office again the next day, and somehow snuck by Sydney, insisting he and I—that we kiss each other just to see what would happen. So. . ."

"Wait! *Please.* I need an intermission before you get to the good part," interrupted Regina desperately. "I need food. Between the alcohol and the titillation, my head is spinning."

Alexa laughed at the strain on Regina's face.

Lauren sighed in disappointment at having to wait to hear the good part, but knew she might as well study the menu. Both Alexa and Regina took their food very seriously.

"Well, it's been a while since one of us had this much to share," Regina explained. "I don't want to miss anything."

After ordering dinner, Alexa ate more than half of hers before she resumed her story.

"So back to my story—when Casey came back the second day, he said we should kiss to find out if there was anything worth pursuing. I guess he sort of blackmailed me into it or dared me. I still can't figure out why I agreed. I started out not really participating, but eventually he—well, he noticed I wasn't really doing much. I—" Alexa paused, trying to think how to describe the moment she kissed him back and lost her grip on reality.

"The next thing I know I was ripping off his clothes and we were heading to the floor. At least we were until Casey changed his mind and stopped."

"Changed his mind?" Regina and Lauren asked in unison, forks pausing midair.

"He wants to be friends first," Alexa stated flatly, frowning at her plate.

Regina and Lauren looked at each other. Lauren

recovered first.

"Well, that's nice isn't it?" Lauren asked Alexa, who gave her an *Are you kidding?* look in return.

Regina watched Alexa frown at her half-eaten dinner. "Why do you suppose he wants to be friends first, Alexa?" She had her educated suspicions, but Alexa was in no place to hear Casey was already starting to fall in love with her.

Alexa shrugged in reply. "Casey said he didn't want to be just a one-night stand—relatively speaking. He kept telling me over and over that he liked me, which is a joke because he doesn't even know me."

When Regina said nothing, Alexa told them the rest. "I took him to Jean's place for hot wings last night. I was going to tell him over dessert about owning the place, just to see how he reacted to the news, but in the end I couldn't do it. It felt too mean to flaunt my wealth trying to scare him away."

"Are you planning on telling him how successful you are before or after you sleep with him?" Regina asked.

"Who says I'm going to sleep with him?" Alexa protested.

Lauren let out a laugh, but winced when Alexa frowned at her. "Sorry. I thought you were making a joke."

And *that* made Regina laugh because Alexa was fooling herself if she thought she wasn't going to end up in bed with Casey Carter. Even Lauren could tell. Casey was pursuing Alexa despite the family complications of Jenna and Seth, and had somehow charmed Sydney in the process of trying to woo her.

The fact that he wanted their sex life to be on his terms was intriguing, but it didn't worry Regina. She knew Alexa would change the situation as soon as she stopped fighting her feelings for the man.

"Alexa, I bet you didn't even sleep last night for thinking about being with Casey," Regina said kindly, sympathetic to anyone who struggled with desire.

Alexa didn't answer immediately. She picked up the wine and drank.

"I've wanted other men I didn't end up sleeping with," she finally said quietly.

Regina and Lauren exchanged a look.

"I think you should go for it," Lauren said, waving her hand to emphasize. "It's been a long time since you had a man in your life, Alexa."

"This from a woman who hasn't had a sexual relationship with a man in what? Six or seven years?" Alexa asked, incredulous it was Lauren encouraging her to indulge.

Lauren lifted a shoulder and waved a hand in the air. "I have a good instinct about Casey. Any guy who wants to be friends before he sleeps with you is at least worth getting to know. I mean, aren't you curious why he wants to be friends first? That's not typical."

Regina laughed, totally delighted with Lauren. For the first time in a while, she was hopeful for both her friends, and maybe even for herself.

"Now don't faint, Alexa—but, well I'm agreeing with Lauren on this one. Casey sounds intriguing, definitely worth getting to know. Of course, it's understandable if you think you'd be more comfortable with someone older."

Regina used her toe to nudge Lauren's leg under the table. "I mean, if you want a man more your own age, I guess Lauren or I could set you up with someone who could take your mind off the fire Casey seems to have lit in you."

Lauren picked up the hint without missing a beat. "I know several men, and they certainly wouldn't be intimidated by your success—at least not much."

Alexa looked between the two women, irritation in her eyes, posture, and the set of her mouth. She tossed back her hair and glared until both of them laughed.

"This is only about Casey," Alexa said tightly.

"You know, it's good to see you heated up about a guy again. I've been worried about you," Regina went back to her food, happy at least one of her friends was taking chances and really living.

Lauren leaned forward to Alexa, not able to hold in her excitement about it all. "We can see you have it bad for Casey, honey. It's all over you. Just do him, and then come back and tell us how great it was. Regina and I can date vicariously through you."

Regina dropped her fork and had to scramble to keep it on the table.

"*Do him*? Did you just tell Alexa to *do him*?" Regina burst out laughing at Lauren's enthusiastic nod. "Wow, I'm speechless, Lauren."

"Alexa is inspiring me," Lauren said, dreamy-eyed over imagining Casey demanding he and Alexa become friends. It was such a romantic thing for a guy to do, especially a guy who was much younger than the woman he wanted.

"*Do him*," Alexa repeated the phrase, all too easily imagining herself being with Casey. Her frustration level grew with every fantasy she allowed herself.

She came back to reality again when Regina and Lauren's laughter became loud enough to draw the attention of everyone sitting around them. Her face flushed as she realized she had drifted away on them like she had with Sydney. Fantasizing about Casey was addictive.

"Fine," she said. "I don't think I have a choice anyway. Just cross your fingers Jenna doesn't find out and kill me."

Chapter 8

While Alexa was having dinner across town, Casey was in the kitchen of Seth's condo loading the dishwasher for the third time, trying to escape the crowded living room and the press of bodies everywhere. Though Seth had said he'd simply forgotten to tell him about the cocktail party, Casey suspected the oversight was probably intentional given the much higher ratio of females to males in attendance tonight.

Several of the older women had wandered into the kitchen, perched at the breakfast bar and talked to him for a bit. They were nice enough, but none were Alexa Ranger, so Casey had a difficult time paying attention for long.

Casey didn't feel bad about his lack of interest. He hadn't seen Seth hanging on anyone he'd invited either, and he damn well knew it was because of Jenna. Why would Seth think Casey would be tempted? Neither of them worked like that.

Tired of being social, Casey retrieved a humidor from the pantry and withdrew a solitary cigar from it. The polished mahogany humidor had been the last gift Susan had bought for him. Though she hadn't liked the cigars, his wife had wanted him to have the beautiful cigar keeper.

Casey clipped one end of his last cigar, clamped it between his teeth, and lovingly tucked the humidor back into the pantry.

Slipping out the door off the kitchen, he walked away from the private patio to a quieter area of the condo's shared courtyard. There was a wooden bench in a gravel circle under a magnolia tree about to bloom. He sank down on the bench, grateful to get the pressure off his hip.

Casey lit the cigar lovingly, sighing in ecstasy with the first puff. He hadn't been there three minutes when Seth walked through the darkness to sit beside him.

Casey looked at him through a grayish-brown cloud of pungent smoke, grinning when Seth wrinkled his nose and swiped at the smoke with his hand.

"That's a disgusting habit," Seth pronounced. "I can't believe Susan never made you quit."

"Yes. It is disgusting. I'm using it to discourage the women you keep sending to me," Casey said, flicking the ash off into the gravel around the bench.

"What's wrong with them? Didn't you meet anyone you liked?" Seth leaned back and put an arm up on the bench.

Casey knew Seth meant well, that he probably didn't understand, or at least was pretending not to get it.

"Is there anyone here you'd go out with?" Casey challenged, taking another deep pull on the cigar.

Seth pulled his arm away and stood. "No. There isn't, but that's different."

"How so?" Casey asked. "Hell, Alexa and Jenna are practically twins."

Seth frowned.

"You can't seriously be interested in a woman who's over a decade older than you," he said, running his hand through his hair.

"You know last month when I met Alexa at one of these parties you like to throw? I shook her hand and got an instant hard-on. It was the first time a woman affected me like that since Susan. Even if you set aside the fact that Alexa is gorgeous, she'd have to be butt-ugly before I would pass on the chance to figure out why I had that strong reaction on our first meeting," Casey told him. "I realize her being Jenna's mother makes it a little complicated for you."

Seth nodded. "Well, it would be complicated if I was still seeing Jenna, but I guess that's not the case. I get that you have an unexplainable sex thing for her mother, and God knows, you're a damn pit bull when you have your mind set on something. Whatever—I just came to tell you that you don't have to hide out here in the dark and smoke. Everyone came by just for drinks. They'll all be leaving shortly."

"I'm fine," Casey said. "Enjoy your guests. I do appreciate the thought."

Seth started walking back toward the patio, head down, hands in pockets. Casey thought he looked like a disappointed kid.

"Seth," Casey called out. When Seth turned back, he asked, "Are we good?"

Seth nodded his head, lifted a hand, and headed back to the house at a faster clip.

Casey sighed into the darkness and closed his eyes. When he opened them a couple minutes later, Alexa Ranger was walking toward him with a frown on her face. She was wearing her usual jeans, paired this time with a silky white shirt that practically glowed in the dark. She looked like a sexy girl next door. Casey's body said hello before she even got close to him.

"That's a disgusting habit," Alexa told him in greeting, taking a seat beside him as far away from the cigar smoke as she could get.

Casey sighed again. "So I've been told. How did you find me?"

"Seth showed me how to find you," Alexa said. "He didn't seem very surprised to see me."

"Probably because we just had a discussion about you a few minutes ago," Casey said, flicking ash into the gravel again, taking another drag from the cigar.

"Would it have anything to do with the number of women I had to swim through to get out here?" Alexa asked, crossing her arms.

"It had to do with me telling him I wasn't interested in anyone but you," he said, reaching out a hand and poking her in the side with his finger until she uncrossed her arms.

"Maybe Seth has the right idea about the age range you need to shop in, for female companionship," Alexa said in irritation, as Casey just laughed.

"Too bad. I've found all the companionship I'm going to want for a while," Casey said firmly, "but it will have to wait until some other time. Even Susan would never let me near her when I smoked one of these."

"Your wife was a smart woman," Alexa said, smiling for the first time since she sat down. No woman in her right mind would tolerate the cigar stink.

"Next time I marry, I'm having a cigar tolerance agreement put in the contract," Casey informed her.

"You better go back in the living room and look for someone dumb then. That search may take you a few years. Hurry. You better get started tonight," Alexa said to him, almost laughing now herself.

Casey sighed heavily, the third time he had done so since sitting on the bench.

"Okay, true confessions. I do like cigars, but gave them up when I was injured. Tonight it was the only thing I could think of to keep the women away," Casey explained. "Before the cigar, I was forced to load the dishwasher multiple times just to avoid engaging in boring conversations."

Alexa's laugh echoed through the courtyard. "Am I supposed to feel sorry for you because you had to be social and make conversation?"

"No, you're supposed to be impressed I'm not interested in other women," Casey said, peering intently at her through the smoke. "I'm interested in you, Alexa."

Alexa swore, a nasty habit Casey seemed to bring out of her more frequently. "You know, I have done absolutely nothing to be alluring to you. If I wanted to hold your attention, it would not be difficult to do. You wouldn't be able to look at another woman if I—oh hell, Casey. Flirting with you is not why I came here. I came to tell you something I didn't tell you last night because I didn't want to ruin the fun evening we had."

Casey smiled around his cigar. He'd had a good time last night, too.

"I'm listening," he said, puffing on the cigar.

"I own the restaurant where we ate last night," she said dully, crossing her arms again.

Casey thought about it for a moment, and then laughed. "Okay. I admitted you were right about the wings there being the best in town, and I paid for dinner as agreed. What more do you want from me, woman?"

When Alexa looked off into the dark, the genuine worry on her face did start to concern him. "Just spill it. Put what you're thinking out there. Let's see how bad it is."

"I also own more than half of the restaurant where I had dinner tonight with Regina and Lauren," she said, her gaze finding his in the dark.

Alexa watched Casey puff on the cigar as he continued to listen.

"So it's like this—I own interests in several businesses around Falls Church, including Sydney's. All that isn't even counting my own business, which now is at least three separate businesses rolled into one. I own multiple vehicles: two cars, two SUVs, and the pick-up you saw. My house is not a mansion, but it is a fortress for my private life. I have a security gate and only give the code to family and very, very close friends. I'm not Donald Trump, but I'm doing pretty well for myself."

Casey took his cigar out of mouth and studied it, not meeting her eyes. He had assumed Alexa was more wealthy than he was, but hadn't really given much thought to what it meant to them dating. His interest in her was more basic than what either of them owned or did for a living. On some level, Casey felt sure that Alexa had to know how it was between them, know he was interested in her just for her. She just didn't trust it. Maybe hadn't been able to trust it with a man before.

"So what? Do you think I'm interested in your money more than your other assets?" Casey asked flat out. He wanted to laugh when she swore again using the f-word.

"I never gave it a thought," Alexa said angrily.

"Me neither," Casey replied, rolling his cigar and putting it back in for one final puff. "I'm too busy plotting how to get into your pants, especially after you almost got into mine. Now I admit to worrying about exceeding your previous sexual experiences. In fact, I'm wrestling like hell with that one."

Alexa swore again, using every word she knew.

"Okay. Now I'm confused," Casey said, bending to grind the cigar butt out on the metal strap holding the bench in place. He was trying really hard not to laugh. "Are you trying to scare me away or are you telling me about your wealth to make me want you more?"

Alexa lifted a hand to inspect her French manicure in the dark. "You said you liked me, Carter. I guess I'm telling you the various truths about my life to see what's going to change that."

"Hard to say," Casey said with a shrug. "Your money situation certainly doesn't change what I plan to do to you once I get you into bed." He studied her in the dark. "Does it change your attraction to me that I'm a retired military man who only makes thirty-five thousand a year?"

"I have never needed a man for his money," Alexa said, her eyes hot.

"Then what do you need from a man, Alexa?" Casey asked, enjoying the fire he'd started.

Alexa stood, straining the shirt buttons with her breasts as she tucked her hands in her back pockets. She walked away from the bench to pace.

"I don't know what I need anymore. I haven't wanted anyone in so long I forgot what it was I used to want so badly." She looked at the ground instead of at Casey.

"Yet despite your memory lapse, you do want me?" Casey asked, trying to make it sound like a question, instead of just telling her how it was.

He had stood too long in the kitchen, so he had to lean forward to push himself to his feet. His limp was fairly pronounced as he walked to where she paced.

"Yes, I want you." Alexa couldn't sound happy about it because she wasn't. "But I've wanted plenty of men I haven't slept with in my life, Casey. I don't know if it's worth taking that step with you."

Casey held out a hand. Alexa looked at it for a moment, and then took it reluctantly. Just like the first time there was a tingle of awareness leaping between them as they touched.

"Do you feel *that*, Alexa?" he asked, squeezing and shaking her hand. "I do. I feel it. I felt it the first time I touched you, and I fought it for a bit myself. You have my word that that awareness I have every time we touch is the main reason I want you."

Alexa groaned in defeat and stepped into him, putting her arms around him for a hug. He felt really good to her, and she almost told him.

"You reek," she said instead, burrowing her face in his shirt and running her hands over his hips, sighing at the solid muscles flexing under her hands. If he didn't have the cane, you'd never know the man had a physical weakness at all.

Casey pulled her tight against him and felt her body fit along the planes of his as if they had been hugging for years.

"Sorry I reek," he said casually, kissing her temple. "If I had known you were coming by, I'd have skipped the cigar."

They stood there for a long time, just hugging in the dark. "Alexa?"

"Yes," she answered.

"I have a thing tomorrow night at a VA organization in Arlington where I volunteer. We're supposed to bring our families. Would you like to go as my date? It's military formal, so I have to wear my dress blues. You can wear any dinner dress. Lots of women wear black."

"Don't you want to take Seth?" she asked.

"He has plans. I wasn't going to go this year, but—well, I just thought if you went with me, I might go after all," Casey told her.

Alexa pressed her face into his neck. Long moments passed, and then she finally nodded. She kissed his neck and whispered okay.

"Come on. I'll walk you to the door. You can help fight the women off. I didn't bring my cane outside," Casey joked.

But when they got inside, no one was there. Alexa said good-bye at the door, walking quickly away. Casey watched her hips until she disappeared around the corner of the hallway.

Tired, he walked to his bedroom and picked up his favorite picture of him and Susan in its silver frame.

"You'd like her," he said to the image of the woman who had been his friend and lover for most of his adult life. "I like her a lot. I hope you're okay with it."

Then he walked to the dresser, opened a drawer, and tucked the picture and the past away.

Another woman filled his thoughts tonight, a woman who had come to him and who cared about what he thought about her. He went to bed smiling and happier than he'd been in a long time.

Chapter 9

The spring lingerie pre-launch was Saturday afternoon, so early Friday morning Sydney was sipping coffee while overseeing the mannequin bodies and busts being scantily dressed in the latest styles. Most of Alexa's designers and marketing staff rushed around helping. Various textures and colors of female lingerie covered every available surface.

Through it all, Sydney smiled and sipped his full-fat, half-and-half, mocha cappuccino, happy with the world in general. He would be the first to admit that he enjoyed the drama and last minute rush of the buyer open houses, each and every time one happened.

He had just taken in a mouthful of coffee when he noticed the silence and sudden motionlessness in the open room. All eyes seemed to be focused behind him, so he turned too, promptly choking and spitting coffee on the newly polished wood floor. Someone rushed over with paper towels as Sydney fought to get his breath back.

"Mercy, Alexa," he said, while one of the women slapped him on the back as he choked. "I forgot you could pack so much punch."

"Sydney, that's twice this week you've choked because of me," Alexa said, walking into the room on three-inch black platform heels. The shoes sent a person's eyes soaring up silky legs that definitely did not end at the hem of the short black dress a few inches above her knees. "What? I can't wear a dress anymore? I have a date tonight and no time to go home and change."

Sydney motioned to the dress with his hand. "A date with Casey Carter?" he squeaked.

Alexa nodded.

"He's going to have heart failure when he sees you. I'm gay, and you stopped my heart anyway. Woman, you're still as stunning as ever," he said, motioning to the posters on the walls of her modeling her early line of panties and bras.

Alexa laughed and put her arms around him, kissing both cheeks.

"You're so good for me, Sydney," she told him, squeezing his arms before she turned him loose.

So okay, maybe she had noticed others sneaking some envious looks at her even though they had returned to their tasks. It had been some time since she'd dressed up for work, or anything else for that matter. There was no denying she felt good about herself today.

She loved wearing the shirts and jeans to work, but admitted she had enjoyed the surprise on their faces to see her dressed up. She'd just gotten out of the habit of looking *really good*, that's all.

"I'm going to my office. Lauren is stopping by to check out the date dress at lunch. Can you call in something from Stanley's for us?" she asked, heading to her office.

"Absolutely," Sydney said, watching her saunter away, hips swaying to a beat playing only in her head.

"Holy moly, the model is back," Sydney said to himself when Alexa was out of earshot.

And for that blessing, he would cancel the background search on Casey Carter as soon as he got settled again at his desk.

At five thirty that afternoon, Casey walked into the waiting area of Alexa's business wearing his dress blues. He took his time tucking his white hat under his arm and hooking his cane on his wrist.

"Hey, Sydney, how's it going?" Casey said in greeting.

Sydney raised his head and blinked a couple of times as he looked at Casey. Standing, he held a finger up. "Wait. Stay right there. I don't want to miss this. You owe me for letting you in to see her yesterday, so today I get to watch."

Casey held out his free hand, palm up. "What are you talking about?"

Sydney pressed the intercom. "Alexa, your date is here. He's keeping me company until you're free."

Sydney motioned for Casey to follow him at the same time he pressed a button to open the sliding door to the display room.

"Let me show you some posters of Alexa when she was a model," Sydney said, thinking Casey needed to be prepared. He was fighting laughter already anticipating the surprise in store for both of them.

"Sure," Casey said, shrugging as he followed Sydney into an open display area filled with female busts and mannequins all dressed in underwear. On the wall, displayed on several giant twelve-foot posters, was Alexa Ranger in her underwear—literally *her* underwear, since she'd designed them.

"Wow," Casey said, no other words coming to mind. Alexa had certainly been a stunner when those were taken.

Sydney grinned at the way Casey was perusing each poster. It brought back memories of watching his brother look longingly at Playboy centerfolds.

When he heard Alexa's heels clicking in the hallway, he made sure Casey's back was to the door. Feeling a bit like a director in his own movie, Sydney was actually vibrating with anticipation.

Alexa waited until she was in the room to speak. "There you are. Why—"

When Casey turned around, Alexa forgot what she was saying as her purse slid from suddenly limp fingers to the floor. It was the white hat under his arm, the pressed uniform, the way he looked so—she had no word for it. Handsome didn't even begin to cover it.

When Casey saw Alexa, the cane fell off his wrist bouncing on the wooden floor, and his pristine white hat soon went sliding after it.

"Alexa—" He stumbled a step toward her, then stopped, realizing he had dropped everything.

Sydney caught Casey's arm. "No, no. Here, I got them," Sydney said, swiftly bending and picking up the hat and cane. "Don't wrinkle those pants until you have to."

Handing the hat and cane back to Casey, Sydney's eyes bounced back and forth between them as they simply stared at each other in shock.

Alexa recovered her senses before Casey did, stooped to retrieve her purse, and then walked the remaining distance across the floor to him. In her heels, she looked him levelly in his eyes.

"You make that uniform look good, Carter," she said, hoping she sounded confident and light-hearted, because she wasn't feeling it.

She wanted to throw herself into Casey's arms and cry for all he had given up when he got hurt. Seeing him in his uniform, Alexa suddenly understood what he had been, what he still was in many ways. It was no wonder he missed the military. He was the military, a live walking icon of noble service. Alexa swallowed the urge to cry and smiled instead.

"Do all Marines look as good as you?" she asked, teasing.

Casey only smiled at her flirty question. He was still speechless, lost in the impact of seeing in person what Alexa had tried to explain to him, and teased him about on multiple occasions.

More than just beautiful, she literally had no competition from other women when it came to stunning, mesmerizing allure. The image of Alexa walking toward him in that short black dress, mile-long legs, and sky-high heels was burned into his brain. He'd probably never be able to enjoy looking at another woman again.

"Sorry," he said at last, clearing his throat, and dropping his gaze to her legs. "I'm searching for some compliment to offer you in return, but I think I lost too many brain cells watching you walk across the room to me. What's left is busy wondering what kind of underwear you're wearing under that dress."

"Oh. Oh. I know. I know," Sydney said, dancing with his hand in the air, like an excited kid who knows the right answer to a math question.

Alexa gave Sydney a quelling look. "Shush, drama queen. You've had your fun at our expense." She waved her hand at Sydney in the go-away sign. "I gave you a man already. It's Friday. Go play with him and leave my date alone."

"You used to be a lot more fun when you were younger, Alexa," Sydney said, striding away even as he smacked her lightly on the backside, laughing when she almost fell into Casey.

Casey grinned at Sydney's retreating back.

"Sydney's like a pesky younger brother," he commented softly.

"Something like that," Alexa agreed.

"Did you really give Sydney a man?" Casey asked, offering her his arm. "That's pretty amazing. Was it a perk, like a gold watch for ten years of faithful employee service?"

"More like five years of faithful service. I'll tell you the story when I know you better," Alexa said, hooking her arm through his.

Casey laughed. "I'm not sure I want to hear it. Sometimes ignorance really is bliss. Between the two of us, we're one step away from being a reality talk show host's wet dream."

Alexa snorted as they stepped into the elevator. "You don't even know yet how close that is to being true."

When they got out on the main floor of the building, Casey let go of her arm and took her hand as they walked out the lobby door.

"The only two things I know tonight are how incredibly hot you look and how much fun I'm going to have trying to talk you into bed later. I am so glad I sprang for a limo," Casey said, gesturing to where a driver stood by the open door of a polished white limo.

Alexa looked at him in awe.

"You surprise me, Casey. Every time I turn around, you surprise me."

"Your turn to surprise me back then," Casey said, letting the driver help her inside, while he got the pleasure of taking a good long look at her amazing legs. Good thing he hadn't gotten a good look before she wrapped one around him the other day. He'd have taken her to the floor for sure.

Alexa laughed. "You like surprises, Casey?" she asked.

Casey smiled and nodded yes. "Not that the way you look isn't surprise enough. You look great in jeans and a shirt, but, lady, you look fucking incredible in that dress."

"I know," Alexa said coyly, smiling.

When Casey got in beside her, he reached over and pinched her thigh until she yelped. "You're supposed to say thank you to a compliment, even a crude one."

"Yeah, well men in uniform are supposed to be gentlemen," she countered, laughing. "Pinching is not nice."

"I couldn't be gentle with you tonight if I tried. You're going to have to have that level of control for both of us, babe."

When Casey put a hand on her knee, the heat seared her. Alexa opened her knees slightly and his hand slid down between them and up a little on one thigh. He cupped her leg under the hem of her dress. Alexa bit her bottom lip and looked away from him.

"If you're expecting me to exercise self-control, we're in big trouble. I hope you trust your limo driver."

Casey laughed softly. "You smell like heaven. Is the offer still open to rock each other's world?" he asked, pulling her leg tightly against his, liking the sound of her rapid breathing.

He was so tempted to run his hand all the way up her lovely smooth thigh, to take the edge off her desire for her, to watch it happen as she came apart in his hands.

"Yes," Alexa said, leaning against his arm, inhaling his cologne and wishing they were headed to her house now. "The offer is still open. Tonight. Come home with me. I have to work tomorrow afternoon, but not until two."

Casey moved his hand a little, stroking her knee and just

above it. "Now that I know how busy you are, I'll just take the first week of sex in installments."

He smiled as she pretended to brush lint off his sleeve. They both knew it was just to have an excuse to touch him.

"Still bragging about your sexual abilities? The male ego knows no limits," Alexa declared.

Casey just grinned, thinking about how much he really liked being the object of her flirtatious interest.

Alexa turned her head and spoke softly into his ear.

"I'm wearing a black bustier, black garters, black stockings, and black lace bikini panties that can be ripped off with one hand," she listed, watching the grin fade as his hand tightened almost painfully on her leg.

Alexa inspected her fingernails on the hand she had used moments ago to pet his sleeve, pretending not to notice his new level of body tension. "I thought it was a little too early in the dating game to skip wearing panties," she said matter-of-factly, ignoring the hammering of his heart.

Casey counted to ten. He recited the Marine's Prayer in his head.

Then he made the mistake of staring too long at Alexa pretending to study her nails in the semi-dark of the limo's back seat, as if she hadn't just completely destroyed his peace of mind.

Oh, he knew a dare when he heard it.

There was no other choice but to find out if she was telling him the truth. He just hoped he could control his reaction to finding out.

"Alexa." His throat was so tight with desire all he could manage to say was her name.

Twisting in the seat as much as his injury would allow, he pressed Alexa against the back of it, his mouth urgent and seeking hers, finding hers urgent and seeking in return.

He slid the hand already on her leg up until he felt a garter. He ran fingers over and around the snap, wondering if he could unfasten it without tearing it all to hell. His mouth mated itself to hers until they were both groaning.

Fortunately, a tiny bit of sanity peeked through the lust

for a moment, just enough to let him stop. He cupped Alexa's leg, keeping his thumb stroking the top of the garter.

Alexa had been telling the truth about the garters, which meant she also been truthful about other things. He likely could rip her panties off with one hand, especially with all the adrenalin pumping through him at the moment. Then she'd be walking around tonight among all those other military men with no underwear at all.

Not a good option, Casey decided.

He had barely enough control left to not take her in the back seat of the limo, audience or not, but the first time tonight was definitely not going to be pretty. It couldn't be helped since Alexa was teasing him to the point of madness. He eased away from her carefully, and slid his hand firmly back down to her knee.

Casey's voice was hard when he spoke, all evidence of his lust gone, replaced by a determination and an assured confidence that had shaken the Marines he'd served with over the years. There was a reason he had earned the uniform.

"You need to say good-bye to the pair of panties you're wearing tonight because they're history. You have my word I'm going to rip them off you and completely destroy them first chance I get. Then I plan to sexually torture you until you're begging me to put you out of your misery."

Casey felt justly rewarded for his self-control by a quivering knee under his hand and a mostly silent ride the rest of the way to the Arlington VA Center.

Later that evening, Casey had trouble following the conversation of the newly wounded solider he was welcoming to the center. Instead, he was absorbed in watching Alexa from across the ballroom, standing in a swarm of men in uniform. Most of them were officers.

There had never been less than five or six men around her at any given time. Worse than the number though, Casey could tell from Alexa's light laughter and smiling face that she was enjoying every minute of the attention.

He'd been cornered by the director of the center the moment they came through the door, and ended up seeking out the new attendees. So far, he'd not made it back to Alexa for almost an hour—not that it probably mattered. Surrounded by flyboys and chief petty officers, Alexa seem to be having a grand time without his company.

If this was what Alexa Ranger was really like in public, Casey didn't think he could live with the flirting. Alone in the limo, he'd felt like the only man in her life, but that was probably never going to be the case.

Now he was wishing like hell he had never brought her.

On the other side of the room, Alexa was getting tired of smiling and making charming conversation with every man in the place but her own date. For over an hour, she had been watching Casey moving slowly around the room, talking to various young men on crutches or in wheelchairs.

Even surrounded by handsome men in uniform, Casey stood out to her in his. It was the way he carried himself, she thought. There was just so much pride, so much dignity in his posture. He was absolutely the most masculine man she'd ever gone out with, and she couldn't wait to take him home.

Finally, when Casey seemed to no longer be talking to anyone specific, she excused herself from the group and walked over to him.

"Hey," she said with an easy smile. "I'm looking for the Marine that brought me here. Have you seen him?"

Casey didn't smile back and it sent a little warning alarm through Alexa.

"Why? Don't you have enough military men in your fan club?" Casey asked, unable to keep the mean out of his voice.

"No. I'm missing one Marine. What's your major malfunction?" Alexa demanded in the military speak she'd been hearing all evening. She was intrigued by Casey's show of jealousy, but also hurt by his comments. "You've basically ignored me since we got here. I was just making polite social conversation while I waited on you."

"Polite social conversation?" Casey said in disbelief,

laughing harshly. "It's called flirting, Alexa. And it's disrespectful."

Alexa's hands came to her hips. "Disrespectful? I don't believe this. You drop me inside the door, ignore me for more than an hour, and then have the nerve to chastise me for talking to people? You left me alone, not the other way around. And for your information, I was not flirting."

"Like hell," Casey said. "I heard you laughing everywhere I went. I was on the receiving end of your friendly conversation on the ride over here. I know exactly how you are. You flirt so much you don't even realize it."

"You," Alexa said, poking an angry finger at Casey's chest, "don't know anything about me, and I just became really thankful about that. Rather than stand here and let you keep insulting me, I believe I'll find my own way home."

Alexa turned and started toward the door, shaking so hard she was surprised her teeth weren't chattering. Then she stopped, turned, and walked back to him.

Casey's chin came up when Alexa stood in front of him again. He was right about this. If she wasn't interested in being monogamous with him, then he really didn't want to be in a relationship with her.

"Just in case you try to tell yourself later that I had the hots for some other guy here tonight, I thought I'd set the record straight with witnesses," Alexa said tightly.

Grabbing a couple fistfuls of his uniform, Alexa yanked him hard enough against her to have him dropping his cane with a clatter on the cement floor.

Then Alexa plastered her mouth to Casey's in a kiss so hot and full of genuine longing, it would have melted a glacier. It almost melted her. She hated—really hated—knowing she still wanted him despite his opinion of her.

But she let go finally. What was the use? He hadn't returned the kiss at all.

Fine, she thought. Forget him. She didn't need him or his approval.

"All I wanted tonight was you, Casey Carter. I can't believe you ruined what was between us just because you were jealous. Well, now you can go straight to hell as far as I'm concerned. We are done."

Alexa turned and walked away, her heels clicking on the floor. She didn't look back, and she didn't hang her head in shame. Instead, she wound back the clock inside her to the woman she was before she'd kissed Casey the first time. She didn't need him or his interest to validate her. She knew exactly who she was.

Too embarrassed and prideful to call out to Alexa and try to stop her, Casey started walking slowly after her, but never caught up. He was still mad, but something in the punishing kiss she had delivered, some desperation in her action, had made him regret their fight.

He watched, frustrated as Alexa climbed into a taxi that magically pulled up the moment she got outside. Everything probably worked that way for her, Casey thought resentfully.

When he came back to the ballroom, a fellow Marine and friend had retrieved his cane and was holding it for him.

"Hey, Gunny. Did Alexa have to leave?" Corporal Aaron Franklin asked, noting the frown. "That was some kiss goodbye. You could hear hearts breaking around the room. I'm surprised you're still here after that lip lock."

"Alexa thought I was ignoring her and went home early," Casey said, not willing to spill the whole argument, but unable to keep all of his anger in check.

"I'm sorry you two had a fight. She is some amazing woman. You should have heard the way she grounded that fly-boy zero when he tried to ask her out," Aaron said with a laugh, pointing to a tall, good-looking Air Force officer across the room.

Casey frowned, but was happy to hear Alexa had been turning down dates. He wasn't happy to hear she had been asked.

"He probably thought she was available. Alexa likes to flirt," Casey said sharply.

"I don't know if I'd call what she does flirting," Aaron said, walking along with Casey to the drinks table. "I'd say if she was flirting with you, you'd know it."

Aaron picked up a cracker and chewed as he studied Gunny Carter's set jaw. He didn't blame the man for being jealous, but he just let her go home alone. That couldn't be good. He'd sure hate to see Casey lose the best thing that had happened to him since Aaron had known him.

"You know, Alexa asked a Chief Petty Officer to get her a drink like he was on the fucking wait staff here. He looked like he could have chewed through the hull of a ship. I thought I was going to bust a gut trying not to laugh."

Casey laughed a little at the image himself. That comment might have been fun to hear. He could definitely imagine Alexa's regal but sweet tone delivering it.

Aaron nodded with his chin at a group of Army officers across the room. "Some of the Army guys were bad-mouthing Marines—just joking, you know. I swear the evil look she shot that Army Major damn near knocked the maple leaves off his collar. She's a keeper, Gunny, and damn hot, too—if you don't mind me saying so. You better make up fast before she moves on."

Aaron slapped Casey on the back and headed off to find his wife.

Casey drank some punch and wished it had something stronger in it. Aaron was right. Alexa Ranger was enough of a "keeper" to be worth the fight.

And she was hot too.

Maybe he could understand her flirting a bit with guys who couldn't keep from being attracted to someone as hot as she was. Flirting was probably some sort of uncontrollable reflex reaction Alexa had around men.

He'd apologize tomorrow, Casey decided.

But some things would have to change in the long term. They were eventually going to have to talk about her flirting, which had to stop if they were involved. He took all his commitments seriously.

Right or wrong, Casey didn't think he could even be in a sexual relationship with a woman he didn't trust.

Chapter 10

Alexa found a salon opening Saturday morning and let them spin some magic on her to remove the traces of a nearly sleepless night. By the time she hit the office at twelve thirty, she was at least half way over being mad.

Worse than her sagging appearance, the pressure in her chest bothered her more. She was fighting some insistent urge to bawl that she was definitely not going to indulge—at least not until the buyer open house was over.

When she walked in the office waiting area, Sydney looked at her tight red dress and matching heels with obvious relief. Alexa went instantly back to a full mad.

"What happened? Did Casey call fifty times or send flowers with an apology? I can see on your face you were expecting frump lady to show up today."

Hands on hips, she glared at Sydney, who still hadn't said anything.

"You should know me better. I don't pine for small-minded men. Casey Carter can crawl back into the Neanderthal cave he came out of because I certainly don't need him," Alexa stated, ignoring the voice inside her head calling her a liar.

"Wait!" Sydney called, before she taken too many steps down the hall. "Casey's in your office."

"Oh, fucking hell, Sydney." Alexa swore again and again,

each time more viciously, making Sydney blush with embarrassment.

Sydney held both hands up in surrender. "Look, I'm sorry. I didn't know what else to do with him. He wouldn't say anything other than he hurt your feelings and owed you an apology. After yesterday—well, I couldn't just boot him out."

"Wuss," Alexa hissed at him. "Fine. I have no problem kicking his ass out myself. If he refuses to leave, I'll call the damn police."

Sydney checked his watch to see how much time before the lingerie buyers starting showing up. He hoped Casey and Alexa worked out their problem before then. Actually, he just hoped they worked everything out period.

Yesterday was the closest moment to a happy ending he'd ever seen Alexa Ranger have in her life. Even Paul was dying to meet the man who finally broke through Alexa's protective shell.

Alexa opened the door of her office and walked to her desk, not bothering to spare Casey more than a tiny glance. Casey winced at her coldness, trying to remember why he had come to see Alexa today, and why he'd rashly decided letting her temper cool off first was a bad idea.

She was making his remorse worse by clouding his brain as she walked across the room in a red dress and matching heels. Wanting to know what was under her clothes sure blew to hell his civilized intentions for making peace.

He was wound so tight today, he was afraid to put his hands on her.

Alexa looked at Casey and steeled her heart against his words. "You have two minutes to say what you obviously think wasn't said last night, and then you're leaving."

Casey internally winced at her all-business tone but worked to keep his face neutral.

"I think I covered all my complaints about your behavior pretty well yesterday evening," he said softly. "I haven't changed my mind. You flirt too much. It's disrespectful to me and could be dangerous for you."

"And since I still vehemently disagree with your judgment, we're done with this conversation. Unless you want to hear me swear at you one final time before emphatically stating again that I don't care what you think about me or my social skills," Alexa said.

Ignorant ass, she thought.

She refused to yell at him because she didn't want Casey to know how much he had hurt her or how angry he had made her. In all her life and with all the men she had known, Alexa couldn't remember ever being so angry with one.

Today she was still in shock, unable to believe Casey was really a condescending caveman. She had been making social conversation before he'd even been born.

Ignorant ass, she thought again.

Casey looked at her across the desk. Alexa's eyes were blue lasers boring holes in him. It was obvious she wasn't willing or able to see things from his side. In fact, she was taking female irrationality to a level he'd never seen before, even in a pissed off female Marine.

"Look, I'm truly sorry I hurt your feelings. I didn't mean to do that as much as I obviously did. I was just trying to tell you how your behavior made me feel," Casey explained, trying to break through her coldness to soothe the hurt.

"If you want approval for your emotional honesty, go talk to your therapist. I happen to know a good one if you're still looking for help," Alexa said meanly, leaning back in her chair, unhappily settling for glaring at him. "You obviously need it."

What she really wanted was to throw the paperweight on her desk at his hard head to see if she could knock some sense into him.

"Now you're just being mean," Casey replied. "I'm trying to apologize."

"Doesn't sound much like an apology to me. It sounds like you just want to justify your jealousy by making me feel like I was a bad woman," Alexa said. "Well, fuck that. I don't have to defend myself to you or anyone else."

"That's not what I am doing," Casey said through gritted

teeth, trying hard not to start yelling.

"You know, Casey, I've had people finding fault with me all my life because I have the audacity to act like a man. Newspapers and magazines used to devote great amounts of publishing space debating why I acted as I did. At my age now, and as hard as I've worked to be happy with myself, I've earned my damn attitude. Your negative opinions of my behavior might have influenced how I felt about myself twenty years ago, but I'm not as nice or as gullible as I used to be," Alexa said, her voice hard and flat because she meant every word.

She damn well knew she had lived her life the best she could. She would not shrink herself now into a quiet, anti-social woman she couldn't like, not for Casey Carter or any other man. She wanted Casey, maybe in ways needed him, but not enough to stop being herself.

Casey's elbow hit the cane resting on the arm of the chair. He adjusted its position and then brought his attention back to Alexa.

"I have my own therapist through the VA. He said I needed to soften my personal comments to civilians and work on not swearing so much," Casey told her.

"Hell, don't worry about sparing my sensibilities," Alexa snorted. "I passed up being mad at your insults and went straight to furious at about three o'clock this morning. It cost me a hundred dollars to make sure my emotions weren't showing on my face today so I could look my male buyers in the eyes without wanting to kill them. Truth is, I'm really madder at myself than you. I can't believe I let you close enough to get in a verbal slap so big. It's been a long damn time since I made that kind of mistake."

Casey studied his hands, looking for a way to get through her anger, which was a lot stronger and far more righteous than he'd imagined it would be.

He could see now that there was a lot he hadn't considered last night. He got what she was saying. It wasn't just him Alexa was mad at, but everyone else before him who had tried to shame her because they thought she was doing something wrong.

Too late, Casey realized he really should have let her temper cool off.

"Since it doesn't look like you're going to listen, I'll leave you to your work then. I'm sorry I hurt you Alexa. The idea that all those guys you talked to last night would think you'd make good on the flirting made me crazy. Maybe one of these days you'll be less angry and able to see our fight differently."

Casey pushed himself out of the chair and started walking to the door.

"Wait a minute," Alexa said, rising from the desk. She walked to the chair Casey vacated, lifted his cane from the arm of it, and walked to him. "I don't want to have to explain your stuff being in my office again."

Casey reached out to take the cane, his hand closed over hers where she held it. When Alexa tried to remove her hand, his grip tightened even more.

"I am sorry, Alexa," Casey repeated. "I don't like fighting with you."

"Save your breath," she said, putting a little more energy into pulling on her hand.

"Are you always this hard and unforgiving?" he asked, hurt seeping into the question.

"Yes. You'd know it to be the truth if you ever read my press. 'Cold, hard bitch' and 'incorrigible flirt' are often used in the same sentence," she said tightly. "Are you going to let go or do I kick you in the knee to make you?"

Casey twisted the cane in a single flip, and used it to push Alexa up against the wall. He still had his hand over hers on the cane, and she wasn't strong enough to break the grip with her free one.

"I know you're not cold or hard," he told her, his mouth inches from hers. "The rest of the description is debatable. I might feel differently in few moments, especially if you decide to kick me with those heels."

"Let me go," Alexa demanded, struggling against him and the cane.

"You threatened me and I defended myself. Now I'm

going to apologize again and this time try to hear it. I'm sorry I hurt you, Alexa," Casey said softly.

A muscle twitched in his jaw.

"I can't let you go and you know it's the truth. We're going to have a relationship because we need and want each other. The attraction between us is worth fixing this disagreement. You can be as mad as you want about our fight, but eventually we're going to make up."

"Go to hell. I don't have to do anything," she denied, shaking with anger because she had never allowed a man to physically overpower her before.

Alexa knew she should kick Casey in the knee, or knee him in the balls. Something... anything—to free herself. But she couldn't look at the man without seeing herself walking across the room to him in his uniform.

And she couldn't bring herself to add more hurt to a man who had suffered such a loss of self, no matter how bad he'd made her feel, no matter how much she might think he deserved it.

Which left her where?

Other than pinned to the wall, Alexa didn't know. Casey was stronger than he looked, despite the injury. Unwilling to hurt him, she was virtually helpless to escape. Damn, she had never been so conflicted in all her life.

She hissed when Casey pressed himself a little closer, all but leaning into her.

"I bet you're wearing underwear that matches the red dress aren't you?" Casey asked, the question a sexy whisper on her cheek. "I'm sorry I'm not going to find out until you get over being mad at me."

Casey lightly kissed a spot below her ear, felt her pulse pounding hard against his lips. He pressed his cheek against her neck and felt her tremble. She was so his, he thought, wondering how long Alexa was going to resist what was between them.

"You're meant to be mine," he whispered. "I think I knew that the first time I touched you. Flirt all you want with other men if it gives you some kind of thrill, but don't expect me to tolerate it silently. I guess I'm just the jealous type."

Casey leaned into her hard then, pressing his straining erection against her. "I would hate to believe you're planning to break my heart just to feed that notorious reputation of yours."

When Alexa froze at his words and stopped struggling, Casey leaned in fully and kissed her lips softly, his passion for her restrained in favor of gaining more in the long run. He stepped reluctantly away from her warmth and pulled the cane with him.

"Nothing has changed how I feel about you," he said quietly. "I hope you get over being mad, but I intend to sleep with you anyway. Eventually you're going to have to forgive me so that can happen."

Alexa stayed against the wall, heart beating, mind spinning while Casey walked away.

Through the open door, Alexa heard him talking to Sydney, who came skidding to a halt in front of her seconds later.

"You okay?" Sydney asked, noting Alexa's shock and flushed face.

Alexa nodded and eased away from the wall. "I'm in big trouble, Sydney."

"No kidding, There are two buyers fighting already over wanting an exclusive for the breakaways. I know how you feel about exclusive contracts, but you've got to hear what they're offering," Sydney said, eyes wide as he watched Alexa smooth her hair back into place and walk to her desk on wobbly legs.

"Did you and Casey work out your differences?" he asked casually—or at least, he hoped it was casual.

"No," Alexa said, pulling out a lip-gloss and a hand mirror from her desk drawer. "I don't think Casey cares whether or not we settle our differences."

"Well, I'm sorry for that," Sydney said genuinely. "Casey caught me in a weak moment this morning. My heart fluttered a bit when I saw him in his uniform yesterday. He looked like some movie hero, and he seemed liked so much fun too. So is it over, Alexa?" *Please say no*, he begged silently.

"Over?" Alexa asked, eyebrows disappearing into her hair. "No. Oh, no—it's not over. He used his cane to hold me to the wall while he lectured me about dating etiquette. The only reason I didn't kick free was because I didn't want to hurt him more than he is already. Damn it. I can't believe I wimped out."

She threw the lip gloss and mirror back into the desk drawer.

"His apology—if you could call it one—was more like a declaration of war. I don't think it's going to be over until one of us is left standing over the other's dead body."

Sydney looked at Alexa's body language. On a mad scale of one to ten, she was only at seven, even after being allegedly manhandled and severely insulted. He'd seen Alexa practically maim other guys before for far lesser offenses.

"Casey used his cane to hold you to the wall? How very macho of him. Are you still mad?" Sydney asked, noting the eye daggers and the stomp as she headed back to him.

"Furious," she stated. "But he's probably right, no matter how mad I am, we're going to end up in bed together anyway. I just hope I don't get tempted to strangle him in his sleep. He brings out the absolute worst in me."

Alexa stopped in front of Sydney and put her hands on her hips.

"Do you think I flirt too much?" she asked him, indignant still over the insult.

Sydney choked on a laugh. "That's a joke, right? OMG, did Casey Carter accuse you of flirting too much? That's so typical alpha male. Well, you should be flattered he's jealous. It means he's really into you."

Then Sydney considered how it must have seemed to Alexa—after all the men she'd dealt with over the years without so much as mussing her hair—well, the idea that Casey could ruffle her self-confidence by being jealous was hysterical. He ended up laughing so hard he doubled over with it.

"It's not funny," Alexa said, hands on hips.

"Oh yes, it is. Well, not the flirting part. I just can't imagine Casey had the nerve to tell you how he felt about your flirting. No wonder you're mad. And I'm impressed you restrained yourself. I mean, I assume you exercised restraint since he didn't walk out holding his private parts," Sydney said as they walked down the hall.

"He's an immature caveman and I am fifty damn years old. I am not changing who I am for him," Alexa said tightly. "How does even he know what I said to anyone I talked with last night? He spent most of his time networking with the people he helps there."

She frowned as she shrugged her shoulders, trying to shake away the rest of what he'd said.

"What?" Sydney asked. "What else did he say?"

"Casey said I'd break his heart if I kept flirting," she said, still frowning.

"Well, I believe that," Sydney said easily. "Don't you?"

When Alexa didn't answer right away, it bothered Sydney more than he could explain. Casey certainly had his work cut out chiseling away at Alexa's skepticism.

"No wonder you quit dating, Alexa. Being with too many men has made you cynical. Casey Carter is falling in love with you, honey. Pull up those big girl panties you created for yourself and deal with it because you're probably falling for him, too."

"I am not falling for him. I've done nothing but try to discourage him from the beginning. I certainly didn't ask him to fall in love with me," Alexa said, sounding like a child even to herself.

"Except with your every breath," Sydney told her, totally exasperated, not believing Alexa didn't know the truth about herself—hell, about them.

"You and I are narcissists, Alexa. We're always asking to be loved. You're used to men desiring you like a Rolex watch or a Lamborghini. Maybe you don't recognize real desire or real love, but I do, thanks to you. It's wonderful—and, well awful too—when you fight. Still it's worth it."

He stopped her at the end of the hallway with a strong

grip on her arm.

"The best thing about fighting with someone you truly love is make-up sex," Sydney said consolingly.

"I haven't had any sex yet," Alexa confessed, blushing at Sydney's laugh.

"Don't wait too much longer," Sydney said wisely. "You guys will be breaking furniture and knick-knacks on the way to the bed. Then when it turns violent with need you'll end up walking funny for a week."

"Sydney! Too much information," Alexa protested, bringing her hands to the sides of her head. The similar threat Casey issued was ringing in her ears again thanks to the man now sleeping with her ex-husband.

Sydney just laughed. "Well, it's been a while for you, Alexa. You might have forgotten how intense it can be, and the casual kind is nothing compared to being with the right person."

Sydney turned her around and straightened her clothes from the back and then turned her back to face him again, checking her front.

"Besides, you've never been with anyone like Casey. He's not as refined as the men you're used to sleeping with. Don't expect him to be polite in bed. He looks like the kind who wants to call all the shots."

If Alexa rolled her eyes one more time, she thought she was going to look like she was going through an exorcism. Her head would probably start spinning around on her neck.

"Come on, Sydney. Let's go sell some underwear. I have to stop thinking about sex or I'm going to have a meltdown."

She smacked Sydney's arm when he laughed loudly again.

When they walked through the door into the display area, everyone stopped talking and stared at Alexa, who froze in panic.

Score another win for the Marine, Sydney thought. It was the first time since he'd known Alexa Ranger that Sydney had seen her come unglued in front of a captivated audience. Narcissist no more, Alexa was so worried about her fight with Casey that she'd forgotten about herself.

"They're all looking at the stunning red dress and heels," Sydney whispered reassuringly in Alexa's ear. "You don't have hot-for-Casey tattooed on your forehead."

He patted her shoulder.

"At least not yet," he added, bringing a blush to her face.

Alexa smacked Sydney in the chest with the back of her hand, and walked over to talk to the first buyer she recognized.

Chapter 11

"You were home awfully early Friday night," Seth said to Casey over coffee Sunday morning. Casey only grunted in reply and topped off their cups. Seth hadn't seen him at all yesterday and figured Casey had been hiding in his room.

While he wondered what was up with the man who had raised him, Seth sipped the excellent coffee with gratitude. He'd gotten very spoiled letting Casey take care of the cooking and other domestic chores. Casey had insisted it gave him something to do with his time.

"The way you were smiling when you left here—well, I guess I thought I wouldn't see you for a few days," Seth said around a grin, trying to lighten the mood.

This got another grunt out of Casey.

"We had a fight. Alexa was flirting and I called her on it," Casey said flatly, sipping his coffee and staring at the counter as if he wanted to kill it.

So that's what happened, Seth thought. He chose his words carefully.

"Jenna thinks her mother flirts too much too. I don't see it that way though. Was Alexa touching anyone or letting them touch her while she talked with them?" Seth asked.

Casey thought back. The only person Alexa had touched was him when she grabbed the front of his uniform. "No. I guess not," he admitted.

"Then she was probably just being friendly and making conversation," Seth reasoned.

He met and held Casey's troubled gaze across the table, thinking how strange it was for him to be the consoling one in the matter, especially since he still didn't think Alexa was right for Casey.

"Jenna grew up in the shadow of a famous model turned more famous lingerie designer. I can understand Jenna wishing now and again for a more normal mother. But that's not the reality of who Alexa Ranger is. A successful model's public image is a marketable commodity, and Alexa Ranger has been smart to build her business around her notoriety."

Seth took another drink of coffee while he watched Casey struggling with what he was saying.

"My guess is Alexa's flirting is an autopilot reaction to any sort of attention. I mean the woman is incredibly successful. I wish I had half her social charm," Seth said easily.

Casey scratched his whiskered jaw, and set his coffee cup on the table.

"Let me get this straight. You don't see why I want to date the woman, but you think her flirting is just—hell, good for her business?" Casey asked, totally blown away by what Seth was saying.

Seth laughed a little self-consciously. "It's not as shallow as it sounds."

"Have you ever seen Alexa dressed up—I mean, full-out model mode?" Casey asked.

Seth ran a hand through his hair and wrinkled his forehead. "Come to think of it—no."

"Picture Jenna in that blue dress, and then multiply by ten. Add unshakeable self-confidence, more poise than a queen holding court, and a glint in her eye that says she's not afraid of doing anything she wants to do. And take it from me, the glint is not an idle threat. The woman is— *incorrigible*," Casey said finally, remembering the adjective from her snide comment about being called so by the press. It fit her perfectly.

"So you were jealous and asked her to stop flirting?" Seth

asked around a smile.

He didn't know as much about women as Casey, but even he knew better than to openly criticize a famous woman always in the public limelight. Jenna had shared story after story about how the press had tracked her mother's dating life, not to mention her every business move.

Casey rubbed his unshaven face with a tired hand. Sleep had been impossible last night and he was feeling its loss this morning. "More like I told Alexa she was being disrespectful to me," he admitted.

Seth grimaced. "That couldn't have gone well. Did she throw something at you or hit you over the head with the nearest large object?"

"No," Casey said frowning. "She kissed me with tongue in front of God and everyone at the VA center. Then she told me to go to hell and took a taxi home from Arlington."

Seth picked up his phone, scrolled through the contacts, and held it up so Casey could read the display.

"Best florist in Falls Church," Seth told him. "They always get the words right on the apology note."

That got a laugh out of Casey. "Too late for flowers. I talked her assistant Sydney into letting me wait for her in her office yesterday morning. The apology didn't go well either. She was still really mad and I ended up trapping her against the wall with my cane while she spat insults at me. I don't think she heard a word I said."

Seth's eyes widened. "Shit, Casey. You physically subdued the woman in her own office? I'm surprised we're sitting here having this conversation. You should be in a hospital having your nuts put back in place."

"Tell me about it," Casey said with a frown. "She didn't fight back and I don't know why. It bothers the hell out of me."

"I guess I know where Jenna gets her hardheadedness from now," Seth countered.

"If Jenna is like her mother, you're in for a hell of a hard time when she gets mad," Casey said.

The fact that he and Seth were having similar problems

with women in the same family was probably reason to laugh at the bizarre situation. Thank God his sense of humor was still working. He needed to look on the bright side.

"Alexa and I were joking Friday about how our relationship was the kind of thing you see on a reality talk show," Casey admitted.

"Nah," Seth disagreed lightly. "If you were sleeping with Alexa, and then found out I was secretly sleeping with both mother and daughter, then THAT would make us a good show. Right now we're just like all the other pathetic losers who aren't getting any from their women."

When Casey burst out laughing for real, Seth could tell he was finally making his cousin feel better.

"Since you value your man parts, we know you sleeping with Alexa is never going to be a problem, don't we?" Casey threatened.

Seth just grinned without answering Casey's question. He still couldn't understand what Casey saw in Jenna's mother, but he could definitely see Casey was wrestling hard with it—whatever it was.

And Seth had to admit that it was highly entertaining to imagine his macho military cousin telling a woman like Alexa Ranger that her flirting was disrespectful. Only Casey had that kind of nerve.

Seth recalled all the times that Casey and Susan used to argue. A couple days would go by, and then Susan would suddenly be smiling. Casey would also be smiling, and from Seth's standpoint—gloating. Whatever leverage Casey used with angry women, it seemed to work for him. Seth had no trouble believing that eventually Casey would win his battle with Alexa Ranger, even if his cousin lost a skirmish or two along the way.

"Want French toast and bacon for breakfast?" Casey asked, bad mood lifting at last.

Seth smiled. "Sounds great. I hope you know I've put on a lot of weight in the year you've been here."

"You're four inches taller than me, Seth. When I got here last year, you looked like a walking skeleton. You should come to the gym with me and put some muscle on that frame of yours," Casey told him.

"No need," Seth said, answering a text he received while he talked with Casey. "I don't think I'm going to have to physically subdue Jenna to get her to listen to my apology. I think she's weakening. She actually answered one of the twenty texts I sent her last week."

Casey shook his head at how naïve Seth was about female strength of character, of which he was fast learning the Ranger women had more than their share.

"Seth, let me tell you something. Fighting with a woman who has set her mind on something is harder than fighting a battalion of armed men. The woman is more strategic mentally. Sometimes a physical approach is the only tactical recourse left."

Seth shook his head from side to side and sighed loudly. "Casey, I love you man. Are you going to talk in military euphemisms for the rest of your life?" he asked, being a tad more sarcastic than usual in his teasing.

"Why? Do you want me talk in phone text shorthand instead, like 'OMG, Casey, I am ROFL at your stories about Alexa?" Casey mimicked the text language he knew Seth used with friends.

Seth grinned, happy to see the evil returning to Casey's eyes.

"Yeah, but you need to work on your text vocabulary. I would say—WTF Casey, you going to let Alexa win the fight? OMG, I can't believe it. BTWAGIOW," Seth finished.

Casey paused in turning the bacon that was now sizzling and dancing in the pan.

"You lost me. What's the last one mean?"

"Bed The Woman And Get It Over With," Seth said, laughing. "The sexual tension is killing you."

Casey laughed and turned back to the bacon. "You can say that again."

The doorbell rang and Seth went to see who it was. When he did, he could only gape before his sense of humor caught up. It was like every time he and Casey talked about Alexa

Ranger, she showed up.

This morning she stood quietly waiting in the doorway wearing sunglasses, baggy sweats, and running shoes that had seen some hard use. Looking at the sweats, Seth pondered Casey's sanity again, but smiled at her anyway, getting a fairly dazzling smile in return. Even with the smile, Seth just didn't see the mega beauty in the aging woman Casey claimed was there.

"I guess you smelled the French toast and bacon from the gym. Come on in. Breakfast is almost ready." Seth smiled genuinely at the woman.

At least she was going to completely roust Casey from the blues one way or the other, he decided.

Alexa stepped across the threshold and removed her sunglasses. "Spur of the moment visit," she said.

Seth watched her biting her lip in a way that reminded him painfully of Jenna.

"Nah. I don't believe it. I've known Casey too long. He must be getting better. It used to take two whole days," he said around a lingering smile.

Casey should definitely give lessons on how to argue with women and win, Seth thought.

Alexa had no idea what Seth was talking about it, but she did notice he was being exceptionally nice to her this morning. He motioned for her to follow, and walked ahead of her to the kitchen.

"Make enough for three," Seth said to Casey's back.

Casey turned from the stove and froze seeing Alexa standing beside Seth. Or at least he was fairly sure it was Alexa. The disgusted grunt was instinctual.

"Grunge is a really different look for you," Casey said harshly before he could bite his tongue.

The moment he spoke he saw her eyes darken. He swore inside, but it was too late to take the words back. The well-worn gray pants were all but falling off her, and the shirt was at least two sizes too big and had seen better days. In fact, they looked more like men's sweats.

Alexa's hands came to her hips immediately. She had only

herself to blame. She should have known Casey wouldn't even say hello before launching into insults. Since Alexa had come by to try to get him to be reasonable, she was doubly upset to know rushing over here had been a waste of her time.

Seth had to look away to stop the laugh from escaping. Casey was going to need a metal jock strap to protect his balls if he kept insulting the woman.

"Yeah. Well, Mr. Scruffy, you don't exactly look like the front cover of men's magazines yourself this morning," Alexa told Casey. "Hard to sleep with a guilty conscience, isn't it?"

She looked at his holey, camouflaged tee shirt with undisguised disgust.

Casey knew it would shock Seth if he walked to Alexa and did what he wanted to do—like turning her over his knee, so instead he sighed and turned reluctantly back to the stove.

"You're going to love my French toast," Casey said, ignoring her verbal jab. "It's something I do really well."

"I didn't come for breakfast. I was working out and—"

Alexa stopped and swore because it was really hard to lower her pride.

"I hate this," she said to Casey's back. "You were wrong Friday night, but I—I'm sorry we had to fight so much about it." *There, it's out*, she thought. She was quite proud of herself for being so mature.

"Maybe I was out of line," Casey said quietly. "Maybe I should have listened more when you tried to explain."

Alexa blinked, and then dropped her hands to her side.

Seth watched in wonder. Casey hadn't even admitted to being wrong, he'd just said "maybe". His friends had advised full-out groveling netted the best results. Well, Seth was certainly learning a different technique this morning. Start with an insult, just say "maybe" you were wrong, and glare— a lot.

Alexa continued to stare because Casey hadn't turned around yet. "Are we good then?" she asked, directing the question to his back.

"No. Probably not," Casey said, turning finally to meet her

gaze. "I'm sure it will come up again the next time I catch you flirting."

She breathed in and out for a moment, fighting to find some calm.

Nothing was settled then, Alexa thought. Casey wasn't sorry. He was just trying to make peace with her. She hated to be placated, more than she hated to be publicly shamed.

Seth thought it must be the woman's maturity that kept her from bursting into tears and running from the room. Even he was offended by Casey, and it wasn't his business at all.

"Damn you, Casey. Are you always so sure you're right?" Alexa asked, exasperated at his condescending attitude.

"No. This is why I didn't sleep last night and haven't shaved this morning. Why do you look like hell?" Casey challenged.

"I work out at a co-ed gym," she said, crossing her arms. "I left the tight yoga pants at home this morning out of residual guilt about drawing unwanted male attention— obviously misplaced guilt I see now. I won't make *that mistake* again either. And I repeat, your attitude brings out the absolute worst in me. I try to be rational and reasonable, but it just doesn't seem to work with you."

Casey waved a hand to her horrible clothes. "I know those are not yours. Who do those clothes even belong to?"

"My ex," Alexa said, lifting her chin, daring him to say something nasty.

Casey laughed bitterly, swore richly, and then stared at the kitchen ceiling as if he could find patience among the tiles. He couldn't kill Alexa in front of a witness, and he couldn't drag her off to bed yet for the same reason. All he could do was retreat and save the rest of the fight for another day.

"I hope you're not expecting any sissy, sugar-free syrup. This is a bachelor pad. All we have is the real stuff," Casey told her harshly, his mouth set in a tight line.

Alexa looked at Seth, whose mouth was hanging open as he studied Casey. It was good to know she wasn't the only one shocked by the man's obstinate behavior.

"So tell me, Seth, did I win this round? And if I did, how the hell can I tell?" Alexa asked.

Seth closed his mouth and cleared his throat, a little worried about being dragged into the fight.

"Well," he said carefully, "when Casey runs out of retorts, or military analogies, he changes the subject. Dead giveaway."

"Thanks," Alexa said. "I owe you one."

Then she turned back to Casey, stiffening her back as she prepared to be strong again. One way or the other Casey was going to have to accept who she was or she'd be damned if she would sleep with him.

"Artificial sweeteners will kill you. I either have the real thing or skip sugar altogether. I could use some sugar this morning. And it would be polite to offer me some coffee if you want me to stay," Alexa said, her tone saying it didn't matter to her and she would just as soon leave.

Knowing he could not answer politely, Casey opened the cabinet to the left of the stove, took out a cup and poured a stream of dark liquid into it. Then he just looked at her.

"Just black," Alexa said to the unspoken question.

Casey held the coffee out so Alexa would have to walk to get it. It was petty, but he didn't care.

Seth found himself actually holding his breath, waiting to see who would give in first. Or who would take the first swing. Seth wasn't sure what was going to happen, but he felt something coming.

Alexa sighed and walked to Casey. When she reached out a hand, he moved the cup just out of reach.

"Look, Carter—" she began, only to have Casey swoop in and take her mouth fiercely, possessively, the message in his hard kiss was that nothing between them was over. Not the fight and certainly not their desire. It was a brief, but thorough invasion of her mouth, and it stunned her into complete and submissive silence. When Casey released her, Alexa felt the coffee cup being pushed into her hands before he turned back to the food he was preparing.

Some greater instinct than common sense had Seth walking around the counter to a still-in-shock Alexa and guiding her by the shoulders to a seat on the other side of it.

Good lord, Seth realized, he actually felt sorry for the woman and was going to rescue her. In the split-second before Casey kissed her, there had been a look on his cousin's face that would have rivaled any warrior landing a deathblow to his enemy. He didn't get the how or why Casey felt like he did, but both he and Alexa had seen the depth of it.

"So where do you work out?" Seth asked quietly, trying to steer the conversation to something normal. He could feel Casey vibrating still and figured Alexa could too. The fight was far from over, but Seth was hoping for a cessation of hostilities during breakfast at least.

After she and Seth were seated and, Alexa conceded, out of immediate harm's way, she looked at Seth as if she were seeing him for the first time. He was instinctively trying to protect her from Casey's anger. She reached out and patted Seth's hand in gratitude.

Not that she needed rescuing, but Casey definitely did. Left alone, she might actually have bashed Casey over the head with the coffee cup he had given her. And she would have done so because Casey Carter was a controlling, insufferable barbarian who wasn't using the brain God gave him or the eyes in his head. Still, it was the thought that counted, Alexa conceded, gazing at the young man now seated across from her.

"Jenna doesn't really know you, does she, Seth?" she said to him, not a question really, but more of a comment.

Then she shook her head to clear the tension, and told Seth about the gym. Unlike telling Casey, Alexa found it easy to share with Seth that she'd bought a healthy share of the locally-owned gym for an investment and visited a couple Sundays a month just to see if standards were being kept up. They talked business until Casey brought heaping plates of French toast and bacon to the table.

Alexa took a bite of French toast, closed her eyes and sighed with pleasure.

"You weren't lying, Casey. This really is the best French toast I have ever tasted," she said, smiling at Casey as she licked a line of syrup off her bottom lip with an agile tongue.

Seth squirmed in his seat, uncomfortable with a sudden heightened awareness of Alexa as a woman. When he looked at Casey, his inner laughter quickly diffused the moment. Casey was watching Alexa eat, his eyes traveling with every bite she took. The woman knew it, was enjoying it, and making his cousin pay.

If Seth hadn't been there—well, that made him laugh more, especially when he looked at the woman dressed in the baggy gray sweats. It certainly couldn't be how Alexa Ranger looked for Casey, Seth thought. It had to be something else. Maybe it was because Alexa was the first person in a long time who didn't feel sorry for Casey and was willing to give him a hard time.

Seth was faintly surprised when Alexa gave Casey a light, syrupy kiss after breakfast and ran off. Casey watched her exit with no more than a regretful sigh.

"Why did you just let her leave?" Seth asked, after the door had closed behind her.

Casey looked at him in confusion.

"I know sometimes I miss things happening between people, but come on. There were a couple of moments in the last hour where I thought the two of you were going to forget I was here," Seth explained.

Casey just ran a hand over his face again. "She's still mad. Under the polite civility is a woman who is seething. And truthfully, I guess I'm still mad too. I don't want our first time to be about anger. I'm sure we'll have plenty of those times along the way."

"You are a hell of a role model, Casey." Seth got up from the table, carrying their dirty dishes to the sink. "And though I still don't get your attraction to her—especially in those sweats—I find myself suddenly really, really hoping you get the woman soon. You've certainly paid your dues. You deserve to have sex with her."

Casey laughed. "Please do not ever tell Alexa that." Then

Casey laughed again. "But I feel the same way. She's mine, and we both know it, even if she's trying to ignore it for now."

"*She's mine*," Seth repeated Casey's words as if they were a foreign language. "Damn, you don't say that kind of stuff to her, do you?"

Casey just grinned and sipped his coffee.

Seth shook his head and thought Casey might be inviting World War III into his life with comments like *she's mine*, especially with a woman like Alexa Ranger who clearly didn't belong to anyone but herself.

"Oh, hell. Now you've got me doing it," Seth complained.

"What?" Casey asked, thinking about Alexa and what Seth didn't know was hidden under those ugly clothes.

"Now I'm thinking in military analogies. I hope you transition to civilian life soon," Seth told him. "I don't have genuine experience of the military, so I'm starting to sound like some old war movie veteran in my head."

"Transition isn't easy, but I'm working on it," Casey said lightly, not offended by Seth's complaint. And he was thinking he really did need to work on it more. Despite volunteering at the VA, he was interacting with non-military people on a daily basis.

He needed to *improvise, adapt, and overcome*, he thought, laughing at the way the unofficial mantra of the Marines still seemed to fit his life so well.

He also needed to figure out his work situation. Casey knew he couldn't keep sponging off Seth forever, though he had managed to put aside some savings in the last year. Besides, he knew he was cramping Seth's style, messing up his metro cocktail parties and complaining about his electronics all the time.

Casey sighed. Well, he'd had a whole year of doing nothing, of grieving for his wife, his life, and the rest. It was time he started working on what to do next.

Right after he figured out what to do about Alexa Ranger.

Chapter 12

Casey managed to wait until Friday of the next week to become frustrated beyond what he could stand. By then it had become obvious that waiting patiently for Alexa to come to her senses wasn't gaining him any ground. She hadn't called, texted, or tried to contact him in any way since he'd fed her French toast the previous Sunday.

Casey didn't even know if he and Alexa were still fighting or not, but had he decided it was time to find out.

And also, besides all that, he just simply missed her.

The doorman of her building greeted him with full smile and a cheerful "morning, sir," barely glancing at the cane as he ushered Casey through the door.

Upstairs in Alexa's office Casey found chaos again as he stepped into the waiting area. The sliding door was open and sewing machines were humming much as they had been the first time he'd come by. One or two models walked around in short robes, which they seemed to open on demand for anyone who asked.

He could only assume that beneath the robes was some sort of experimental underwear being examined as needed. Nice work for the underwear inspectors, Casey thought, grinning.

Yet as amused as he was about what the robed underwear models were hiding, Casey could all too well imagine the woman down the hall opening her robe for him just because he asked.

In the last week, he'd lost count of his regrets about not dragging Alexa to the floor when he'd had the opportunity to do so. Now Casey was determined to never pass up the chance again. That determination brought him back to why he was currently standing in the waiting area.

"Excuse me, sir," a deep voice said from nearby. "Can I help you?"

Casey looked in the direction of the voice and saw a mountain of a man sitting at Sydney's desk. It seemed Alexa had hired a new guard dog.

The man was clean-shaven and dressed for the office in a pristine white dress shirt and tie, but he still looked like a mixed-breed bullmastiff at a thoroughbred dog show.

Sheer curiosity had Casey pausing in his quest.

"Good morning. Where's Sydney?" Casey asked politely.

"Sydney is out. My name is Allen Stedman and I'm assisting Ms. Ranger today. Is there something I can do for you?"

Casey took a couple of moments just to study the man.

Allen Stedman was likely six foot four. He was younger, taller, bigger, broader, and much more intimidating than Sydney—or Casey for that matter. But Casey could instantly tell Allen wasn't nearly as assistant savvy yet. Sydney would already have been standing in front of Casey instead of remaining behind the desk.

To get by Sydney, a person had to literally run over him. Then again, given the sheer size of Allen Stedman, if he did come after you, you probably weren't going to get by him either.

Casey played over several possible ways to get by Stedman before settling on the same ruse he'd used with Sydney.

"My name is Casey Carter. I just happened to be in the neighborhood and thought I'd stop by to see Alexa."

Casey made a big show of leaning on his cane while he talked and noticed Allen's eyes automatically softened in sympathy. Not that Casey needed the sympathy, especially on a good day like today, but he was not above using it to get around her new assistant. Besides, it was always interesting to watch the reactions people had that he walked with a cane.

"Are you a friend of Ms. Ranger's?" Allen asked, shifting his eyes from the cane to Casey's face again.

"We're dating," Casey said, shrugging and smiling.

He shifted his weight and tried purposely to look as unsteady as possible. Giving Allen a hard time was actually sort of fun. He'd spent eighteen years challenging and testing young Marines, and he missed it.

Allen crossed his arms, revealing muscles that belonged to a weight lifter. Casey fought not to laugh. While he wouldn't willingly challenge the kid to arm wrestle, neither was he overly impressed with his big-dog stance. Having done security for most of his career, Casey had learned early that muscles were only as good as the brain that controlled them.

"I don't recall a boyfriend being mentioned in my briefing," Allen said.

"We're fairly new as a couple," Casey told him, biting the inside of his bottom lip to stifle the grin.

"How new?" Allen challenged.

Casey had to think for a moment. Even though he personally counted the day he met Alexa and considered their relationship two months old now, it didn't fit his story.

"Two weeks," he told Allen, smiling as he dated their relationship to the first day he came to the office.

"I'm sure Sydney or Ms. Ranger would have mentioned a boyfriend if your story was true," Allen said.

"Well, actually—Alexa and I recently had a fight," Casey said, careful to remove the smile from his face. "I've been pretty mad at her. Alexa is a great woman, but she flirts a lot."

Casey noticed Allen was either shocked by the comment or shocked Casey made the comment.

Or impressed with his show of balls. It was hard to tell.

"I don't like it when she flirts with men other than me," Casey told him, shrugging as if it was a guy thing and Allen should understand.

Casey could see the wheels churning as Allen Stedman continued to look at him in disbelief. And he could also see Stedman contemplating how best to eject a man with a cane from the office. Casey gave him points for even considering it. Most security people would never take on a person with a disability, even if the person could be a potential criminal.

"You and Ms. Ranger are fighting? After only a week of dating?" Allen asked with a smirk, obviously not believing the statement.

Casey laughed, wondering what the man would think when he discovered that part of his story was absolutely true. He smiled and offered another shrug.

"Well, frankly I thought we made up Sunday when Alexa came by for breakfast. She liked my French toast and kissed me goodbye when she left."

Allen blinked a couple of times, uncrossed his arms like he wanted to believe Casey, and then crossed them again. Casey grinned as he watched Allen debate about what to do. It was probably a case where the truth sounded stranger than fiction.

"Seriously. I'm telling the truth. You can ask Alexa yourself," Casey said, purposely limping to a chair, feeling Allen's eyes on him. He wanted to laugh but restrained himself. "I'll wait."

Once seated in the chair, Casey noticed Allen seemed to relax his idea of bodily throwing him out of the place. After a few moments, Allen finally uncrossed his arms and pressed the intercom.

"Yes, Allen?" Casey heard Alexa answer.

Casey watched indecision race across Allen's face.

"May I ask what you had for breakfast Sunday morning?" Allen finally asked, his gaze locked in silent battle with Casey's.

Casey could hear Alexa laughing through the intercom. "A bagel and cream cheese," Alexa lied, surprise evident in her voice. "Why?"

"I guess I misunderstood something Sydney told me.

Sorry to have bothered you during your meeting." Allen released the intercom button and glared hard at Casey. Before he could speak though, the intercom buzzed again immediately.

"Allen?" Alexa called in her business voice, but Casey could tell she was trying hard not to laugh outright as she spoke.

"Yes, Ms. Ranger?" Allen answered, his eyes still on Casey. "I forgot to mention a man named Casey Carter might stop by. He and I have some unfinished business. Casey has a tendency to just show up when the mood hits. I apologize in advance if he gets rude with you. He's a former Marine, and not always polite."

Allen narrowed his eyes at Casey in warning. "I'm not worried, but thanks for the warning. What would you like me to do with Mr. Carter if he shows up?" Allen asked.

Casey laughed out loud. He already knew what Allen Stedman wanted to do to him. It was being communicated in every glance.

Alexa's answering laughter drifted through the intercom.

"Wow. Let me think—no, never mind, that's illegal in Virginia. I guess just send him back to my office. He's very stubborn. I've discovered it's best to just suffer through his persistence and hope he leaves quickly," Alexa said with a sigh.

"I'm sure I could persuade him to be less stubborn if you wanted," Allen told her, his eyes narrowing on Casey sitting relaxed in the chair.

"Aren't you a darling? I'm sure you could with all those muscles of yours," Alexa purred. "And I appreciate the offer more than I can say. However, don't let the limp fool you. The man is positively lethal with his cane. I know this first hand."

"Very well. I'll keep an eye out for him. Do you need anything else?" Allen asked.

There was a long pause before Casey finally heard her sigh.

"Only if you can perform an exorcism. I think I might be possessed," Alexa said, giving in to the laughter she'd been fighting.

"Sorry. Outside the office, my skills only extend to flattening unwanted intruders into pancakes," Allen told her.

Casey heard Alexa sigh again. "I much prefer French toast to pancakes, sweetie. Oh wait, silly me! I had French toast for breakfast on Sunday. *It was so long ago, I forgot*," she emphasized, raising her voice so that it projected loudly out of the intercom.

Casey shook his head, rolled his eyes, and sighed himself. It didn't surprise him that a woman like Alexa would blame him for not seeking her out sooner. The woman could simultaneously annoy and entice him with that sassy mouth of hers.

Allen finally grinned a little as he started figuring it all out. When he did, Casey saw a real guy with a sense of humor peeking through. Truthfully, he liked the fact that Stedman was seriously protecting Alexa. Go figure. Still, Casey could have done without hearing Alexa call the kid 'darling' and 'sweetie'.

"I'll keep a sharp eye out for Mr. Carter." Allen released the button and lowered himself to the chair.

"You'll wait fifteen minutes, and then I'll let you go back. She's meeting with her officers. Sydney says they chat about fun stuff the last fifteen minutes of the meeting, so you won't be interrupting any important business by that time."

Casey saluted Allen and smiled, eliciting a genuine laugh.

"I served one three-year tour in the army," Allen told Casey. "I got out when I was twenty-two to become a professional weight lifter. When I found I couldn't purchase dress clothes that actually fit my lifting body, I decided to pursue clothing design. I recently finished my degree. I guess this job is sort of an internship."

"What was your job in the Army?" Casey asked. But what he was really wondering was how anyone could make the leap from the military life to clothing design.

"I was an MP." Allen said, grinning when Casey belly laughed. "Now tell me the truth—are you really Alexa Ranger's boyfriend?'

"The dating campaign is still in progress. The rest I said is truth. I did feed her French toast Sunday and we are fighting. I'm crazy about her—or just plain crazy. It's hard to tell some days."

The typical male confession got another genuine laugh out of Allen, and Casey finally relaxed for real.

"Are you replacing Sydney?" Casey asked Allen.

"No—well, maybe. Sydney is a friend. We met working out at the same gym. As I understand it, Ms. Ranger wants Sydney to scale back and put more time in on his own design work. The SydneyB clothing line has a chance to go international. Whether I replace him or not is still undecided. I hear there's a couple people here who want the job." Allen looked at the computer, frowning.

"You get my vote," Casey said, checking his watch and seeing his waiting time was up. "You didn't let the cane stop you from challenging me. That's impressive. I was a Combat Engineer, but did several stints as a Marine Security Guard during my eighteen years. I got busted up during the last one. I'm retired but thinking about doing some sort of security business for a living."

"If you ever get something going, let me know. I'm not opposed to a little moonlighting now and again. Until I get famous, being a designer is mostly a hobby," Allen said, rolling his eyes. Then he looked at Casey with a smirk. "If you continue fighting with Ms. Ranger, I still might have to eject you sometime. Then you could see my other skills. I'd probably even enjoy showing you."

"Warning noted," Casey acknowledged easily, walking down the hallway.

Casey tapped on Alexa's office door, opened it enough to enter, and then simply walked on into the room. He didn't wait for an invitation even though it was rude. He enjoyed irritating Alexa. There definitely was a payoff when her eyes sparkled in challenge.

Four attractive women seated at the small conference table near the window turned their full attention to his entrance.

All of them were smiling except Alexa, who was all but laughing. It was hard not to be charmed by the picture they made. Doubly hard not to rush over and kiss Alexa's laughing mouth.

"Sorry," Casey said smiling, obviously not meaning it. "Am I interrupting?"

"Always," Alexa said. "Since when do you care?"

"Well, it's hard to care about a woman who would lie about the best French toast she ever tasted," Casey told her, smiling.

Alexa laughed. "Consider it partial payback for all the insults you've heaped on me. We're not even yet, so you'd better start praising me a little more if want to lessen my retaliation."

Casey came over to the table and stood near Alexa, waiting to be introduced.

"Casey, this is Karen Fortran, my CFO. Next is Ginger Alton, Marketing Director. And then Cindy Reed, Overseas Sales," Alexa said.

Casey nodded to them all. "Good to meet you."

With the introductions, he had the humbling and uncomfortable realization Alexa really had been conducting a business meeting, and he really was barging in on her.

Again.

Casey knew he was going to have to stop surprising her at work, but he didn't know how else to see her.

He looked at Alexa apologetically. "Would you rather I wait with Allen until you're free? I really don't mean to interrupt your work."

"No. We're done." Alexa said, surprised at his apology. "Who are you and what have you done with Casey Carter? He's a rude man, but I kind of like him."

The women all giggled, but Casey laughed. "He's still around, just trying to play nice in front of your staff."

"It's working. They're very impressed," she told him.

Alexa looked at his freshly shaven face and trimmed hair, thinking Casey looked very civilized, except for the glint of something wicked when he looked at her the way he was now.

"How about you?" Casey asked, lifting his hand to Alexa's cheek simply because he had to touch her beautiful smiling face regardless of the sassy mouth. "Are you impressed yet?" Alexa couldn't speak with her heart in her throat, so she turned her face into his palm and kissed it as if she'd done the action a thousand times.

Casey leaned down and lightly kissed her mouth in return, wishing like hell they didn't have an audience.

"Hi," he said to her softly. "Sorry I didn't come by sooner. You could have called me, you know."

Alexa rewarded him with a mischievous, happy smile that made the trip to see her suddenly worth every moment he'd spent talking himself into it for the last four days. The fight might not be over, but she seemed to be in a different place about it at last.

"I thought we were having a stubborn contest. I wanted to win for once," Alexa said to Casey, making the women at the table giggle again.

"You did. That's why I'm here," Casey conceded, stepping away from her and walking over to sit in one of the chairs in front of her desk.

Alexa laughed and turned to the others. "I think that's all for today. I'm sure Mr. Carter and I have given you plenty to discuss behind our backs now."

All the women laughed at her comment as they got up to leave, and each fervently denied she would gossip about it.

Casey smiled at the women but gave Alexa a wicked look. "No, don't tell them to be discreet. I want them to talk about it. I need witnesses who can vouch for me with Stedman. He almost threw me out of the office when you lied."

Alexa laughed and followed the women to close the door behind them. She noticed their heads were already together as they went the down the hall. It had been some time since she'd generated internal gossip, especially over a man. It was kind of fun to have the attention again.

When Alexa looked back, Casey was sitting comfortably in a chair, just waiting for her. Despite his tendency to try to control every situation, he was also turning out to be the least self-absorbed, most patient man she'd ever known.

Even though she was still plenty mad at him for calling her a flirt in the derogatory sense, if Casey hadn't come to her, Alexa would have gone to him within a day or two. In the internal debate Alexa kept having about her budding relationship with Casey, the physical desire to have sex with him was winning hands down over her irritation at his lack of understanding about her character.

Maybe it was naive to think Casey might eventually accept who she was, but it was the hope she clung to, which made her wonder if at fifty she had learned as much about men as she thought she had. Maybe Regina was right about her being the ultimate optimist, though she'd never thought of herself that way.

Instead of arguing about their disagreement, all she really wanted was to hug Casey and show him how happy she truly was to see him. The knowledge had her sighing. Casey had been nothing but polite in front of her staff, grudgingly winning her admiration again. Damn the man for making her feel so conflicted.

Alexa sighed and walked the short distance to where Casey sat.

"Got room in your lap for me?" she asked.

Casey smiled in welcome and patted his right leg. "Sit on this one. This is the good leg."

Alexa eased herself into his lap and ended up squealing when Casey lifted both her legs and swung them over his other leg as well as the arm of the chair. Her long legs dangled, but not uncomfortably. Her bottom was snugly tucked high in his lap.

"Certain things are going to get uncomfortable in a couple of minutes, but my legs will be fine," he told her, making her laugh, and at the same time addressing her worry about hurting him.

Casey put his hand on her thigh but removed it before he gave in to the urge to stroke up the inside. That would lead quickly to doing something rash, but damn—it was tempting.

To distract himself, Casey brushed her long hair back behind her shoulders, noticing once again how incredibly beautiful Alexa was.

Her throat tightened when she felt Casey moving and stroking her hair. Alexa was nervous sitting in Casey's lap, but at the same time it felt completely right as well. She couldn't remember ever feeling so unsettled with a man in her life.

"I just needed to be close to you for moment," Alexa explained, putting an arm along the back of his shoulders. "I'm still upset at you, but—." She stopped, not knowing how to finish to sentence.

Casey laughed, but there was no real humor in it. He stroked from her shoulder down to squeeze her hand, before moving his hand to her stomach.

"Welcome to my world. I feel the same way about you," Casey told her, toying with the buttons on the light pink shirt she wore. "So are you ever going to sleep with me, Alexa? Or do anything else in a bed with me? I'm dying here, lady."

Alexa sighed heavily, finally giving in to wanting to know what those strong, capable fingers would feel like on her. She knew her voice would give it all away when she spoke but no longer cared if Casey knew how much she wanted him. She watched his fingers plucking at the buttons. He was waiting on her now, just like he'd been waiting since Sunday.

"As far as I'm concerned, you could rip those buttons off and we could take this to the floor right now in the office," she whispered, teasing him. Or at least she was pretty sure she was teasing.

"No, not here," Casey answered quickly. But in contrast to his answer, he swiftly unbuttoned the first three buttons of her shirt and slipped his hand in to cup a breast covered in soft cotton.

Lace one day and plain white cotton the next, Casey thought, dizzily betting himself Alexa would make the simple bra look sensational.

Alexa groaned as Casey stroked a sensitive nipple to attention with his thumb. She let her head fall to his shoulder and sighed brokenly, feeling his body hardening under hers. If Casey decided to take it to the floor, she was definitely going.

For Casey, Alexa's broken sighs were like winning the lottery—and he badly wanted to cash in the winning ticket. Casey pulled her closer, holding Alexa as if she were already his, because she was in ways he couldn't have explained to anyone—not even to her. What he wanted today was a hell of lot more than a quickie on her office floor.

"Take me home with you, Alexa. Let me show you how good we can be together," he demanded.

Casey pulled his hand from her breast and used it to cup her face while he kissed her with all the longing he felt. And her kiss gave him back the answer he sought before he was able to hear the words.

"Okay," Alexa said against his mouth when he broke the kiss. "Let's go. I'm done for the day now."

She started to move away, but Casey stopped her.

"Wait," Casey said, buttoning her shirt back up with a regretful sigh. "If you go out of here with so much as a hair out of place, Stedman will turn me into a human pretzel."

"Don't worry," Alexa said, leaning back into him, nipping his bottom lip as she kissed him again before swinging her feet to the floor. "I'll protect you from my assistant. Besides, Allen's a big teddy bear or I never would have considered dating him."

When Alexa started to walk away, Casey grabbed the back of her shirt and pulled her backwards. "Say what again?" he asked.

Alexa laughed and reached behind her trying to smack his wrist. "Let go of me, heathen," she said, laughing.

"Explain the dating comment," Casey demanded, grabbing her hand and pulling her back onto his lap.

"Sydney offered to fix us up, but I turned down the chance," Alexa said, laughing and shrugging. "I don't let people set me up with dates."

"Stedman's what? Twenty-five? Twenty-six? He's probably not even as old as Jenna," Casey said. "Are you freaking kidding me?"

Alexa bit her lip as she studied Casey's set jaw. She was going to have to develop better filters when she talked to him about her life. He had no sense of humor about the men who passed through it.

"Okay, so Sydney thought I needed to date a younger man. But by the time he mentioned Allen as a possibility, I had already had dinner with you."

Alexa poked Casey in the chest, but got only a grunt in reply.

"Look, I'm trying my best to be honest with you. I would never date someone half my age. Thirty-eight is the absolute threshold of youth for me. I'm still trying to deal with how young you are."

Casey sighed heavily. It seemed to be a side effect of his association and constant frustration with Alexa Ranger. "I've got to get a handle on this jealousy thing before it drives me crazy. Maybe when I've been inside you a few hundred times, my confidence level will let me hear you talk about other men without wanting to kill them or you."

Alexa bounded off his lap to stand in front of him. "You are some piece of work, Casey Carter. I may not be perfect, but I'm at least a serial monogamist. I don't cheat when I'm dating someone."

"I didn't say you would cheat. It's just you're really beautiful, and obviously desirable to any number of men of any age."

Casey sighed again. It shouldn't be that hard for her to understand his point of view.

"Hell. It's bad enough I'm going to need a large quantity of alcohol for our sex talk," Casey said.

When Alexa huffed and looked at him blankly, Casey looked back sternly. "Don't give me the look, Alexa. I do believe you take intimacy seriously or you wouldn't have stopped or let me stop when I asked you to the other day. And I need to tell you a little about my physical limitations, or at least what I think are my limitations. I never really got to do many test runs after my surgery. Susan got really sick really fast."

Her heart immediately contracted with sympathy for him and his wife, for what they lost, and what they had missed. Alexa leaned down again, took Casey's face in her hands, and touched her forehead to his in understanding. One minute she was livid at him; the next she was aching to soothe him.

"Damn it, Casey. Try to stop insulting me, okay? You are a good man. Part of the problem is I'm jaded, cynical, and way too used to being alone. I'm probably not a good enough woman for you, but I want you in my bed anyway."

Casey scooted forward in the chair, ran his hands possessively around her hips, over her backside, and then rested them at her waist.

"Not good enough for me?" Casey protested hoarsely. "How in the hell can you say that when you could be going home with the weight lifter out there? I'm not even sure what I can do in bed anymore. The only thing I can guarantee is my enthusiasm. I want a chance to try."

Alexa sighed against the top of his head when he leaned forward to lay his head against her stomach. She felt the warmth of him through her shirt. The inevitability and rightness of their intimacy hit her full force. If there was heartache afterwards, she'd just have to deal with it.

"You make me crazy," Alexa told Casey, all teasing gone from her voice. "Trusting the attraction between us is not easy for me. You're the first man I've wanted in years. I hope like hell you can truly believe I'm not a bad person before we have sex. I don't want to sleep with a man who thinks so poorly of me."

Casey groaned against her belly, and then laughed when she pulled out of his arms.

"Just hold my hand when we walk out, okay? I want Stedman to know you're taken so he can give up any fantasies he may have about dating you," Casey told her.

"In case you haven't noticed, this is not high school," Alexa said snidely, retrieving her purse from the desk, but also walking around to take his hand when she saw the earnest look on his face. She felt silly doing it, but then felt righteous when Casey smiled at her and tightened his grip. What was it about him that made her feel so full of possibilities? And he seemed to be able to talk her into things more than anyone, even Sydney.

As they were leaving, Allen smiled at Alexa and smirked at Casey when he saw them holding hands. "Did you blackmail Ms. Ranger into holding hands, Gunny?"

"You're so mistrustful, Stedman," Casey told him with a grin. "I like that about you. Stay that way."

"Hey," Alexa said, smacking Casey in the chest with her purse. "Allen is my employee. If anyone gets to harass him, it's me."

"You can have a turn next Tuesday," Allen told her lightly. "Sydney will be out again."

"Fine," Alexa said, pretending to pout. "Put an appointment on my calendar."

"Yes, Ms. Ranger," Allen said, dipping his head to hide a smile.

In the elevator riding down, Casey played with her fingers. "So which vehicle did you drive today?"

Alexa ignored Casey's question.

"Why won't Allen call me Alexa? I hate it when he calls me Ms. Ranger. I feel like I'm his mother," she said instead.

Casey pulled her into his arms and held her tightly. "Good. I want you to feel like his mother. That way I'll look like a better deal to you."

Casey kissed Alexa hard, his tongue hinting at what was going to happen soon, before turning her loose.

Alexa narrowed her eyes and brought a hand to the back of his head.

"You know, you use a lot of caveman tactics on me. I'm not sure I like it. But in the interest of being fair, I want to try it myself. Back up," she ordered.

Casey took one step backward and felt the elevator wall. "What are you—?"

The rest of what he'd been going to ask disappeared in the heat of Alexa's mouth, the slide of her tongue, and then got completely lost as her sexy moan of desire vibrated against his lips.

Her hands moved over him and around him with the sure intent of arousing him as much as possible. He felt it in her touch. When Casey felt her skim the front of his jeans with an open palm, he thought he'd go mad.

Before the elevator could travel two floors, Casey was shaking with desire and once again hard as a stone for her.

Alexa freed his mouth and pushed her hips against Casey's until she could stroke against the bulge in his jeans.

"I'm so glad we're the same height," she whispered frantically, diving back into his mouth for more. She moved her body against Casey's with aggressive strokes of her hips, setting his loins blazing even through all the layers of their clothes.

Fighting the haze, Casey grabbed Alexa's arms hard to push her off of him, seeking a reprieve from the inevitable explosion mere moments away.

When Alexa looked at him, dazed and lustful, he gripped her arms hard, closed his eyes, and swore viciously. "I want you so bad, I almost don't care. But we have to stop before we end up in a damn Internet video. There's a surveillance camera in the elevator."

Casey's hands were trembling as he held her. She blinked at him but said nothing. Casey wasn't even sure she heard him.

"Are you okay? Talk to me, Alexa." Casey shook her a little to get her to focus.

Alexa let out a breath while her brain tried to understand why she wasn't still moving hard against Casey. She was throbbing and hurting in places she'd long forgotten were part of her. She cleared her throat and met his gaze.

"Wow, I guess I like acting like a caveman too. Now I can see why you do it," Alexa said reasonably. She reached out a hand and ran a palm down his shirt, delighting in the hardness of his chest, the unevenness of his breathing.

Then reality sunk in and his words penetrated the haze.

"What? Did you say there's a camera in here—*in the elevator?*"

Casey eased his grip on her arms then, turned her around, and pulled her back against the erection that painfully longed for renewed contact with her hips. Both of them groaned as their bodies instinctively fitted themselves together again even in the new position. If he had to stop their lovemaking one more time, he was going to lose his sanity completely.

He put an arm around Alexa's waist to hold her in place against him and then pointed to the camera in the corner. "I hope you trust your building security," he whispered in her ear.

Finally, the full reality of the situation hit Alexa's brain. She pulled out a cell and punched a number.

"Lenny? Hi. It's Alexa Ranger. Look I—I didn't know there was a camera in the parking garage elevator. My boyfriend and I were kissing, and—oh, you blanked it. Do I want you to delete it? Yes, thanks. I appreciate it. I—we're new and just got a little carried away. Yes. Thanks again."

Alexa closed her phone with a snap and blew out a breath. Fifty years old and she was making out in a public elevator. What had been she thinking?

She was already taking Casey home with her where they could do what they wanted in private. What if Casey hadn't stopped her?

Embarrassment had her face turning pinker than her shirt.

Casey laughed to break the tension. He should have just let nature take its course, he thought. The last thing he wanted was for a passionate woman to be embarrassed about her desire for him.

"Boyfriend?" he repeated her term for him, smiling. "You told the building security guy I was your boyfriend. Great. Now I have another witness."

Alexa elbowed him and walked out of the elevator into the parking garage. She took a deep breath and tried to forget how turned on she had been in the elevator.

Casey stepped out after her. He motioned to vehicles with his cane. "Surprise me, honey. I need a big distraction to take my mind off my physical frustration."

Alexa dug in her purse and pulled out a shiny red key fob. She lifted it high above her head to reach two rows over. Casey dropped his cane when he saw the lights blink.

"That's—that's a Ferrari," Casey said reverently. The woman owned a cherry red Ferrari convertible.

"It's an F430 Spyder," Alexa told Casey, liking the respectfulness of his tone. "It's my *girlie car.*"

"You consider a Ferrari to be a girlie car?" Casey asked. "I was impressed with the pickup. Now I'm just speechless. What else do you own?"

Alexa flicked her hair back. "Besides the Ford and the Ferrari? I own a BMW and two Lexus SUVs I use for business."

She picked up his cane and handed it back to him. Then she held out her car keys.

"Want to drive?' she asked with smile. "It's an automatic and I trust you."

Casey didn't blink, just stared at Alexa for a very long time.

She was stubborn, flirty, and mouthy. She also kissed with total abandon, set him on fire with her hands, and would have rocked them both to orgasm through their clothes if he hadn't stopped her. He got another quiver just thinking about them kissing in the elevator.

And now—now she trusted him to drive her Ferrari.

There was no doubt Alexa Ranger was driving him crazy. He'd have to deal with the fact he was falling in love with her later.

"You drive the car," Casey told her quietly, taking her hand and tugging her along as they walked. "I can barely walk now thanks to the raging, relentless hard-on you gave me in the elevator. The only thing I'm interested in driving is you. And when we get to your place, I intend to drive you over every edge I can—providing you don't incinerate me first. I never went up in flames so fast just kissing before. It was shocking, Ms. Ranger."

Alexa decided it was best to not comment. She was still a

little shocked as well by how carried away she'd gotten. Her face started to heat again just thinking about it.

Casey smiled at her flushed face and opened the driver's door. When he was seated next to her in the passenger's side, Casey turned his head, happily appreciating the gorgeous woman she was and the picture she made behind the wheel.

"Alexa, you look like you belong in this car," Casey told her sincerely.

"I thought so too," Alexa said, surprised at his instant understanding. "That's why I bought it. It just seemed right, you know?"

Casey nodded. "That's the best reason to do a lot of things," he agreed softly.

Because she knew Casey was really talking about them, and because she was fervently hoping he was right, Alexa's heart did the flipping thing again as she eased the car out of the parking space.

Chapter 13

As they pulled into her neighborhood, Casey saw that Alexa lived in a gated community with a live guard. She had yet another security gate on the area around her house, and told him she had an electronic door lock that only worked with the key inserted. All of which meant Alexa had not been kidding when she had described her home as a fortress.

"So exactly who are you keeping out with all this security?" Casey asked.

Alexa looked at him as she raised the garage door. "Is that criticism I hear in your tone? I thought as a military guy you would appreciate it," she said.

"I do," Casey replied, "but—well, it seems like a lot, even for a well-known model turned lingerie designer."

Alexa pulled the car into the attached garage and turned off the ignition while she pondered how to answer.

"I guess I don't need the security as much since I quit actively dating. For many years, I wanted to keep out the media people who just wanted to get a picture of the man I brought home for the night. Truth was I went home with my date when I was inclined, not the other way around. The only men who came to my home were Jenna's father and Sydney. I have always felt a need to protect my family from my public life," she explained.

Alexa looked out into the dark garage, lost in thought,

realizing how tame her life was now compared to even five years ago. "I wasn't always successful in keeping my private life private, but I tried. The security helped me feel like I was doing that."

Casey reached over and took one of her hands in his. "It wasn't a criticism, just a curiosity type of question."

She smiled and shook her head. "Sorry I'm so glum."

Casey squeezed her hand in support, and it turned her smile into a genuine one.

"I haven't been asked anything about myself in a while. And I don't mean to be defensive over everything you ask. My *don't-give-a-damn* is honed from years of practice," Alexa stated bluntly, hoping her laugh softened the pronouncement a bit.

"I know you've had a very different life than mine. I'm far too curious about you to not ask questions," Casey warned, playing with her fingers. "I like you and want to get to know you."

Alexa did laugh openly then. "Your mind is clouded by lust, Casey. We'll see how you feel in the morning."

Casey grinned at Alexa, hearing the unspoken fear in her voice. He had his own worries, but no doubts about being with her.

"Morning, huh? Are you already asking me to spend the night?" he joked.

Alexa smiled back. "Why? You fishing for an invitation already?"

"Hell yes," Casey replied quickly. "But I need more than one night. I want to spend the weekend. I'm even wondering if I can talk you into taking the day off tomorrow."

Alexa laughed with genuine amusement at that one.

"No man is that good in bed," she warned, amused at his smug grin. "I have a business to run. I work when I want to and need to. Men are fun, but they don't distract me from my greater purpose. I'm a mother and business owner, as well as a woman."

"Sounds like a challenge to see if I can change your mind about which priority should come first," Casey said, lifting her hand to his lips for a kiss.

Alexa laughed again at his macho bragging. "Been there, seen that movie. Orgasms don't last that long, Mr. Carter."

Casey laughed hard at her statement, his whole body vibrating with excitement. "Wow, you definitely are jaded and cynical. Or maybe you've just never had *really, really, really* great sex. I plan to rock your world lady—not bragging, just fact—but I admit it will probably take a few times. I need the weekend. I'm a bit out of practice."

"Well, you're in luck," Alexa said, laughing. "Pleasing me in bed will be easier than you think. I have a short fuse." She paused to consider what she'd just told him. "Does this count as our sex talk?"

Casey barely kept the rolling laugh building inside him from escaping. The woman was so damn forthright. It was hard to frown when he was so tempted to pull her across the console into his lap.

"No. I want to know how many men you've been with, but at the same time, I really don't. I'm having a morale dilemma, so I'm stalling," Casey said.

"You mean *moral dilemma*, don't you?" Alexa asked with a giggle.

"No. I mean *morale*," Casey said easily. "There have only been six women in my sex life. When I found Susan, she was it for me. And honestly, she gave me everything I wanted. I never looked beyond her—until I met you."

Alexa could only look at Casey and sigh. He had so much to give a woman whose heart was as open and trusting as his seemed to be. She wondered again why he wasn't pursuing someone a lot younger than her. He could have a wife and children if he wanted them, not just settling for sex with an older woman like her. *It isn't too late*, the voice inside reminded her.

She could still send him away, but now she didn't want to.

Alexa looked at the man holding her hand as they sat in the car. All she could think was how great it would have been to have met Casey twenty years ago. Instead of her fifty-year-old self, Casey would have been sleeping with a very different woman tonight. He was certainly not getting the nice version of her for sure.

"Do you seriously want to know that answer?" Alexa demanded softly, making Casey laugh again.

"I'm not naïve, you know," Casey told Alexa. "Given the differences in our ages, and the fact you never married, it's only reasonable to assume you've been with more partners than me."

Alexa snorted at his statement. *Here comes the judgment,* she thought.

"How magnanimous of you, Mr. Carter. So do you want a drink first to brace yourself?" Alexa asked with a smirk.

Casey held Alexa's gaze trying to determine if she was worried or not about what he thought. He decided he couldn't tell. Either he was too nervous to figure it out, or Alexa truly didn't care.

In the end, he decided neither would change their reality. It was a waste of time to worry about how many men had been in her bed before him.

"Am I going to need a drink to hear the answer?" he asked finally.

"Depends. Are you a person who peels off a band-aid slowly or just rips it off all at once?" she asked, stalling.

Casey contemplated the warning, recognizing it for what it was. He watched Alexa tracing the steering wheel with her hands as she waited for his response. He badly wanted those capable, confident, experienced hands on him, stroking him as boldly as they had every other time she'd touched him. *That* was the real answer—and the only one that mattered.

"If the number of men is anywhere under a hundred, I swear it will not change my mind about nailing you," Casey promised, gaining another lusty laugh from her.

"*Nailing me?* Yet another of your lovely sex terms that does nothing to entice me into bed with you," Alexa said to him sarcastically. "Well it seems you're in luck again, Mr. Carter. The number is just a little under twenty-five. I'm not completely sure. My sex life covers several decades and I wasn't exactly keeping a count."

"Well, hell. Twenty-five is not many," Casey said with a grin. "Most men I know average in the twenties. If I hadn't been faithfully married, I probably would have hit that number, too."

Alexa snorted at the almost disappointed look on Casey's face. "Good to hear that as a healthy, sexual fifty-year-old woman I haven't exceeded the average male quota for sex partners. What number did you think I would say?"

"Looking the way you do?" Casey asked, checking her out completely with a long sweeping gaze. "I'd have believed a much higher number with no trouble at all."

Alexa was grateful for her sense of humor or she'd probably put him in taxi and send him home. "So am I supposed to be flattered or insulted by your conclusions, Casey? Sometimes I just can't tell with you."

"Take everything tonight as flattery. I'm about to raise your number of partners again," Casey said, pulling her toward him and kissing her lightly as she laughed.

Alexa leaned back in her seat, her initial desire waning a little at Casey's questioning. He was right to force the discussion, but it bothered her more than she admitted to him. She would like a little more time to think about the differences in their lives, especially how they would translate to the bedroom.

"Let's take a tour, and then I'll feed us. You're welcome to stay as long as you want tonight. So I'm the first woman since Susan? I guess that explains why I have a sense I'm about to make you an adulterer. I'm even feeling a little guilty."

"It's okay," Casey assured her, opening his door. "Susan would approve of you."

Alexa got out and gave him a disbelieving look "Really? Your wife was into sharing you with other women?"

"No. Susan would have castrated me for being unfaithful, but after being diagnosed with cancer, she made me promise to keep on living if she died. Tonight you're helping me keep a promise," Casey said, following her to the utility room door.

"Yes. I guess I am," Alexa said at last. "But for the record, you're doing a pretty good job of moving forward on your own. I think it says a lot about your relationship with her that you're willing to look for another one."

"You know, I don't think I've ever had a woman say nicer, more approving things to me than you do," Casey said as they walked into her kitchen. "It's one of the reasons I like you so much."

Alexa snorted and narrowed her eyes at him. "That's not what you told me last week when you used your cane to hold me against the wall of my office."

"Well, I've never had a woman be colder or harder than you are on me either," Casey informed her. After a bit, he shrugged his shoulders. "I guess you're just passionate and outspoken."

"So carefully speaks the man hoping to get laid tonight," Alexa exclaimed, with a pealing laugh that echoed off the walls of her usually empty kitchen.

Casey narrowed his eyes, choosing not to be offended. Their sex talk made him feel like a kid compared to Alexa in some ways, but he was looking damn forward to demonstrating just how much of an adult male he was.

"Honey, I'm beyond hoping and into *damn-well-going-to-get-laid* mode tonight. If I were you, I wouldn't even count on having dinner until after the first couple of times," Casey told her.

Alexa brought her hands to her hips, and lifted her chin. "You obviously don't understand my need for food."

Casey waved at her stance with his cane. "No, but I get the hands-on-hips thing you do when you're feeling stubborn. So let's just make the preliminaries as quick as possible. I'm not waiting much longer to be inside you. My patience is strained to the limit."

"Live and learn, Carter. Accusing me of being stubborn is not helping your cause," Alexa warned. She certainly wasn't going to admit to the little buzz going on all over her body causing moisture to pool between her legs just at the idea of Casey not wanting to wait.

At thirty, she would have thrown caution to the wind and

just jumped him. At fifty, she knew better, knew to take the time she needed to avoid adding one more man to her list of regrets.

The house tour took less than thirty minutes since Alexa avoided the master bedroom. And Casey never asked about it either.

Eventually they wound back up in the kitchen, with Casey sitting at a spacious dining table while Alexa set about making them something to eat.

"On Thursdays, I usually meet Regina and Lauren for dinner. But I have the makings of ham and cheese omelets if that sounds okay?" Alexa offered.

Casey nodded. Food was optional for him. All he wanted was her.

"Regina? That's the famous Dr. Logan, right? I read some articles about her on the Internet. They say she's brilliant but notorious in her field. Is she as scary smart as they say?"

"Yes," Alexa said easily. "But she's awesome, too. She always says what she means. You'd like her. She swears as much as you do."

Casey laughed at the veiled criticism.

"Tell me about Lauren," he ordered, liking the way Alexa smiled when she talked about her friends.

Alexa lifted her gaze from the skillet and thought for a moment.

"Lauren—how do I describe her? Lauren McCarthy comes from an old school Falls Church family. She was a patient of Regina's, like I was. After she finished treatment, Regina asked to bring her to dinner. That was, I guess, six or seven years ago now."

Casey grinned. "Sounds as rich as you. How old is she?"

"Forty-two, but she looks younger. She keeps men at a distance, so don't get any ideas," Alexa said, laughing, unconcerned at Casey's pretended interest in Lauren. "Regina on the other hand is forty-seven and would bed you in a heartbeat."

"I'm definitely not experienced enough to take on a sex therapist," Casey said with a laugh. "Besides, I'm really into older lingerie models at the moment. Or at least I will be tonight."

Alexa giggled at his innuendo. "You're terrible, and I can't believe I even laughed at that joke."

Casey grinned. There was no better seduction than making a woman laugh.

"Lauren's part of your business, isn't she?" he asked, changing the subject before he was tempted to interrupt her cooking.

"Lauren has a family trust fund, which means she never has to work for money. Instead, she does a massive amount of charity and fundraising work, more work than many people do in regular jobs."

Alexa reached into the cabinet for plates as she talked. "Since Lauren doesn't date, for personal reasons I can't really share, she has a lot of free time. For fun, she learned to make organic soaps and scents in her kitchen. They're all quite good."

"You wear one of them, don't you?" Casey asked.

"Yes. The others are just as good, and now I'm going to sell them. We'll have to look into a way to mass-produce them if they take off. Strange as it sounds, I'm giving Lauren her first real paying job," Alexa said, smirking.

"You make running a business seem like the most natural thing in the world," Casey said to her. "In fact, you do everything with grace. I like watching you move through your life. It inspires me to keep thinking about starting my own business."

Alexa carried the plated food to the table. "I inspire you?" she asked, surprised by his comment.

Casey nodded his head yes as he tasted the first bite. "Yes. You're a good cook, too."

"Thanks for both. I don't know if anyone has ever said they were inspired by me," she told him, taking the seat next to him.

"You have every right to be proud of your achievements, Alexa," Casey said sincerely. "And you manage to inspire me while simultaneously driving me crazy. I'm coming to think of it as just your natural multi-tasking talent."

Casey said the last around a grin and a mouthful of omelet.

"Oh, there you are," Alexa said, forking up her own food and chewing. "I wondered where the rude Casey Carter had gone. You're a real Jekyll and Hyde kind of guy, aren't you?"

"Which do you like best?" Casey asked in what he hoped was a sexy tone. "I'll be any kind of guy you want tonight."

"Finish your dinner," Alexa ordered, barely stifling a grin. "I can't flirt when I'm hungry."

After dinner, they went for a tour of the garages and vehicles, and then for a short walk in the gardens Alexa was still in the process of developing. She even showed Casey the tree house Jenna designed and helped build as a child.

Back in the house at last, Casey laughed as he walked through her living room holding her hand. Alexa had done just about everything possible to delay the inevitable.

"Are you done stalling now?" he finally asked, calling her on it.

When Alexa tried to pull her hand away from his, he held on tighter. His patience was gone. He wanted—no, needed to be with her.

"I wasn't stalling. I was being hospitable," Alexa defended.

"A fancier phrase for *stalling*, but still the same thing," Casey agreed. "I was in the elevator with you this afternoon, remember?"

Alexa dropped her gaze from his and swore. "So what if I am stalling? Don't you think I have the right to be a little nervous? You're much younger than me. We disagree over some pretty big things. I still haven't completely decided if this is a good idea or not."

Casey laughed and pulled a reluctant Alexa into his arms. He dipped his head and hungrily sought her mouth, slipping his tongue in to dance with hers until they were both weaving back and forth, fighting to stand up.

"Fine. While you're debating the wisdom of sex with me, be hospitable and finish the house tour," he said as he freed her mouth. "Show me the master bedroom, Alexa." He kept her hand captured in his, not willing to let her run from her feelings or him.

Alexa nodded and led him down the hall, crossing the threshold into a room containing an unmade queen bed and yesterday's clothes in a heap on the floor. The dark woods of the furniture and soothing white bedclothes were immensely inviting. There were pillows on the bed and more on the floor.

"I wasn't expecting company," she told him with a shrug.

Casey laughed. "Good to know you have some normal faults. It makes you a little less intimidating."

"I'm not intimidating," she protested.

"Yes, you are, but it's not going to keep me out of you," he told her with a laugh.

Casey pulled her around to face him, holding her in his arms as he held her gaze. "Kiss me, Alexa. I want to be with you, and whatever happens this time, we're not stopping."

He closed his mouth hungrily over hers again. When he broke the kiss this time, Casey sat on the end of her bed, then lay back, pulling Alexa down on top of him, dragging her body across his until she was draped there.

"Prone at last," Casey said with a laugh. "Now kiss me like you mean it, or at least tell me what you're afraid of."

"I'm not afraid," Alexa denied, "just—just nervous."

Casey moved one of her legs between his, until his erection was directly under her thigh. He felt a tremor shake her. "See how much I want you, lady? Granted, it's not going to last long the first time, but there's only one way to get to the second and third times. Let me inside you, Alexa."

With every movement, Casey made sure she brushed against him. The contact was exquisite torture.

"You said," she breathed hard, "you said you had some limitations."

"Hip replacement. Not all positions are safe. I'll let you know what's okay as we go along. You can trust me to tell you," he said quietly. "I'm a very honest man in bed."

Casey moved his hands to her backside, cupping her

through her jeans and holding her.

"*Woman On Top* can be good," he suggested, moving her hips across the front of him until he felt her heat directly on top of his erection. "But it doesn't seem fair to make you do all the work the first time. Maybe later."

Casey watched her sigh and close her eyes in pleasure as she tried to get closer to him through their clothes. He was going to thoroughly enjoy banishing every concern she had about him.

Thankful for the last year he'd put in at the gym, he rolled them over on the bed until Alexa was completely under him. Putting both his legs between hers, he pushed his now aching erection down firmly into the center of her heat. Even through their jeans the contact was electric. She groaned and arched hers hips up to get closer to him.

"Okay, *Man On Top* is as fucking awesome as I imagined. I think we've picked a winning position for our first time, honey."

Holding Alexa in place with his hips pressed down on hers, Casey raised his upper body and made short work of the buttons on her shirt. He didn't slow his efforts until Alexa was bare except for the plain cotton bra she wore.

Later he would remember this and think about how much fun he was having with her. Her face was flushed and he could still feel her hesitation. It was like undressing the sexy girl next door instead of the lingerie queen who had kissed him senseless in the elevator. God help him, he liked the idea of being with both. The woman beneath him was so damn interesting.

"I like how strong you are," Casey told her, his voice rough now with lust, husky with approval. "I like how our bodies match up so well. I like how absolutely unashamed you are of being turned on by me. It's all I can do not to rip off the rest of your clothes."

He bent his head to her neck, ran a trail of burning kisses from ear to collarbone, and then farther down to a center point between her straining breasts. "You are absolutely the most beautiful woman I've ever seen."

Casey reached down and lifted both her legs under her thighs, encouraging her to wrap them around his waist. When she did, he pressed her into the bed and kissed her deeply, groaning into her mouth. "One day I'm going to find the right words to tell you how much I love having your long legs wrapped around me. It's the sexiest thing I've ever known."

"Casey," she choked, and had to clear her throat to get his name out clearly. "I want you so badly. Get me out of these damn clothes."

Laughing at her honest command, he rolled them to their sides. He pushed her shirt down her arms and reached behind her to unclasp her bra.

Alexa struggled to unbutton her cuffs while he was sliding the jeans from her hips and down her legs. He kissed her stomach above the plain cotton panties she wore, and she bucked.

"No," Alexa pleaded. "Too much. I need you—"

"—inside the first time," Casey finished. "I know, honey. I feel the same way."

When Casey finally stripped her down to her underwear, Alexa rolled to her knees and made short work of stripping his shirt from him. She paused only to run her hand down the front of his chest, admiring the taut nipples and tight abs she found along the way.

Her hands shook in anticipation as they unfastened his jeans. She was working on the zipper when Casey finally stopped her with his hand.

"It's too dangerous for you to touch me. Next time," he promised, all but destroyed by her trembling, eager touch.

To show him her compliance, Alexa moved her hand to his shoulder while he pushed his jeans and underwear off together. She heard him retrieve a condom from the pocket before tossing them in the floor.

"Do that now," Alexa said firmly, staring into Casey's eyes. "Next time I want to do it for you."

"Okay," Casey agreed harshly, pulling her close again and kissing her fiercely. He rolled on the condom while he watched Alexa remove her underwear.

When she was completely naked, he pulled her into his arms again. "I'm not going to be able to wait, or be gentle. I'm too far gone, so just let me apologize in advance if this goes badly. You can kick my ass later."

Alexa touched her fingertips to his lips, stroking them to silence. "I thought Marines were the strong silent type. You talk more in bed than any man I've ever known."

Casey smiled and rolled them again until he was back on top and between her legs once more.

"No, Marines are the loud, passionate, get drunk, and go for it type," he corrected.

"Really? Could have fooled me," Alexa said, laughing.

She lifted a leg, sliding it slowly up the back of his good one, and finally hooked it across his hips letting her knee rest in the small of his back. "Go for it then," she demanded.

"Oh, hell," Casey said, sliding as slowly as he could into her wetness, noticing all the little resistances of her along the way. The pleasurable heat of her had him groaning.

Before he was even all the way inside, Alexa arched and called, "There. There, Casey. Harder."

He stopped and backed off, and when he slid in again, it was all the way and in perfect sync with the arch of her hips against his. He repeated the action twice, moving as hard as he could with his heart hammering against her breasts. He felt Alexa pulsing in release around him. Her body gratefully responding to his.

"Got to love a woman with a short fuse," he growled in her ear, letting himself happily pound and stroke the rest of her climax away as he found his own release.

"You were right about your enthusiasm. I actually felt you emptying yourself inside me," Alexa told him afterwards, kissing his cheek and stroking his face. "I love the way you feel. Now all I can think about is doing this again with you."

Casey kissed her below her ear, and then moved to her mouth with gratitude.

"That's a good thing, honey, because we're just getting started," Casey promised, reveling in the answering shiver that shook her body beneath his.

Chapter 14

After the first time, there were two others that night, each more vigorous than the last, until they both finally fell soundlessly asleep around ten with the bedroom lamp still burning.

Alexa was used to sleeping alone, so she woke up surprised when Casey adjusted her in his arms. Looking at the clock on the nightstand, she saw it was only two. It had been almost a year since she'd been in bed with a man, but it had been much longer since she'd woken up with one. Much, much longer than that since a man had pleased her so thoroughly. Maybe never.

A satisfied sigh slipped out. It was apparently loud enough to have Casey opening his eyes.

"Hi," he said, smiling, tugging her closer.

"Go back to sleep. It's only two," Alexa told him, brushing a hand across his forehead and through his hair. "The light woke me."

"Too late, I'm completely awake now. Anything you want to do?" Casey asked sleepily, moving a leg across hers.

"No," Alexa said with a laugh. "You've worn me out. My fifty-year old libido isn't up for an all-nighter. I warned you to pick a younger woman."

"When the hot burning fires are banked, that's when the real magic can happen," Casey said softly, tracing her lips with his finger.

Alexa smirked and patted his erection with the palm of her hand.

"This is as impressive and promising as it was the other three times, but I seriously need some rest, Carter."

"Just once more, Alexa. I need you again. Do you want to hear me beg?" Casey asked. "I know how to beg really well."

He moved a hand to cup her breast and stroke her nipple with his thumb, causing her to release a series of broken sighs as a tight bud formed instantly.

Alexa couldn't hold back the moan rising up in her throat. Casey was drawing responses from her that she hadn't felt for decade or more, but there were still limitations to what she could accommodate.

"Casey," Alexa said softly, laughing at his earnestness. "I simply don't think I can do this again."

"Can you still get pregnant?" Casey asked seriously, peering into her face, trying to see the answer there.

"No," she said, surprised at the shift in topic. "No chance of that. I had surgery in my late twenties. Disappointed?"

"Relieved," he clarified. "I don't want to use a condom with you this time. I want to feel all of you."

That got her attention. "Why?"

Casey just raised his eyebrows in reply.

"Sure, I guess it's okay," she said at last, because it was what she wanted. She just hadn't made complete peace with it yet.

Casey rose over her and pushed her completely to her back, pressing her down into the mattress and the pillow they had been sharing. "Trust me, Alexa. I won't hurt you. I just want us to be completely connected."

He held himself off her with one arm while he ran a possessive hand down her side. "After this, I'll let you sleep all you want. Maybe even during."

"During?" she asked, looking at Casey in mild alarm.

It already baffled her how he could talk about nailing her in one breath, and then sweetly beg to be inside her the next. Now he was telling her she could sleep while they had sex.

She couldn't keep up with him or his thinking.

Casey tilted just enough to stroke a hand down her stomach and between her legs, groaning softly at what he found there.

"See? You're still wet for me and I want inside again. I'm willing to beg if that's what it's going to take," he whispered, burying his face in her throat as he stroked.

"Fine. Whatever," Alexa said, moving her legs to let his hips slide down between them. "Go slowly."

"Don't worry, I plan to," he said, his voice a laughing whisper in the dark.

Casey entered her body a little at a time, stroking and praising every inch he gained until he was seated inside as far as possible. He could feel Alexa adjusting to his length, accommodating his hardness, and struggling against taking him. It said a lot about her that she didn't complain even though he could tell she wasn't completely comfortable.

"Look at me, Alexa," Casey commanded, which she did with her blue eyes stripped bare of everything but an acknowledgment of what they were doing together. He stared at her for a long time before he could trust himself to speak sanely. Vulnerability looked so damn good on her.

"You feel more amazing than any fantasy I had about you. I love being inside you. Thank you for letting me be with you," he said roughly.

"You're welcome," Alexa replied politely. "I guess." She closed her eyes and swallowed hard. "You—you feel amazing, too. I almost never do this without protection."

"Thank you for that as well—and for trusting me not to hurt you," Casey said, pushing into her a little more, bumping against the core of her in the process, emphasizing the fact he was thrilled to be filling her completely.

He was rewarded by a sigh as she relaxed a little more around him.

"Being inside you is very important to me. I don't take it lightly, Alexa," Casey said, kissing her temple. "Whatever you believe or don't believe about men in general, you can one hundred percent take my word on this being the truth between us. It's not about your cars, your wealth, or anything other than the fact that you make me feel like life is worth living again."

Casey lay down on her fully, letting her cradle his weight as he kissed her cheek. "It's nice being inside you without the overwhelming desire I feel for you most of the time. I like the way you take me in and make room for me inside your body."

"Are you just going to stay hard inside me for the rest of the night?" she asked quietly, shifting against his possession, making even more room, though she couldn't say how it was possible. He just laughed at her playful insults.

"I'll stay as still as I can for as long as I last. Then I'm going to hold you while you sleep in my arms," Casey promised.

"And if I want something more than that?" Alexa asked, eyes shining, body trembling under his.

"This raging hard-on I have belongs to you. If you want, I'll happily pound you hard enough to break both you and the bed," Casey told her, wanting to laugh when she trembled at his words. Alexa was proving to be a hell of a woman to conquer, he thought, wondering if he was going to be able to be as still as he promised.

"I think I like the staying still part this time," Alexa said meekly. "Pound me tomorrow after I've had some rest."

Casey's heart contracted at her willingness to be vulnerable with him and tell him the truth.

"We'll compromise. How about this?" he asked, bending down and sucking an aroused nipple into his mouth. He sucked hard until she arched, and then released her nipple only to roll it between a finger and his thumb until she groaned. "I bet I can ignite your fuse without moving at all."

"Damn it, Casey. What are you trying to do to me?" Alexa demanded, exasperated not with what he was doing, but that he was calling all the shots, had all the control.

Casey didn't comment, just bent his head to the other nipple and gave it similar attention. When Alexa arched again, he sucked even harder, not releasing her this time. When he felt her twisting and thrashing to the point she was lifting both of them from the bed, Casey brought his attention to her mouth. He stroked hard in and out with his tongue until Alexa exploded around him, pulsing and throbbing. Her heart continued to hammer hard beneath his even after she'd calmed.

"What—" she stammered, had to clear her throat to speak, "what about you?"

Casey kissed her temple and put his face on the pillow beside her ear. "I have everything I want just being inside you, but thank you for asking," he answered softly on a laugh. "Sleep now. I won't wake you again."

"Casey," Alexa began, unsure what to say to him. She'd fallen asleep still connected after sex, but she'd never had a fully aroused man just resting contentedly inside her before.

"Shush. Just sleep. Trust me," he ordered, pleased when she did.

When Alexa woke in the morning, Casey was not beside her, but she heard the shower running.

Looking at the clock, she saw it was seven fifteen, already later than her usual rising time.

No workout today, she thought, pushing her tired and aching body upright. Climbing reluctantly from the bed, she pulled on yoga pants and a tee, headed to the guest bathroom, and then to the kitchen to make coffee.

Casey found her in the kitchen, staring at the coffee pot, hair mussed and face still foggy from sleep. It was his fault she looked so tired, he thought, fighting not to smile too much about it.

He walked slowly to Alexa and pulled her into his arms for a hug.

"Morning," Casey said.

"Good morning," she replied, hugging him back, and leaning on him a little. "You smell nice."

"You smell sexy," he said, kissing her neck as she pulled away. "Are you going to work today?"

"Important meeting this morning," Alexa said quietly, turning and reaching into a cabinet to pull out two matching mugs.

Casey sighed as she poured dark, fragrant liquid into both mugs. "Damn. I guess I wasn't good in bed after all. Well, you did try to warn me."

"Come with me," Alexa offered, the words tripping out, fueled by the urges developing much farther south.

Casey grinned over his mug, his eyes flashing. "Every time I can," he promised.

Alexa slapped his chest with the back of her hand. "Fool. I meant come to work with me. I can probably get away at lunch."

Casey's eyes grew thoughtful. "How about I pick you up at lunch? I have something I want to do. Am I spending the weekend?"

"Up to you," Alexa said with a shrug.

"Alexa," Casey said firmly, shaking his head from side to side. "Do you want me to spend the weekend or not?"

"Does my attorney need to draw up a contract? What do you want from me?" she demanded on a laugh. "We talked about this yesterday."

"I said I wanted to stay. Now I need you to ask me," he ordered. "Just ask me to stay the weekend."

"No," she replied back. "I already did. I'm not going to beg."

"Alexa, we're about to christen your kitchen floor. I'm still stirred up from being inside you for hours while you slept under me. I'm going to have to pound you this time."

"That was not my fault—" Alexa began, and then changed her mind about arguing when Casey set his still full coffee cup on the counter.

"Would you like to spend the weekend with me?" Alexa asked quickly as his arms came firmly around her, causing her to slosh her coffee over the side of the mug.

"Yes," Casey said. "But now I'm even more stirred up. I don't know if I can wait until this afternoon."

Her backed her against the counter, moved the coffee from her hand to the nearest flat surface, and leaned into Alexa for a kiss that shared a whole lot more than just a taste of coffee.

"I knew this would happen. I want you even more today. What time is your meeting?" he asked.

"An hour from now," Alexa said, using her hands to stroke his back while his hips pressed into hers. She straightened and spread her legs to pull him between them.

Casey groaned at the deepened contact. "I can wait a few hours. I'm sure I can. I may be insane by that point, but I can wait. I need to go home, pack a bag, and run an errand. I'll ride with you to work and take a taxi. I'll come back at noon."

He picked up her coffee and handed it back to her. Then he picked up his own.

"You make good coffee," he said, thinking how it would be to wake up with her every day.

"Basic survival skill," Alexa said, refilling her mug and heading to the bedroom. "Give me a few minutes to shower. I'll be quick."

"Can I watch?" Casey asked, smiling over the mug at her.

"Next time," Alexa promised, finally smiling herself. This morning she didn't trust him, but worse, she didn't trust herself. If it wasn't for the marketing meeting about Lauren's scents, she'd have taken Casey back to bed to see if he tasted as good as he smelled. She sighed at the depth of her longing. Maybe her shower needed to be a cold one.

When she emerged from the bedroom a half hour later, Casey was sitting on the couch in her living room, flipping through a business magazine. "I'm ready," she said.

"That was fast. And you still look amazing. Tired—but amazing," he told her.

Alexa smiled and offered him a hand to pull him from the sofa.

"So what are you driving today?" he asked, not able to keep the excitement from his voice.

Alexa tilted her chin down to smother a smile. "Are you just having sex with me for my vehicles?"

"No," Casey denied, shaking his head. "But they're a real perk."

"BMW," she said flatly, slapping the keys into his palm. "You're driving this time. I'm exhausted. Some horny Marine kept me up all night."

"Lucky you," Casey said, grabbing her hand when she laughed. "Have I told you I love that sassy mouth of yours?"

"Good thing," Alexa said, leading him through the maze of her house to the garage. "I'm too old to change my personality, even for great sex."

"Great, huh?" Casey grinned. "Honey, you'll be adding adverbs to that adjective before you have a chance to talk to Regina and Lauren about it."

He unlocked the passenger door and held it open for her.

"You honestly think I'm going to tell my friends how good you are in bed?" Alexa asked, hands on hips again.

Casey smirked. "Of course. And when I piss you off, they'll be the first to know that too. I was married. I know how it works."

Alexa dropped her hands and sighed. "It's true," she admitted, climbing into the car while he laughed.

Casey put the key in the ignition and waited in awe as the soft leather seat adjusted itself perfectly around his rear. "Oh, hell. I didn't know what an opportunist I was until this seat molded itself to my ass."

Alexa laughed, "So you *are* sleeping with me for my cars?"

"Maybe," Casey said, backing out of the garage and smoothly rolling down the driveway. "I hope that's not the case. I'll let you know for sure in a few days."

"Again, this is not a good way to win points with me," she chastised, laughing. Her ego didn't dent so easily. "So I'm competing with my cars," she mused, smiling to herself. "We'll see about that."

Casey never heard her threat because he was totally absorbed in driving the car through Falls Church morning rush traffic.

Alexa leaned her head back and fell asleep on the way.

At her building, Casey kissed Alexa goodbye and got off the elevator at the main floor. The doorman was flagging a cab for him as the elevator doors closed.

Alexa rode up to the office alone, missing Casey already.

She was lost in a fantasy thinking of last night when Sydney spied her.

He looked at his watch and then narrowed his eyes. "You're late, but at least you finally got laid," Sydney said, picking up his coffee with a grin.

"*Got laid*?" Alexa repeated. "What is it about men and their unflattering euphemisms for sex?"

"Well, what do you want to call it?" Sydney asked with a shrug. He tapped on his PDA. "Marketing meeting is in fifteen minutes. Want me to delay the meeting time?"

"No," Alexa barked, then softened her tone as she realized she was on the verge of yelling for no good reason. "No. Sorry for yelling. I'm just tired. The meeting is the only reason I dragged myself here today. I need about ten more hours of sleep."

"Hmmm...you're awfully grumpy. Carter must not have been as good as he looked," Sydney said with a laugh.

"Fat lot you know," Alexa said, her mouth twisting into a playful snarl. "The man finally let me sleep after the fourth time. Hell, there could have been a fifth or sixth time. He was still up for it when I passed out."

"So you're mad because Casey didn't fall asleep before you?" Sydney asked, feigning confusion, when he secretly wanted to do a happy dance and twirl Alexa around the waiting area.

"No," Alexa said, turning to stride down the hallway. "I wanted him to stay with me today, but he had an errand to run."

"Honey, you can't bring a lover to work like he was a purse dog, otherwise Paul would never leave my side."

Sydney took a sip of his coffee and thought about it for a while.

"Though after four times last night, I can see why you might want to keep an eye on Casey. If word ever got out to the other women here, well, things might get ugly for you," he joked, pretending to shiver at the potential violence of women fighting over Casey's affections.

Alexa raised a middle finger salute over her shoulder.

Sydney was the only person who reminded her occasionally that beautiful was good, but it wasn't always enough. She both loved and hated him for it.

"Hey," Sydney yelled at the finger. "You weren't the only one who got lucky last night."

"Stop bragging and have someone get me a large coffee. Then come talk to me about business. I want you to sit in on the meeting about Lauren's scents."

Alexa walked on not glancing back, not wanting to see the I-warned-you look she knew was on Sydney's face.

"Bossy today, aren't you?" Sydney yelled down the hall. Then the light bulb turned on in his brain. "Oh, *that's it*, isn't it? I was right. Carter was just as bossy in bed as I suspected."

Sydney heard her office door open, and then heard some stomping across the room. *Direct hit*, he thought, laughing. He shouldn't tease her, really shouldn't. But it was a lot of fun to see Alexa Ranger meet her match at last.

Sydney picked up the phone. "Ellen, is Jeannine with you? Can she make a coffee run? Somebody is a little down today. Yes. We will need sprinkles, lots of them. And whipped cream too. Yes I know, but it's one of those days. Yes. Thanks."

Sydney picked up his PDA, his own coffee, and hummed all the way down the hall.

Chapter 15

Casey looked up at the steel and glass monster, wondering how a creative person could voluntarily work in a modern professional building so cold and unwelcoming every day.

Maybe to some it was a feat of creative genius. To him, it was no more attractive than a hangar or a Quonset hut, which were about as ugly as buildings could get.

Though Casey didn't dwell on his military past very often anymore, today it was on his mind because of what he had to do.

As a Marine, he had served in many wars and altercations and managed to survive. There was the Gulf War, Somalia, and Afghanistan. Not to mention the six times he had handled security for embassy duty, if you didn't count the last one in Djibouti where being thrown by a bomb had taken out his hip.

He'd even survived that, though it had cost him his military career.

Today he wondered what price he was going to have to pay for the fight he was about to have. He wished it didn't have to be a fight, but if Alexa was right about her daughter, then it was probably going to be one.

Still, after seeing Alexa's vulnerability last night, he'd decided it was worth risking this conversation, no matter what the outcome.

There was no doorman to greet him in front of the metal monstrosity, but just inside there was a round receptionist area where a woman hesitantly greeted those who entered. In his military mindset, the receptionist area reminded him of a foxhole.

Casey shook his head to clear out the past and brought his attention to the task at hand.

"Casey Carter. I have an appointment to see Jenna Ranger at ten. I made it just a little while ago," he told her.

"Yes, Mr. Carter. If you take the elevator on the left, Ms. Ranger's office is in Room 337," she said with a sympathetic smile, sneaking a look at his cane.

Casey smiled and nodded as he headed off. Normally, he would have been either irked or intrigued by the sideways glance, depending on his mood. His mind was on bigger matters this morning.

Outside Jenna's office, he took a deep breath and then knocked. He wasn't surprised when she personally opened the door moments later. If she was anything like her mother, Jenna Ranger would never have yelled for him to come in unless she had to do so. Virginia manners had been bred into her.

"Hi, Casey. You didn't need to make an appointment. I'd have seen you anyway," Jenna said, smiling. "Come in and sit. Can I get you some coffee or a water?"

"No, I'm fine. Thanks." He chose to sit in a dark leather chair with chrome legs. It reminded him of the furniture in Seth's condo. It was comfortable, but not very appealing to his nature.

"It's nice to see you, but I should warn you before you sit down that I think your cause is already lost," Jenna said firmly.

"I certainly hope not," Casey said fervently, working on producing a genuine smile.

"Look—before you start campaigning for Seth, I think you should know he and I are truly finished," Jenna said softly.

Casey watched Jenna walk back to her chair, another leather and chrome version, even if it was the executive one.

"I'm genuinely sorry to hear it," he replied. "I know Seth doesn't show his feelings well, but he really does care about you a great deal."

Jenna shrugged and sighed. "I've concluded Seth and I are just not suited," she said philosophically, looking at the desk because it was too hard to look into eyes so similar to Seth's and say the words. "I'm already dating someone new. I think Seth should do the same."

Inside Casey winced, but he only shrugged as he replied. "I guess that's up to Seth."

Jenna nodded. "Well, I appreciate you coming by. It's nice of you to want to do this for Seth. Mama told me you even came to see her. I saw your cane in the office."

"Yes," Casey said, sucking in air, knowing her statement was his best invitation to just spill it. "That's actually part of what I came to see you about."

Jenna wrinkled her face in confusion. "The fact you left your cane in Mama's office? She already explained Seth hadn't put you up to coming. I'm not mad at you."

"Try to hold that thought. You know, you look a lot like your mother when you get confused," Casey said to Jenna. "Do you do the hands-on-your-hip thing, too?"

Jenna blinked a few times, trying to find the sense in what Casey was saying. Why was he so fixated on comparing her to her mother?

"Okay. Let's try this explanation," Casey said when he saw she hadn't picked up on his hints. "I left my cane in your mother's office when I came to see her, but it wasn't about Seth."

Jenna nodded wisely, hoping she looked properly sympathetic. Seth had said Casey was worried about not having a job.

"Were you looking for a job in Mama's company?" Jenna asked.

"Me work for a lingerie company? Not hardly," Casey denied, snorting at the thought.

When she continued to look confused, he decided to just confess. "Oh hell, look I'm—shit, I'm interested in your mother."

Jenna blinked several times again, looking at Casey with new eyes, finally noticing his nervousness, and the slight flush on his face.

"Why? Mama's menopausal, you know. I think she takes supplements to control the symptoms," Jenna said, trying to shock him.

"So?" Casey asked. "What does that have to do anything?"

"She's given up men too," Jenna told him.

Casey looked at Jenna, gauging her discomfort with his revelation and decided it definitely wasn't safe for him to defend Alexa's sexuality to her daughter.

"I'm planning to change her mind," he said after a few moments, proud of how innocently hopeful it sounded.

"Okay. Explain yourself. What do you mean *interested in her*?" Jenna demanded.

Casey blew out the breath he was holding and just let the words follow it. "I want to date your mother. I'm hoping the idea doesn't bother you."

"*Of course it bothers me*—for goodness sakes, I'm dating Seth." Jenna startled herself with her pronouncement. It didn't help when Casey just grinned about her answer.

Jenna shook her head. "No. Wait, I didn't mean that. I'm *not* dating Seth anymore. Damn it, Casey. This is complicated."

"I agree," Casey said with a nod. "The connections make it a little bit complicated, but I want to date her anyway."

"So what do you want from me? I'm not her keeper," Jenna protested, her frustration taking over. "Wait. Are you asking for my *permission*?"

"No. And hell no. I'm not asking for your permission. I have enough problems getting Alexa's permission. I'm asking if you're going to be okay with it," Casey said, exasperated. "I know your mother worries about what you think about her. She's not chasing me. I'm chasing her. If you're going to be mad at someone over this, be mad at me."

Despite her initial repulsion, it was very interesting that Casey was willing to confront her. That certainly hadn't been the case before. Most of the men her mother dated couldn't have cared less what she thought about the situation.

Jenna rose from her chair to pace behind her desk to the window and then back to sit at her desk again as her brain struggled to take it in. She looked at Casey, who now sat with his gaze on her desk while he waited on her to respond.

Well, this would teach her to be so self-absorbed, Jenna thought. Just when she was sure she'd reached adulthood, something always catapulted her back to childish behavior. She hated feeling like a child. Now she had let both the Carter men make her feel that way.

So don't, she scolded herself. *Stop reacting the same way. You're a logical woman. Think logically.*

She turned to face Casey and crossed her arms while she studied him. When had Casey even talked to her mother enough to be attracted? It had taken her a couple of months just to introduce them. Wait, she thought. Was Casey the reason for her mother's flushed face when she first met him? If so, it must have been some meet and greet between them.

Jenna watched him toying with the end of his cane. If that was the case, then why hadn't her mother said anything about being attracted to Casey? *Probably because she knew you would be upset,* her inner voice concluded. Jenna sighed at the truth.

Had she really told Casey her mother was menopausal?

Childish, she thought. *Very, very childish.*

Jenna closed her eyes in embarrassment. She had to get over this thing about her mother dating. It wasn't about Casey. Casey was a good man. There was no reason to be all crazy about a few dates anyway. Look how it had worked out between Seth and her. She had even made her Mama promise to start dating again, which Jenna knew was the right thing for a concerned daughter to do. *Time to be a real grown up,* Jenna decided, taking a deep breath.

"So does Mama know you're here?" Jenna demanded.

Casey flushed and shook his head no. "I'm still walking,

aren't I?"

Well at least Casey understood the soggy ground he was standing on. It made Jenna laugh. "Boy, are you going to be in trouble when she finds out," she said, taking great pleasure in getting to inform him.

"Thanks, but not a news flash. I was kind of hoping that if you didn't want me dead, you might be willing to just keep this little visit between us," Casey explained.

Jenna ignored his pleading look. Seth had made her impervious to the Carter charm.

"Did Mama tell you I have a test for men who want to date her?" she asked.

"A test, huh?" Casey echoed, not for moment believing her story, but grateful Jenna was starting to be friendly to him again.

Jenna shook her head. "What's the thing you most like about my mother?"

"Her sassy mouth," Casey said, not missing a beat, and giving Jenna a hard glare, which she merely returned with a knowing grin.

"What's the thing you hate about her?" Jenna asked with a laugh.

"Who are you? Freaking James Lipton? Same thing, especially when she's flirting," he said, gripping the end of his cane. "Want to hear what my favorite curse word is next?"

Jenna laughed loud and long. The man was already jealous. Great, she'd let Casey Carter dig his own grave. Her mother hated jealous men. "Congratulations. You passed the test. You may now date my mother."

"I can tell you're still pissed. Why are you not killing me?" Casey asked, surprise overriding his common sense.

"I'm trying to grow up," Jenna said truthfully. "Run while you can. My attempts at maturity usually don't last long."

"Not yet. I need to know some other stuff. Why are you not bringing up our age differences, the fact that I'm unemployed, or the obvious?" Casey asked, patting the cane.

Jenna bit the inside of her cheek to keep from laughing again. Well, damn. Maybe she wasn't as impervious to Carter charm as she thought. The man was insecure, but brave as hell. It was hard not to be impressed.

"Okay, you're right. Maybe we should talk about those concerns. First, I figured eventually Mama would have to stop dating stuffy older guys with no fun left in them. Second, neither Mama nor I need a man for money." Jenna put both arms on her desk and met his dark brown gaze with her own direct blue one. "Lastly, I'm absolutely sure a cane hasn't slowed you down much. The satisfied look in your eyes already tells me you're pretty sure my mother is just as interested in you as you are in her."

She only liked him more for the wicked twinkle in his eyes that confirmed what she was saying.

"I'm not blind, Casey. I can see why Mama would like you. Besides, you look like an older version of Seth," Jenna said with a shrug, thinking Casey ought to know his own appeal.

"I genuinely like your mother," Casey told her, meaning every word. "I think your mother likes me back. I don't want to be a man Alexa won't tell her family and friends about. I also don't want to make you or Seth uncomfortable, but it's not like I planned to be attracted to her. Seth has already tried to hook me up, but I'm not interested in other women."

Jenna huffed and looked away. "Did Seth think Mama was too old for you?"

"Yes. I think our age difference bothered him more than the family connection," Casey said.

"He obviously doesn't know my mother. She's ageless where men are concerned. I can see in your face you don't think she's too old," she said.

"No. I think she's just right," Casey said truthfully.

Jenna shrugged. If Seth was against the relationship, that was just one more motivation she had to make herself okay with it. She would not let Seth hurt her mother's feelings with his disapproval.

"If Mama wants to date you, I'm going make myself be okay with it one way or the other," Jenna said with absolute sincerity. "I love my mother, Casey. I'm done giving her a hard time about the men in her life."

Casey sighed, feeling even more genuine regret that Seth and Jenna had broken up.

"You know, Seth arranged a cocktail party with fifteen or twenty women trying to get me interested in one of them. They were all attractive and very nice women. You know what I asked him?"

Casey waited a moment to be sure Jenna was completely hearing him.

"I asked Seth why he thought I'd be interested in any of them if he wasn't."

Jenna held Casey's gaze for as long as she could, any longer and he'd see the truth about how she still felt about Seth. The relationship was over between them, but she wasn't yet over Seth.

Casey stood. "The thing you need to know about the men in my family is we bond to the women we choose. Maybe you're not interested in Seth anymore, but I can vouch for the fact Seth isn't interested in anyone but you."

Jenna smiled and stood to see him out. "If Seth was ever interested in me, I could never tell it, Casey. He mostly ignored me while I worked hard all the time to get his attention. It was emotionally exhausting and I had to stop."

Casey nodded his acceptance of her explanation and walked to the door. He stopped at the threshold. "So about me and your mother—if you happen to stop by your mother's house this weekend and I just happen to be there—?"

"I'll try to be an adult," Jenna answered, cutting him off and biting her lip to keep from laughing again. "Stop worrying. I'm sorry I got so upset when you first told me. I'm going to be okay whether it works out or you go down in flames."

"Just for the record, I am not going down in flames. I'm a very positive thinker," Casey told Jenna. He was thinking he positively was getting back inside Alexa first chance he got, but he wasn't telling her daughter. "Thanks for seeing me. I just wanted to—well, you know."

"Yeah, I know," Jenna said, patting his arm. "I won't even

call to harass Mama until tomorrow. That will give you the rest of the day to confess about coming to see me."

"Gee, thanks." Casey said with laugh. "I don't suppose we could keep this a secret."

"Oh, please," Jenna said with snort. "This is way too good. Mama will be embarrassed beyond belief you came to see me about dating her. I'm not above enjoying seeing Alexa Ranger squirm. Kiss my Mama for me, Casey—if she ever lets you."

Casey just sighed and walked away. His discussion with Jenna had gone better than he had anticipated, but now he had to tell Alexa what he'd done before Jenna did. There would probably be more hell to pay with mother than with daughter.

He could only hope the makeup sex would be good.

Chapter 16

In the waiting area of Alexa's office, Casey dropped the duffle with his clothes into one chair and himself into another. He was beat from running all over town and trying to get back to her office by noon.

There was no one manning Sydney's desk and no activity at all anywhere. He was trying to decide what to do when he spied the intercom. Casey got up and walked to the desk to sit in Sydney's chair, and then pressed the button.

"Yes?" Sydney said, answering.

"Honey, you need to get this intercom replaced. You're starting to sound like Sydney," Casey said, grinning as he listened to Sydney laugh.

"Alexa, I think this heavy breather is your pervert, not mine," Sydney told her.

Casey laughed, and yelled through the intercom, "I hope like hell there's not a room full of people back there."

"Relax, Gunny. Get your ass back here. I'm tired of trying to cheer this woman up. She's been nothing but gloom and doom all morning without you."

"Right away," Casey said, releasing the intercom and rising.

He walked slowly back to the office and found Sydney and Alexa at the conference table pouring over notes and what looked like advertisements.

"I'm doing it again," Casey said. "You can tell me to wait, you know. I don't mean to keep interrupting your work."

"You're not," Sydney said firmly. "I'm running her off and handling the rest of this myself. Alexa's too depressed to handle anything today. Take her home and put a smile on her face."

"I am still in the room, Sydney. You don't have to arrange *everything* in my life," Alexa said, looking up from her work, her eyes softening when they landed on Casey.

"You need a keeper and Carter seems to want the job. Be nice to him, Alexa."

Sydney started gathering up the papers on the table, stacking them in neat, orderly piles.

Casey smiled at Alexa as he walked to the conference table. "If you can absorb the money loss on your investment, the offer I made you on our first date is still good," he said, coming over to run a hand down her hair.

Alexa looked up at Casey's twinkling eyes and laughed. "No. I need the money. It keeps me in sexy vehicles so can I lure younger men into my bed."

"Wow, tough call. Hard to believe any guy would look at you and only see a great car in his future," Casey said, piling the various stacks into Sydney's arms.

"Alexa has been in a sour mood since she came in without you this morning. So I'll just leave you two alone with your innuendo and head to my desk. Alexa, see you on Monday. You can be late. I moved all the morning meetings to after lunch. Have a good weekend, you two."

Sydney vanished out the door.

Alexa wilted in her seat. She put her arms on the table and laid her head on them. "I need a nap."

Casey looked at her. "Hmmm...are you too tired to fight with me?"

"Why? Did you do something in the last four hours that might make me want to hurt you?" Alexa asked, but without much venom.

Casey walked to the other side of the table and sat. He reached across and could barely touch her fingertips.

Stretching a couple of times in different directions to be sure, he finally settled in the chair.

She laughed. "What are you doing?"

"Just making sure you can't reach me," Casey said, leaning back and grinning.

"Spit it out," Alexa ordered. "You have the guiltiest expression I've ever seen."

"Do you want the band-aid peeled off slowly, or should I just rip it off?" he asked, stalling.

"How bad is the news?" Alexa asked, narrowing her eyes.

"I told Jenna about us," Casey said, watching the information being processed and anger light up her eyes.

Oh hell, he thought.

"Look, I didn't want to get caught at your house and it be one of those awkward moments where Jenna rushes out crying, or worse, yells at you. So I thought I'd just go see her and let her yell at me first, maybe get it out of her system," Casey explained.

Alexa rose from the table and walked across the room to the farthest wall, as far away from Casey as she could get. Several minutes ticked by while she tried to think of a rational way of telling a man who had given her the best sex of her life to go to hell. Nothing evil enough came to mind.

"*What* were you thinking?" Alexa demanded, turning to glare at him across the room. "Do you honestly believe I need anyone's permission to sleep with a man, much less my daughter's? You obviously don't know me if that's what you think."

"That's not what I thought," Casey agreed, trying to keep his tone soothing. "I was using insider info Seth shared about Jenna not liking the men you date. I just thought I would spare you criticism about me. I wanted her to know this was more my idea than yours. If your daughter was going to be upset about it, I wanted her to be upset at me, not at you."

"Well, don't do me any more favors," Alexa spat. "I wasn't worried about telling Jenna. I was just waiting until I was sure it was going to be necessary."

"That's why I did it. I thought it was necessary," Casey

said, wincing as he realized too late his statement was like pouring gasoline on a fire. Just because he thought it was necessary didn't mean Alexa did, but damn it, she should be agreeing.

"I didn't mean to butt in between you and your daughter. I just didn't want to be secretive about dating you. I wanted to spend the weekend with a clear conscience about your family." Casey crossed his arms. He could be as stubborn as she about something this important to both of them. She needed to get used to it.

"I'm so angry I could throw something at you, and at the same time, I'm incredibly embarrassed you would do this behind my back," Alexa said, crossing her arms.

"I'm sorry, I didn't mean to embarrass you," Casey said. "Jenna warned me you'd feel that way, but I guess I didn't believe her."

"Great. Even my daughter gets that much. Why can't you? What else did Jenna say?" Alexa asked, throwing her hand up on the wall, leaning on it with her face buried and with her back turned to Casey.

"Jenna said she wouldn't call to give you a hard time until tomorrow. She told me I had the afternoon to confess," Casey said softly, worried when Alexa wouldn't even look at him.

"Did you tell her I'd slept with you?" Alexa asked.

"Give me some credit," Casey said harshly. "I told her I wanted to date you and I hoped she'd be okay with you if we did."

"You asked my daughter's *permission* to date me? I'm fifty damn years old!" Alexa declared, her voice squeaking in shock. All anger was wiped away in utter disbelief.

Casey couldn't help but laugh and wished he could take a picture of how she looked when she turned back to face him. He was sure Alexa would laugh about it one day. "No. Hell no. That's what I said to Jenna when she asked the same damn thing. I told her I liked you. I was not asking her permission to date you."

"I'll never hear the end of this. She'll tell Regina and Lauren. She might even report it to the papers just to spite me. Oh, dear God." Alexa put her face in her hands and shook her head back and forth.

Casey laughed because he couldn't help it. "You're being too melodramatic. Don't you even want to know what she said about *us*?"

"No," Alexa said through her hands. "There can be no 'us' after what you did, so it doesn't matter."

Casey laughed more. "Jenna said she would be okay with us dating if you were okay with it. She said she loved you."

"I love her too," Alexa said, lifting her face and dropping her hands. "You—I hate right now." She made sure the last statement was delivered with an icy blue glare.

Casey grinned, trying to stifle a laugh, but lost. "Fair enough," he said on a sigh. "How long are you going to hate me?"

"Until I get over being angry," Alexa told him righteously.

Casey pushed himself up from the table and walked slowly to her. She backed up against the wall.

"It would not be smart to touch me right now," she warned, blue eyes flashing, sparking with temper still.

Casey laughed nervously, but kept walking closer. "You already know I'm more brave than smart. I've apologized. Now I want makeup sex."

"You are out of your freaking mind. I'm serious, Casey. *Keep your damn distance*," Alexa ordered.

Casey walked up until he was mere inches away from her. "I'm your hero, Alexa. I deserve a hero's reward, so I want a kiss."

"Hero? You're my nemesis," Alexa corrected, tossing her head and sending her hair flying. "I am *not* kissing you."

"Hurt me then, because it's the only way you're stopping me from kissing you," Casey said, moving in closer still as Alexa all but climbed the wall behind her trying to escape. He wanted to tell her how arousing it was and how it just made him more determined. She would have knocked him flat for sure if he did.

"I'm sorry for embarrassing you," he whispered, fighting to keep his hands to himself. "But not for talking to Jenna. It was something I felt I needed to do. I never meant to hurt you."

Casey leaned in and placed his lips on her neck, just above the pulse that pounded furiously still. He brushed his mouth back and forth all the while inhaling the ginger and peaches scent that mixed so well with her heat. His body took the final step into her when there simply was no choice about it. He groaned in relief to finally be touching her again.

Alexa drew in a breath when Casey pressed into her. Indignation warred with arousal, but ultimately lost to the simple need to feel him next to her again. She swore softly, damning him to hell, but let Casey press his hardness into her softness, closing her eyes on her own sigh of relief.

Casey felt her body give in to his but wisely said nothing. Instead, he brought trembling hands to her waist and held her hips while he pressed into her.

"Am I still invited for the weekend?" he asked quietly.

"Would it matter if I said no?" Alexa asked in return, the sting of surrender making her tongue sharp.

"Yes," Casey said. "If the invitation is rescinded, I'm taking you now—up against this wall if necessary. I'm dying to be with you again. I've had a taste and I want more. Lots more, but I'll settle for what I can get."

Alexa thought about it. And it wasn't easy to think with him rocking against her. He stopped rocking when she didn't answer after thirty seconds.

One of his hands moved to the snap of her jeans, and a few seconds later Casey's hand was sliding down the front of her, inside her clothes. Then two of his fingers unerringly found their way inside her, sliding through the wetness both of them knew belonged to him.

Alexa arched against his hand and he all but lifted her up as he stroked. He groaned at her response.

"Casey, stop that," Alexa ordered.

"I wanted to do this in the limo," he whispered, enjoying her wetness, thrilling with each arch against his palm. "I had a hard time talking myself out of it."

"Stop teasing me. You can come for the weekend," she

said finally, her breathing hitched and unsteady.

"Okay," Casey agreed. "But you can do that now while I watch. I owe you for making you so mad after our first night together. I didn't mean it to work out this way. I'm sorry as hell about it."

"I can't have an orgasm in the office," Alexa protested. "I—"

What she was going to say was lost as Casey put his mouth to her neck again and sucked there while she squirmed. Then he moved to her mouth, his tongue stroking in time with his fingers.

Less than a minute later, she exploded violently in his hand. He lifted up gently, his fingers strong inside her, and held her throbbing against his palm as wave after wave rolled through her.

"God, I love that short fuse of yours," Casey said. "Take me home with you, Alexa."

"Okay," she said, dazed with lust, dizzy with climax.

Casey looked at her dazed face, groaned, and took her mouth in a searing kiss. He eased his hand out of her clothes, zipped, and snapped her back as if nothing had happened. He kissed her hard then and stepped away quickly.

"I need to go wash my hand before I'm tempted to lick my fingers. If I do that, we'll end up locking the office door and staying here all afternoon. This floor would be hell on my hip. Be right back."

Casey walked away to her restroom.

Alexa heard the water running in the sink as she slid bonelessly to the floor. "Holy hell," she said to the empty room.

How was she ever going to win an argument with a man that calmed her with orgasms?

When Casey came back, he could barely stop laughing long enough to help Alexa up from the floor.

Sydney's snicker as he said goodbye to them had Alexa turning pink and wondering if she looked as guilty as she felt.

Casey pretended not to notice her pink face or Sydney's knowing look. Instead, he picked up his duffle bag and gave

Sydney a sharp salute before they left.

"If you'd stop feeling guilty about us, you wouldn't be so embarrassed," Casey told her, holding her hand in one of his, and his bag and cane in the other, as they stepped into the elevator.

Alexa looked at him in disgust. She closed her eyes and banged the back of her head on the elevator wall as she swore at him.

"That's anatomically impossible, but we'll figure out a substitute later. I've been studying the Kama Sutra, looking for variations on the seven safe positions for me. I think I've found several that will work. I can't wait to try to them with you," Casey said reasonably.

He was enjoying her embarrassment as much as he had enjoyed her climax. Alexa really did bring out a wicked side of him.

Alexa dug in her purse for keys and slapped them into his hand. "Here. Play with my car and leave me alone for a while. I don't want to talk or flirt. I'm still really mad at you."

"Great," Casey said happily, as they walked to BMW. "I get makeup sex later."

"No. I want a nap," Alexa said with pout. "And I will seriously hurt you if I don't get one. I may take that cane of yours and beat you in your sleep as it is."

"I can see that orgasmic high didn't last you long. Sorry, I'll do better next time," Casey told her, trying really, really hard not to laugh.

Alexa rolled her eyes, climbed in the car, and glared at Casey when he got in beside her.

"I must be insane to be taking you home with me," Alexa said, looking at him and wondering how Casey Carter had gained so much control over her so fast. "I don't even like you most of the time. I can't believe I had sex with you. Sometimes you can be so charming, but mostly you're— you're a bossy, control freak."

"Have you been reading my bad press?" he teased.

Alexa drew in a breath and let it out slowly. She counted to ten, and then to twenty, just to be sure she wouldn't launch into a tirade in the parking garage.

Casey's eyes darkened as he studied Alexa's pink face and fractured breathing. He wanted to soothe her as much as he wanted to do a hundred other things to her. Loving this thorny woman was not going to be easy, but it was going to be a lot of fun. For both their sakes, he hoped to eventually figure out how to not make her stark raving mad every ten seconds.

But there was already one reality between them Casey had absolutely no doubts about at all.

"Alexa, sleeping with me is the best decision you ever made. I'm the man you've been looking for, and honey, I want everything you've been saving up."

"*Honey*—you are full of shit," Alexa drawled, with Virginia in her voice and loathing in her tone. "I don't see how your ego even fits in this car."

"Good point," Casey said agreeably. "With all the space yours takes up, we'll drive the pickup next time. It has room enough for both our egos."

There was another round of swearing, following by some head banging on the seat back, accompanied by a grin from Casey that said he knew she didn't mean it.

There was also promise in Casey's eyes to prove what he said was true, but neither was going to mention it until they were alone again.

Tired of being mad and getting no benefit from it, Alexa turned her head to the window, closed her eyes, and to her utter surprise fell dreamlessly into sleep.

She didn't stir until Casey woke her to code them into her neighborhood.

Chapter 17

Though Casey had let her nap when they got home, he had later exhausted her again. They had fallen asleep early in the evening after a particularly energetic round of lovemaking.

When Alexa woke again, it was just after midnight. Casey's head next to hers on the pillow confirmed she wasn't merely having an erotic dream. As a lover, the man was close to being insatiable. She marveled that Casey had gone so long without a woman in his life—without sex.

No, *companionship*, she thought correcting herself, not able to suppress an amused sigh remembering their first heart-to-heart talk. It was another of Casey's euphemisms for sex, but at least a nicer one. She'd probably never hear the word again without laughing.

Alexa had also come to think fondly of *getting nailed*, as he so crudely put it. For a man with a physical limitation, Casey could still pound himself into her until she was begging him to stop. The man could give her more and stronger orgasms than she'd ever had with anyone else. If doing so caused him any pain, she doubted Casey would ever tell her.

And that's what bothered her.

Her worry over his injury had morphed into genuine concern. Her version of being careful had naturally translated itself into complete physical surrender to him. As a result, Alexa knew Casey was developing some wrong ideas about her. It wasn't her nature to be passive—in bed or out—but she was afraid of doing something to hurt him. She couldn't seem to help feeling that way, and she couldn't seem to ever quite forget about his hip.

When Casey opened his eyes, he found himself looking into Alexa's worried ones. She was also frowning, which was not exactly a strong endorsement for his lovemaking.

"I hope that frown is from a bad dream and not from something I did," Casey said, reaching out to put an arm around her.

He smiled when Alexa shook her head.

"Or from something I didn't do," he added, "though if you think of anything else you want from me, just say the word."

Because the first word that came to mind for Alexa was *companionship*, she laughed, but it came out like a snort.

"You remind me of a man when you laugh, especially the snorting," Casey told her, laughing himself. "Like someone just told you a dirty joke and you can't decide whether it's okay to laugh or not. So instead, it comes out in a snort."

Alexa looked at him and shook her head. Being with Casey seemed to have robbed her of her normal reactions to things.

"You know, you sound so much like Regina sometimes, observing and analyzing everything. You should become a psychologist or a psychiatrist," she told him.

Casey hugged her and dipped his head to tuck it under her chin, a bit ashamed. "I didn't mean to insult you. I just tend to notice everything. My mind comes up with crap constantly, but I try only to let about ten percent of it out of my mouth."

Alexa giggled into his hair. "Well, at least that partially explains why you talk so much during sex."

Casey flushed, reached around and pinched her naked backside until she yelped. "Every time you're mean to me, I'm going to pinch you. One day maybe you'll learn to be nice."

"Don't bet on it," Alexa said with a laugh, putting her

arms around him to hug him close.

He pinched her, berated her, and insisted on her giving up control way too much to him, but still she liked him. If it was a foolish thing for an older woman to do with a younger man, she would just have to deal with the fallout later.

"One day I may get the nerve up to hurt you back, Casey Carter. I might not settle for returning the pinching," she warned.

Casey's head came up on that comment. "What's stopping you from retaliating?"

Alexa lifted a shoulder and tried for light-hearted. "Hard to stay mad enough when you punish me with *really, really, really* great sex," she told him, hoping to tease his mind off the subject.

Casey rose up on one elbow to stare at Alexa in the semi-dark. They'd found a nightlight they used now, so they wouldn't have to leave the lamp on. They both liked to see each other. Neither liked the pitch-black.

"Are you holding back because of my disability?" he asked, searching Alexa's eyes for the truth in case she decided not to answer truthfully.

Alexa answered first with a snort. "I would hardly call a man disabled who can make good on his threat that I would walk funny for a week after sex with him."

"That wasn't my question," Casey said.

"What do you want me to say, Casey?" Alexa protested. "Of course I worry a little. I don't worry a lot. Maybe I'm being a little careful. We're still fairly new to each other. I think of it as learning about you. Don't all new lovers hold back a little?"

"Don't hold back with me," Casey ordered, wrapping a strand of her hair around his finger and tugging. "I want your passion and I want all of it. I'd rather you hurt me than hold back."

"That's just silly," Alexa told him.

"Promise me," he demanded, not able to keep the deep hurt from showing.

Alexa noticed Casey was giving her what she'd come to

think of as his Marine look—obstinate, determined, and unbending. There was no counter-logic he could hear in that mental state, but she was learning how to get around him. She sighed and nodded.

"Okay. I'll try," she promised, only willing to commit to what she knew for certain she could do.

Casey lay back down on the pillow and stared at the ceiling. "I wondered why you were being so submissive in bed. I was having too much fun to question it. But I want the hot, unrestrained woman who kissed me in the elevator, Alexa. Don't give her up just because you're worried. You'll be cheating both of us."

Alexa rolled to her side and ran a hand over his chest and stomach.

"Sir, yes, sir," she mocked, hoping to put anger in his voice again. His disappointed pleading was killing her. She let her hand creep south to soothe and rub.

Casey gave her a look that said he wasn't getting over his mad that easily.

Alexa just laughed because she knew better. And it wasn't going to take that much either. She wasn't the only one with a short fuse.

"Since our discussion probably qualified as another fight between us, you get makeup sex again. Though I have to say you are wearing me out with this arguing stuff."

She leaned into him for a kiss.

"And this is absolutely the last time tonight," she told him, wrapping her hand tightly around an erection that was hot, hard, and already insistent in her palm. She watched his face as she stroked him, watched his eyes darken.

When he whispered her name, she slid herself over his body, guiding him inside her, and rearing up when she felt him go deep. Alexa stilled her body above his for few moments, enjoying the way Casey was bucking beneath her, trying to get in deeper still.

Good, she thought darkly, wanting him to know what it was like to be controlled by desire, to be possessed by the person you were with. This was what he did to her.

"You want to know how I feel about you?" she asked him, more than a little warning in her voice. "You want my unrestrained passion? Fine. Here it is."

Alexa moved her hips back a little, and then drove down on him hard enough to move him up the bed. Casey stiffened beneath her stroke and arched, giving her all the hardness she sought.

She repeated the process again, at first moving slowly and strongly, and then moving swiftly as Casey's body broke in release beneath hers.

Then she kept moving on him long past the time he had exploded within her, ignoring everything he said or did, forcing him to remain semi-hard inside her.

Alexa rode him until she found her own release, until using him to satisfy herself gave her back a sense of control, and then once the orgasm passed she simply collapsed on his chest.

His swearing broke the silence. His heart hammered against her in the aftermath. His chest rose and fell with the effort to breathe normally.

Alexa eventually felt Casey's quivering arms come around her to stroke her back. She purred in contentment.

"Sorry," she said at last, "I heard you talking, but I didn't get any of it. You'll have to tell me again if it was important."

"I don't remember and it doesn't matter," Casey said hoarsely. "I'm sure I lost a few brain cells. I've never had two orgasms before."

Alexa snorted, feeling proud of herself. "Good for you. I thought I was being selfish."

"You were," Casey agreed easily. "And I liked it. Next time, I plan to make it more difficult for you. You surprised me this time."

Alexa sighed against him. "I really am going to walk funny for a week, aren't I? Sydney will give me hell."

"We're both going to walk funny," Casey told her. "And I've never been happier about sex in my life. I can't believe it's this great when we're just getting started. I can't wait to see what happens in six months or a year."

Alexa rose up and looked at him. "You're kidding me. I've never had a sexual relationship get better over time. Seriously?" she asked, her eyes searching his for teasing and finding none.

What she saw in his face caused her to shiver instead.

Casey didn't answer Alexa. There was a lot he could have said about love and a long-term sexual relationship. And he would tell her eventually, or better yet show her. For now, he just stroked her back and smiled as she lay back down on him and fell asleep.

Chapter 18

Casey woke up alone Saturday morning. He didn't hear the shower running, but thought he heard soft music playing somewhere else in the house.

And he smelled *pancakes*, he concluded, sniffing the air. Alexa was cooking breakfast.

He smiled and pushed himself up in bed, wincing at the stiffness and throb in his hip. It hurt like hell but made him laugh as he remembered last night. She'd kill him if she knew.

The funny part of the pain lasted only until he walked to the bathroom. Casey wanted to go looking for Alexa and pancakes but realized he needed to stand under a hot shower until he could at least fake not hurting. The moment the hot water hit his lower back and hips, he felt immediate relief. Casey took his time, and when he got out he was almost a good as normal. Definitely was going to need the cane today though.

When he walked to the kitchen, what he found was Alexa standing in the arms of a very attractive gray-haired man dressed in expensive jeans and polo shirt. They were laughing and hugging. The intimacy between them was obvious. Casey looked inside for the jealousy he normally would have felt over the situation, but surprisingly he found none.

Maybe the shock of seeing Alexa in the arms of another

man was too great.

Or maybe he just wasn't able to believe that Alexa could ride him to oblivion, drive him to multiple orgasms, and find anything else worth having without him.

The man noticed Casey before Alexa did.

"Good morning," the man said with a guiltless smile. "You must be Casey. Alexa was just telling me you were here."

Alexa smacked the man on the arm with a spatula she was using to turn pancakes.

"Alexa was just telling you to mind your own damn business," she corrected.

Casey looked between the man and Alexa. Nope—no jealousy, he concluded.

Before he could examine it further, a female arm found its way around his waist. He stumbled a little sideways in surprise, but the woman caught him and kept him upright.

"Good morning, Casey," Jenna said with as innocent a smile as she could manage. "I'm so glad you could *stop by* for breakfast."

When she winked, Casey decided he definitely needed coffee to deal with all this.

"I'm not sure I'm talking to you," Casey said, using his cane to prod Jenna as she walked by him.

Jenna laughed, sounding exactly like Alexa as she headed into the kitchen.

"You got me into serious trouble with your mother yesterday. Weren't you taught to be respectful to your elders?" Casey demanded.

"If Jenna lacks manners," the gray-haired man said, frowning at Jenna. "That's probably my fault. I spoil her. Her mother is the disciplinarian."

"Morning kiddo," he said, hugging Jenna back when she hugged him tightly.

"Morning, daddy," Jenna said, reaching up to kiss his smoothly shaven cheek.

Ah, Casey thought. *Daddy.* This was Jenna's father.

Casey's eyes softened then as they took in Alexa's back and her head bent over the pancakes. She had yet to look at

199

him. Instead, she poured another cup of coffee, put the cup in the Jenna's father's hand, and pointed to him.

"Take Casey coffee and go introduce yourself," Alexa ordered Paul, ignoring his knowing look. She didn't need her ex-husband gloating over her new boyfriend spending the night.

"Paul Ranger," the man said with an easy smile, handing Casey the coffee. "We sort of snuck in on Alexa last night. Well, Jenna snuck in this morning early. I had some work in Baltimore and the plane was delayed. I called Alexa's cell but she never answered. Anyway, it was about two when we made it to the house. I hope we're not interrupting your weekend."

Casey set the coffee on the dining table and put out a hand for Paul to shake. "It's a pleasure to meet you."

Paul smiled again and took Casey's hand. "Same here," he replied.

Casey was so absorbed in checking out Paul Ranger that he totally didn't see the other man walk up to his side.

"Carter, are you putting moves on my man?" Sydney demanded in a loud voice, making Casey jump for real.

Paul's grip on his hand was the only thing that kept him from banging into the dining table with his bad hip. Casey glared at Sydney and swore.

"Sydney, behave," Paul ordered, his voice lowering and his gaze darkening.

Sydney waved his hand like it was no big deal.

"Honey, Carter and I are old friends now. He knows I'm just teasing," he said, defending his actions, making smooching sounds by Casey's ear as he passed.

Paul dropped Casey's hand and punched Sydney hard in the arm as he walked around them on his way into the kitchen laughing.

Casey wasn't sure what to think about Paul taking up for him.

"Damn it, Sydney. You scared the shit out of me," he said, making Sydney laugh harder. "You're lucky I didn't take you out with my cane."

Casey walked slowly past Paul and into the kitchen as well.

"Get your coffee and get out," he ordered. "I haven't had a chance to say good morning yet."

"Wow, you're really grumpy without coffee. Reminds me of someone else I know," Sydney said to Alexa, walking away with a smile. "I bet mornings are some fun around you two."

Casey watched Sydney leave before he turned his attention to Alexa.

"Gee, is there anything you might want to tell me, Alexa?" Casey asked, leaning against the counter, bracing himself on his cane.

"Last night was wonderful?" she suggested, keeping her focus on the pancakes.

"Thanks—but no. That's not it," he said, fighting a laugh now himself. Alexa was flushed and nervous, obviously more embarrassed about the crowd this morning than she was about anything that happened yesterday.

"How about my ex-husband and Sydney are partners?" Alexa suggested with a grin, deftly sliding more pancakes onto the mountain already stacked on the platter.

Laughter from the dining table had Casey biting back another smile.

"No, that's not it either, but I did figure that out too," he said.

Sure. The puzzle pieces were falling into place inside Casey's mind. The man Alexa had given to Sydney was her ex. And Alexa still loved Jenna's father. You could see it in the hugs. But Casey had filed the info away already because he would need several more years of therapy if he thought about it for too long.

He reached out and gently tugged the ponytail Alexa wore this morning. Then he looked down at her yoga pants, the tight top with thankfully—a bra, because he was going to kiss her like he wanted to and nature would take its course.

Besides, there was no getting around making his intentions clear.

The people sitting at Alexa's dining table were expecting

a show, and he was more than happy this morning to give them one. He let her pour more batter first.

"Stop," Casey ordered, using his best and most commanding Marine voice. "Kiss me good morning. If you don't, I'm calling the press. They'll be on your doorstep before breakfast is over."

Alexa put her hands on hips and glared at him. Only Casey could see she was putting on her fair share of the performance.

Jenna giggled and said "Uh-oh."

Casey stepped into Alexa and tugged her head back by the ponytail he tugged on earlier, kissing her deeply until her hands moved to his hips, holding him in place against her.

"Good morning. You could have warned me we'd be having company for breakfast," he said when he broke the kiss.

"Well, I would have if I had remembered," Alexa told him, smacking Casey with the spatula hard enough to have him calling out in pain.

She tossed her head and sent the ponytail swinging as she shifted her attention back to her task. So far, she'd smacked just about everyone with the spatula this morning. It made her feel marginally better about forgetting she'd invited Paul and Sydney to come for the weekend.

"No one currently sitting at my table considered I might have company for once. They just waltzed right in during the middle of the night, expecting pancakes the next morning," Alexa said sharply.

"Oh," Casey said, pretending to be chastised, when what he really felt was relieved. "Well, that's a good reason then. I'm sorry."

He stepped away, patting her on the shoulder in mock apology.

"Let's not call this minor skirmish a fight, okay? I'm still recovering from making up yesterday. I can barely walk this morning," Casey said, sighing loudly.

Alexa laughed and turned multiple shades of pink.

Casey sighed again, but for real this time, wishing they

were alone so he could show Alexa he was teasing. He wouldn't need to walk if they were spending the day in bed.

Jenna had taken a drink of coffee only to spit it on the table laughing when she realized what Casey had said. Grabbing a handful of napkins from a nearby rack, she set about cleaning up the mess.

"So where's my thank you for starting the fight yesterday?" Jenna asked Casey, when he finally walked back to the table and claimed his coffee again.

After he sat, Casey pointed his cane at Jenna. "I'm not as nice as your Dad and Sydney. You might want to wait until I've had my coffee to harass me. Your mother almost killed me yesterday because of you."

"Sir, yes, sir," Jenna said with mock salute. "Will hold all smart remarks until after said coffee has been drunk."

Casey looked at her in disgust, and then to Alexa who was standing at the stove not bothering to stifle her laughter anymore. Then Casey looked at Paul, feeling genuine empathy for the man having had to deal with these two sassy women all these years. No wonder his hair was solid gray.

"I'm sure you were a great parent, Paul," Casey told him. "And I know damn well Jenna didn't get her sassy mouth from you."

Casey picked up his coffee and drank while Paul and Sydney both just beamed at him.

Jenna smiled and winked.

When Casey grunted, everyone at the table laughed.

Alexa brought the coffee pot to the table, purposely refilling Casey's first. When Casey thanked her, she kissed the top of his head. Then she poured for Paul and Sydney, afterward handing the now empty coffee carafe to her daughter.

"Make some more," Alexa said archly, giving her daughter her best mother glare.

"Yes, Mama," Jenna replied meekly, sticking out her tongue to Casey.

"Yeah. Who's in trouble now?" Casey asked wickedly, gloating.

"Don't start," Alexa said, smacking Casey on the back of his head, listening happily as he called out in pain. "We will have civilized and polite conversation over my pancakes."

"Ouch. I can't believe you smacked me again. Have you had any coffee yet?" Casey asked irritably, rubbing the back of his head.

"No," she hissed, tired of taking care of other people. Two nights of no real rest were taking a toll.

Casey scooted back and jerked her down into his lap, not letting her resist. He pulled his coffee over closer. "Drink, Alexa. I value my life and everyone else's at this table."

"I think I hate you," Alexa grumbled, picking up Casey's coffee and drinking.

Casey grunted and settled her better in his lap. "Fine," he said, sighing heavily. "Drink the damn coffee. Maybe you'll like me after."

Out of the corner of his eye, he saw Paul and Sydney exchange some sly looks.

Jenna came back to the table with the giant platter of pancakes and another containing ham. She made one more trip for pancake syrup and toppings, and another to bring a now full coffee carafe back, along with a coffee cup for her mother.

Alexa slid off Casey's lap and into a chair next to him. He reached over and patted her leg in approval, eliciting yet another sigh from her. This one felt a lot like contentment to her, though a much better kind than she had known for many years.

Looking around the table, Alexa had to admit her odd family seemed more complete with Casey there.

Jenna shoveled a giant bite of pancakes into her mouth, closing her eyes in pleasure. She looked at her mother, recognized the mental debate going on, and gave her a thumbs-up sign.

"I'm glad the pancakes are so good," Alexa said dryly, rolling her eyes at Jenna's lack of manners.

Jenna looked at Casey who was now deep in sports conversation with both her dad and Sydney.

"Yes, Mama. The pancakes are good." Jenna looked at Casey again, and then swung a knowing gaze back to her mother. "Everything is excellent this morning. Don't you think?"

Alexa's throat got really tight. Her daughter actually approved of Casey. All Alexa could do was nod in reply. If she tried to talk, she was going to cry.

Jenna patted her mother's arm and went back to eating. She knew her mother needed to be ignored until she'd had time to collect herself.

Casey felt Alexa's emotions shift and turned to look at her.

"Are you okay?" he asked, concerned about her again. He hadn't seen Alexa off-balance except with him. God help him, he actually preferred her sassy mouth.

Alexa nodded to ease Casey's concern, smiled a little, and turned her attention to her pancakes. She reached over and patted his leg and then picked up her fork.

Now all eyes looked at her, and Casey noticed every gaze held the same question. Humility was cause for concern in a woman like Alexa. Not wanting to embarrass her further by asking more questions, Casey put one hand on her leg in support, and went back to his conversation with the guys about the obscene amount of money athletes were paid.

Jenna looked at Casey's hand on her mother's leg, and then at the flush of pleasure on her mother's face. That's the way it should be, she thought. Who wouldn't want quiet support and understanding from someone who really knew you?

Unfortunately, when Jenna thought about such intimacy for herself, she could only see one man's hand on her leg, which was too bad. Just like it was too bad Seth Carter wasn't more like the man who'd raised him.

It had taken all of ten minutes to see Casey understood her mother, accepted her, and wanted the best for her. And her mother and Casey barely knew each other by most dating standards. *Maybe it happens faster when you're older*, Jenna thought.

Or maybe she just sucked at dating.
Jenna sighed and kept on eating.

Chapter 19

In the family room at the back of the house, Casey sat on a couch that seated five people with Alexa's leg pressed to his. While it wasn't the way he'd originally planned to spend Saturday evening with Alexa, it wasn't bad. She had rounded out the family group by inviting her friends, Regina and Lauren, over to meet him.

Paul and Sydney had made a pizza run earlier for dinner. Now Paul and Regina were engaged in a death match over air hockey. Paul scored the winning slide and gloated, while Sydney cheered him on.

Regina swore, gave them both a middle finger salute, and stomped off to use the restroom.

Alexa had been right. Casey liked Regina Logan. The woman had fire. Too spirited and outspoken for him— Alexa's sass was more than he needed—but he could see the woman had a giant personality and guts in spades. Regina would have made a damn good Marine, providing she hadn't gotten busted every ten seconds for venting her temper.

On the other hand, Casey wasn't sure Lauren even had a pulse. She was the most congenial, easy-going person he'd ever met. Lauren McCarthy glided around the room smiling. She seemed to enjoy the competitive friction in the crowd, but didn't engage in it. Lauren stood to the side, helped people with their drinks, their game remotes, their—well, their whatevers.

In fact, Lauren reminded Casey of a tamer version of his wife. Susan had also been nurturing but had a sassy mouth like Alexa's when you riled her. Lauren probably never swore.

Casey looked with greater appreciation at the woman seated beside him, suddenly immensely appreciative of Alexa's faults along with everything wonderful. Alexa was a challenge, but a hell of a lot more fun than she was work.

"Why aren't you over there beating Paul?" Casey asked her. "Your friends and your daughter are getting slaughtered. Womanhood is going down the toilet while you just sit here and watch."

Alexa yawned and arched an eyebrow.

"It's your fault I'm a walking zombie. I'm still hung over from two late nights in a row and more sex than I've had in a decade—maybe two," she whispered, making Casey laugh at her grumbling.

Casey put an arm around her shoulders and pulled her close to his side. He felt a little guilty for wearing Alexa out, but it would have been impossible not to be happy she was tired because of him. Not one of his more sterling character moments, but hey—he was a guy.

"Here, baby, sleep on me. You need to rest up for when company leaves tomorrow," he said in an answering whisper.

Casey kissed the top of her head when she leaned on him.

Alexa turned her head, giggled against the front of his shirt, and then snorted.

Regina plopped down beside Alexa. "Did I just hear you snort?" she asked a now laughing Alexa.

Regina looked at Casey. "You must be really funny. Alexa only snorts when something is hilarious. Lauren and I used to compete at telling her jokes trying to get her to do it."

Casey looked at Alexa. "You snort all the time with me. You must think I'm hysterical."

Alexa laughed, snorting again. "I do. But I hate snorting," she said. "It's so not elegant."

Casey thought if Regina rolled her eyes any higher, they'd

go through the top of her head. Damn, if he didn't like the woman.

"Well, hell. Of course, we wouldn't want to be less than elegant when we laugh," Regina said dryly, sipping her drink.

Alexa looked at Regina and her drink. "Straight coke," Regina said. "There's nothing in it. Two and out already." She crossed her chest with a big X. "Swear to God. It's just a stress reliever."

Alexa leaned over and hugged Regina, almost making her spill her coke. "I love you. I don't mean to nag."

"Good friends ask," Regina said, patting Alexa's cheek.

Then she turned to the man Alexa was currently glued to on the couch.

"So, Casey," Regina said conversationally, "did you get all the testosterone in your family? If it's too personal a question, you don't have to answer."

Casey looked at his lap, pretending to study his crotch with great interest, and then looked back at Regina.

"How can you tell?" he asked. "Is there some sort of test?"

Regina threw back her head and laughed loudly.

Jenna came over and pinched Regina on the arm. "Quit harassing Mama's boyfriend. If I can't do it, you can't. I'm the one Casey came to see about dating her."

The entire room got silent.

"Ooops—" Jenna said, realizing what she had just announced.

"Give me a push up off this couch, Alexa," Casey said. "I have to go beat your daughter."

Alexa patted Casey's leg, narrowing her eyes at Jenna. "No, that's okay. I'll take care of this one."

Jenna started backing up. "Mama. No, Mama. I'm sorry. I swear. I never meant to announce it."

Alexa jumped up from the couch and ran after her daughter, chasing her around the air hockey table while Jenna squealed and screamed. Paul and Sydney started taking bets, and to Casey's utter surprise, Lauren wanted to put money on Jenna.

"Lauren's going to lose her money," Casey said to Regina,

shaking his head.

His gaze fixed on Alexa, who looked like she was contemplating vaulting over the air hockey table. Casey laughed when she faked it and Jenna squealed in alarm.

"Alexa is the most stubborn person I've ever met. Jenna's only chance is to talk her mother down from being mad before she catches up to her," he said.

"Boy, you sure came up to speed fast," Regina answered, smiling at Casey. "My money's on Alexa too. Same reasons."

Casey laughed again. "I'd never bet against Alexa anyway. I'm in love with her," he said to Regina, needing to try it out.

"Duh," said Regina, laughing. "Alexa is probably the only person in this room who hasn't figured that one out." She reached over and patted his knee, a huge smile on her face. "We all approve, Casey Carter."

Casey smiled back at Regina, sincerely hoping it was true.

"Hey," Alexa yelled from across the room, now sitting on top of a wiggling, squirming, and mostly repentant Jenna. "I'm being a hero over here and you're making time with Regina? What's with you, Carter?"

"Nothing's going on here. She's the one who patted my knee. I didn't touch her. I swear," Casey vowed, crossing his chest with an X like Regina had done earlier. "Come on, Alexa. You know you're the woman I love."

Alexa smiled and it was dazzling. She twisted Jenna's arm a little while her daughter laughed. "Apologize to Casey for your bad manners," she ordered.

"Do I have to?" Jenna asked, squealing and pounding the floor with a free hand like a losing wrestler.

Casey laughed but started feeling sorry for Jenna. Now he knew for sure Alexa could have fought back with him any number of times. Lucky for him she hadn't. She could have seriously hurt him.

"I forgive her, Alexa. It was an honest mistake. Let her up," Casey pleaded on Jenna's behalf.

"See," Jenna said plaintively, giggling against the floor. "Thank you, Casey."

Paul walked over to look at his daughter and her mother

locked in battle on the floor. He stooped down, bending one perfectly creased knee until he was almost eye level with Jenna.

"Obey your mother, Jenna. Apologize to Casey. Then you can get even and tell us all about it," her father said, giving Alexa a wicked look.

"Gee, thanks for the support. This is why she's so spoiled, you know," Alexa said, disgusted.

"I know," Paul said easily. "I love my daughter. What can I say?"

Jenna lay on the floor in surrender now, wondering how she'd let her fifty-year-old mother beat her in yet another physical fight. *Talk about embarrassing,* she thought.

"I'm sorry, Casey. Really, really sorry," Jenna said, immensely relieved to feel her mother's weight lifting off her hips.

"Apology accepted," Casey said with another laugh.

Jenna stood, brushing a hand over her clothes to remove the evidence of being ground into the floor. "I am also really sorry I ever gave Casey permission to date you, Mama. He needs to find a nice woman. Someone who doesn't abuse her daughter."

Jenna broke into a run again when Alexa started to step toward her once more.

With her repentant daughter now in full retreat, Alexa walked back to Casey, who pulled her down beside him. He could feel her vibrating. If they were alone, he would have found out what it felt like to be in the middle of that, maybe share it with her.

"You could have yanked that cane out of my hand and kicked my ass any time you wanted, couldn't you?" Casey asked, narrowing his eyes as he studied her.

Alexa was pretending to be fascinated with her manicure, refusing to answer him. Casey recognized the stalling tactic. It made him remember their limo ride and that she was a woman who told the truth.

"Thank you for defending my honor," Casey said softly and sincerely, watching her reaction. He wasn't disappointed.

For all the attention she got, Alexa was starved for genuine praise.

Alexa blushed both at what Casey said and the way he looked at her so proudly. Then surprising everyone, including herself, she turned around, grabbed Casey's shirtfront, and kissed him hard while she hung on.

"Hero's reward," she said roughly, when she let him go.

Regina was snickering. Casey was smiling.

"So, Alexa," Regina began. "Are you allowed to kiss Casey that way? I never quite got if Jenna gave him permission to date you or not."

"Wait. I want to hear this too," Lauren said, squeezing down on the other side of Alexa.

Casey patted Alexa's knee, feeling the vibration. "This is my fault," he said. "I'll tell the story."

For the next twenty minutes, Casey had to listen to everyone laughing at what he'd done. He ended up arguing with Jenna, who—naturally—wanted to make herself seem to be the angelic daughter, rather than the blackmailer who had forced him to confess.

After the laughter died down, Jenna was still laughing about Casey coming to see her.

Eventually, Sydney couldn't stand hearing Jenna brag about it anymore. "Oh, grow up little girl. You weren't the only one Casey asked about dating your mother. He talked to me first."

Jenna froze, her eyes widening in shock. She looked at Sydney, and then put a hand over her mouth, only half managing to stifle her gasp.

Across the room, Alexa turned her gaze to a now full-out blushing Casey.

"Oh, hell," he said, feeling Alexa's hand tighten painfully on his leg.

"Ooops," Sydney exclaimed, wincing at what he'd done.

Paul crossed his arms and bent his head so Alexa wouldn't see him laughing and get mad at him too.

"Is there anybody you haven't asked?" Alexa demanded, wishing the fire from her eyes could burn holes in Casey.

Lauren and Paul both raised their hands.

Casey looked at Regina strangely, wondering why she hadn't raised her hand too.

"I'm counting our little talk," Regina told him around a grin.

"Traitor," Casey said, admiring her balls and grinning in return.

Casey looked at Alexa, trying to gauge if she was a little mad, a lot mad, or furious again. There were no signs of blushing embarrassment this time. He took that as a good sign.

"On a scale of 1–10, how mad are you?" Casey asked at last.

"Eleven," Alexa said, crossing her arms.

Casey sighed. "Fine. Looks like we're having makeup sex again. You're wearing me out, Alexa."

Lauren didn't know what Casey was insinuating, but it didn't sound flattering to Alexa. So she passed Alexa a small throw pillow, which Alexa promptly started using to smack Casey repeatedly across the face, chest, and anywhere else he didn't have his hands.

Lauren and Regina rose and crossed the room out of the line of fire.

Everyone laughed as they watched Alexa pulverize Casey with a pillow while he apologized over and over.

Lauren smiled. "Casey's more than a boy-toy, isn't he?" she asked.

"He's probably the love of her life," Regina said softly. Then she turned to Paul and Sydney. "You're going to be demoted to Man #2 and Man #3. It looks like Mr. Carter is taking the Man #1 position."

"Yes," yelled Paul and Sydney in unison, which brought on a high-five for saying it together.

Regina rolled her eyes. Then she looked at Jenna. "So how do you feel about this?"

Jenna watched fascinated as Casey gritted his teeth, took the pillow beating for a while, and then wrestled the pillow from her mother, only to give it back after a short period.

And every time he gave it back, her mother used it to beat him more. Was the man crazy?

"I feel sorry for him," Jenna said. "I think I even want to intervene right now. Are we one crazy family or what?"

She put her hands on her hips and looked at the rest of them. "Well, are you going to help me save Casey?" Jenna asked.

Four heads shook slowly from side-to-side.

"Wimps," Jenna scowled, and pushed up her sleeves. "I'm not afraid of her. Casey has his cane. Surely, between the two of us, we can tame one measly fifty-year-old woman."

She walked across the room. Moments later she was squealing and running, as her mother was once again in hot pursuit. Casey just seemed to be laughing and enjoying the show.

Regina looked at Lauren. "You might get to arrange a wedding soon."

"Goody," Lauren said, clapping her hands. "I wish it were mine."

Regina put an arm around Lauren's waist. "Well, you never know. If Alexa can find love after all this time, maybe it can happen for us, too."

"You're next then," Lauren told Regina. "I'm still not ready."

Lauren couldn't feel ready for love, she thought, when the only men that ever attracted her were womanizing cheaters. It may have started with her cheating ex-husband, but her bad luck spanned all the way to the weird thing she currently had for self-professed married womanizer, James Gallagher.

"Of course you're ready—you're just scared to trust yourself. But thanks for thinking of me," Regina said to Lauren. She knew it would take an absolute miracle for her to find a man willing to get involved in her crazy life.

"Come on," Regina said to Lauren. "Let's go help. If we sit on either side of Casey, Alexa will get jealous and come run us off. That will give Jenna time to escape. Maybe Alexa's jealousy over us will balance out that nasty temper of hers."

Lauren had to work hard not to stare at Regina with her

mouth open in shock. Regina thought Alexa had a bad temper? That was the pot calling the kettle black, Lauren mused, smiling. In her opinion, it was a toss-up who was more high-strung, the former model or the notorious sex therapist.

When the two women lined up cozily on either side of Casey, he looked at them strangely.

"We're saving Jenna," Regina told him. "Play along."

Casey stretched his arms out and hooked one around the shoulders of each woman.

"Hey, Mama," Jenna called. "Regina and Lauren are flirting with Casey."

Alexa stopped stalking her daughter and turned her attention to the women on the couch. She walked back and stood in front of the three of them.

"Move it, girls," she ordered, plopping herself down beside Casey again when room was made for her. "I swear I can't leave you alone for a second, Carter. You have no right to ever accuse me of flirting."

Regina pointed to the now abandoned air hockey table. Lauren nodded, and they both left.

"Now you know how I feel when you flirt," Casey told her when they were alone. "Except I wasn't flirting. I was just making *friendly conversation*."

Alexa reached, got the pillow, and smacked Casey again. "Oh, shut up."

"If only you were this bossy in bed. A man can dream," Casey said wistfully, thinking of her midnight ride. There probably would be nothing like that tonight. Pity.

"If only you were—oh, my god, I can't even think of an insult bad enough," Alexa fumed. "You drive me crazy."

"I live to please," Casey said easily, his hand coming to rest on Alexa's knee. "I love your crazy life, by the way."

"Thanks," Alexa replied, smiling at everyone in the room. "I like it, too."

Another wave of tiredness hit her. Alexa kicked off her shoes, curled up on her end of the couch, and put her head in Casey's lap, using the pillow she'd previously pelted him with. She felt him laugh under her cheek and didn't mind.

"Now I really need a nap," Alexa told him. "Guard me. I love them, but these people are nuts."

"Okay," Casey said. "I'll guard you."

He stroked Alexa's face until she relaxed, and marveled at how she actually fell asleep while the family chaos went on around them. When he sighed this time, it was in happiness and gratitude, wondering how he'd managed to get so lucky with a woman one more time in his life.

Chapter 20

Two weeks later, Casey was again sitting at Alexa's kitchen table watching her cook and listening to the results of the marketing tests for Lauren's natural line of scents. He had so much admiration for how Alexa handled every creative endeavor, every opportunity for growth with the same enthusiasm. The longer he knew her, the more he liked her.

"So *Desire* was the complete favorite among the male test group. Lauren said you can mix vanilla with anything and please men. *Revelation* was second with its ginger and peaches scent. *Pleasure's* citrus tones came in last in both the male and female focus groups. Still, I can see Jenna wearing that one over the others. Maybe it needs to be marketed to younger women."

His attraction to her was growing as well, Casey thought, admiring the stretch of her jeans over her backside, feeling an answering response in his own body.

They'd been inseparable for nearly two weeks. He'd seen Alexa now in every way possible, and he liked them all. A future with an aging Alexa Ranger did not intimidate him. Not only did Casey want to watch the lines beside her eyes deepen over time, he wanted a matching set. He thought with her sense of humor and as often as they laughed, Alexa would probably give them to him.

Unaware of Casey's study, Alexa set two heaping plates of pasta covered in marinara on the table before jogging back to the counter to retrieve the shredded parmesan and pepper flakes.

She slid into the chair next to Casey and attacked her food. It took a few moments for her to realize Casey wasn't eating.

"Something wrong with the pasta?" she asked between bites.

Casey shook his head no. He badly wanted to lick the pasta sauce from the corner of her mouth and taste it on her tongue. Instead, he made himself settle for wiping it away with his thumb for her.

He'd done all he could to sate himself, but desire for Alexa still grabbed him with an iron fist. But even that was dwarfed now by the emotion rolling through him like a wave each time he thought about his relationship to her. The tightness in his throat was constricting as he tried to talk.

"I have to tell you something, Alexa," he said quietly. "I'm not going to be able to wait any longer."

"What's wrong?" Alexa asked, pausing mid-bite, suddenly concerned that Casey was being so mysterious. Casey was not mysterious by nature. He was plain-spoken to a fault, a trait she both admired and hated.

Her instant worry made Casey laugh. "Don't look so worried. No one's dead or dying," he said, picking up a fork and taking a bite. "This is very good. I'm afraid all I have to offer in culinary skills is excellent French toast."

Alexa waved her fork over her plate. "I took cooking lessons when Jenna was in middle school. She was gaining weight from eating junk food. It was a result of responding to heavy mother guilt at the time, but I've been very glad ever since. I like cooking, but it's not fun to cook for just yourself," she said, drifting off and taking another bite.

"I promise to be properly appreciative if you want to cook for me for the rest of your life," Casey said, keeping his eyes on his plate. He was too nervous to look at Alexa, and it didn't improve when he saw her fork come to rest on her plate out of the corner of his eye.

Alexa took a deep breath, her heart pounding. She wasn't really ready for this conversation, but it wasn't like she hadn't seen it coming. And with Casey, she had learned there was no avoiding something he wanted to get clear.

"I believe this is one of those times I would rather you just rip the band-aid off quickly," she said, using their code for brutal honesty.

Casey made himself raise his gaze to hers. "I love you, Alexa."

Alexa was already shaking her head from side-to-side before Casey had finished saying the words. "You can't. You hardly know me. It's only been a few weeks."

"I knew you were going to say that," Casey said sadly, wanting to hear she loved him in return and knowing it wasn't going to happen. "I guess—I guess you're right. It's too soon, but I needed to tell you. It was weighing on me to feel it and not say it."

"Maybe you're just—" Alexa stopped when his gaze met hers again. There was nothing but honest emotion in it.

What could she say? Deny it was true? Maybe it was. Casey had known love before. He knew what it was like to love and be loved in return. She was the one who didn't know what it was like.

"I don't know what to say to you," Alexa said finally, sadly.

Casey reached out a hand and rubbed her arm to comfort her. "You don't have to say anything. I just needed to say the words out loud so they wouldn't drive me insane. I won't beat you up with it or make you feel guilty for not returning the sentiment."

Her answer was a giant sigh.

"I'm not just using you, Casey. I do care about you," Alexa said in her defense. There was a slight burning in her eyes and a flutter of nerves in her stomach.

"Yeah," Casey said easily, "I know that, honey."

Casey also knew Alexa loved him back on some level, or at least he strongly suspected it was the case. Because he ultimately wanted to marry her, he hoped it wouldn't take Alexa too long to figure it out.

"Great pasta," he said, going back to eating as if nothing out of the ordinary had been said. "I care about you too, Alexa. You're a good woman—even if you do flirt too much."

Casey smiled across the table.

Alexa picked up her fork and gave Casey a look, one that usually sent people who knew her scurrying off to avoid the imminent explosion. She knew Casey was mostly unaffected by her temper, and she wished that fact didn't turn her on so much.

"Don't start with the insults or I will never cook for you again," she told him.

"Flirt with me later and I might get over it," Casey offered, trying to distract her from the seriousness he had introduced by admitting he loved her. He would certainly tell her again, and he intended to keep telling her until Alexa believed him, and loved him back.

"Leave me alone and eat," Alexa ordered, concentrating on her food and hoping the butterflies in her stomach didn't argue much with the pasta she was now forcing herself to consume.

Later that night, Casey was once again happily buried deep inside Alexa and moving to the rhythm of the new life he'd found with her. It was beyond Casey to do anything other than whisper his love over and over in Alexa's ear while she shattered into brilliant star fragments pulsing around him.

"Casey," Alexa whispered back brokenly, tears streaming, body shaking as he emptied himself within her depths.

"Ssssh. . .sleep honey," Casey said eventually, his heart still pounding against hers. "I've got you."

Alexa couldn't bring herself to be irritated at his possessiveness or even the control he exercised over her. She was emotionally exhausted, blissfully sated, and at the same time, incredibly sad that she couldn't instantly give Casey back what he wanted.

The last thought she had before sleep was Casey always seemed to be one step ahead of her in pretty much everything that happened between them.

The next day Casey purposely kept things light and teasing, trying to break through the sudden reserve in Alexa's interactions with him. He tagged along to work with her but left, promising to return for lunch. When he returned, they opted to walk to a nearby restaurant and enjoy the unusually warm weather for autumn.

They were waiting to cross a busy street when Casey felt the little girl brushing by his leg as she passed him. She was barely a toddler. He dropped his cane to go after her as quickly as he could. His hip twisted painfully as he snatched her up in his arms, but he was glad he'd at least been able to catch her.

Alexa stepped off the curb, chasing them both into the crosswalk. Casey was reaching out with the child, passing her to Alexa, when a car hit Casey and knocked him forward in the street. He hit the pavement and lay without moving.

Alexa called his name in shock. The mother of the child rushed up and scooped the now screaming child out of her arms.

Alexa stumbled forward to join the driver of the car, who had also rushed to Casey's side. Blood flowed from a gash in Casey's forehead. Acting on instinct, Alexa pulled off the sweater she was wearing, folded it, and held it firmly to the gash to try and stop the blood flow. She was shaking badly and it was hard to keep the pressure firm.

People talked around her, but she couldn't hear them, couldn't take anything in but how Casey looked lying in the street. How much time passed, Alexa wasn't sure, but eventually there were several EMTs crouched beside her. Pulling herself out of her stupor as best she could, she answered questions about what had happened.

The mother of the little girl Casey had rescued was also there answering questions, filling in the gaps.

Alexa told them about Casey's military injuries, including

his hip replacement, so they stabilized his pelvic area before moving him.

Trembling, she watched Casey being loaded into the ambulance, and then gratefully let them tuck her in beside him with relief that she wasn't going to have to leave him. At the hospital, they wheeled Casey away to the emergency room, leaving her alone in the waiting area holding a bloody sweater in her hands.

One thought kept running through Alexa's mind over and over. Casey could die without knowing how she felt about him. She should have tried to explain better, told him how much life he'd brought to her. The last and only man she had ever said, "I love you" to had been Paul.

The men she had dated in between Paul and Casey had been interesting, some even fun. But until Casey, no one had touched her heart. No man had challenged her views, much less fought her for control.

And Casey Carter was the only man she'd ever shared the nuances of her business with comfortably.

She hadn't told him any of this, and now she might not get the chance. Tears streamed at the thought. Why hadn't she told him how she felt?

Sydney obviously had been right about how jaded and cynical she had become. She probably wouldn't have recognized real love if someone had handed it to her wrapped with a big bow.

She would give anything now to trade places with Casey and spare him yet another huge physical setback in his life. Seeing him broken and twisted in the street, Alexa had gotten a glimpse of what Casey must have endured when he was originally injured.

She rubbed her stomach to soothe her jangled nerves. Her worry was so overwhelming, it was all she could do not to start tearing the waiting area apart. Alexa closed her eyes and shivered. It was all too easy to imagine the doctor coming to tell her that Casey was dead.

She raised the bloody sweater to her face and cried into it softly.

Her stubbornness had cost her dearly this time.

Sydney got there first and pulled the bloody clothing from her hands before gathering Alexa into his arms. Alexa let herself rest against him, wishing it were Casey holding her instead.

Not long after, Seth and Jenna came running into the waiting area as well.

Seth went immediately to check on Casey's status and then came over join them.

"Alexa?"

She pulled out of Sydney's arms, stood up, and walked into Seth's arms, which came around her instinctively.

"They say Casey is still being examined," Seth said.

"He ran into the crosswalk to save a little girl," Alexa choked on a sob. "I couldn't stop him. I couldn't get to him in time. A car hit him. He was unconscious when we got here."

Seth closed his eyes and took a deep breath to steady himself. Casey was all the family he had left in the world. He couldn't lose him too.

"Is the little girl okay?" Seth asked tightly, needing another focus.

"I think so," Alexa said, pulling back. "The mother was still there when we left in the ambulance."

"That will be the first question Casey asks when wakes up," Seth said, hugging her to comfort both of them.

"How did you all know it happened?" Alexa asked, realizing she hadn't called anyone. She'd been too much in shock.

"Someone recognized you," Sydney said. "A woman called the office and told me what happened and which hospital he was taken to. My instincts told me it wasn't a prank call. I called Seth and Jenna on my way here."

Alexa nodded. She walked back to take a seat, reaching out automatically to pick up the bloodstained sweater and clutching it to her chest. "I watched it happen and I still have trouble believing it. One minute we were laughing and going to lunch. The next I was in the street watching Casey's head bleed."

Alexa put her head in her hands. "How can that man be hurt again? Hasn't he suffered enough in his life?"

She left her face in her hands and wept, uncaring what any of them thought about it.

"Mama," Jenna put her arms around her mother. "Casey would have gone after the little girl no matter what you did. Every soldier is a hero. Isn't that what you always told me?"

Seth came over and sat next to Alexa.

"Jenna's right." He reached out and took Alexa's hand in his. "Besides, I'm not too worried about a bleeding head injury. No one has a harder head than Casey."

Alexa laughed a little, sniffing back as many tears as she could.

"That's the truth," she said, studying her hands. "His leg was—I think Casey may have broken his hip again."

"Maybe they'll rebuild him better," Seth said, trying to look at the bright side. "Maybe he'll be able to move faster the next time he has the urge to save someone."

A doctor in a white coat walked into the waiting area. "I'm looking for the family of Casey Carter."

Alexa and Seth both stood. "That's us," Seth said, putting an arm around Alexa.

"Mr. Carter has a severe concussion. We've not been able to bring him around yet. This is not good, but his vital signs are okay. However, the hip replacement is shattered and needs to be replaced. I'll need one of you to grant permission for us to do the replacement surgery."

Alexa cleared her throat. "We want him to have the best model on the market. Money is not a problem. Just fix him the best you can."

The doctor looked at her. He knew her from somewhere but couldn't place the woman. Seeing the bloody sweater clutched in her hands, he nodded.

"The best is a titanium model. It's very expensive, but adjusts to the individual in a unique manner, sometimes allowing a larger range of motion than traditional replacements. Several people who have received them have walked unassisted afterward."

"That's what we want," Alexa said, looking at Seth. "Are you okay with this?"

Seth nodded down into her face. "Whatever you want to buy Casey is okay with me," he said roughly, kissing Alexa on the forehead. "He deserves the best."

Alexa closed her eyes and swallowed hard, fighting the urge to cry again.

"Make him bionic," she said to the doctor and felt Seth laugh a little at her side.

The doctor smiled. "Well, I can't promise bionic, but I'll do what I can," he said, walking back through the door to the treatment area.

Chapter 21

No matter what anyone said, seven hours later they still couldn't talk Alexa into leaving the hospital. So they called a second shift of Regina and Lauren to stay with her while the rest went home to change clothes and eat.

"Casey's going to be fine," Regina told Alexa. "The surgery went well. There's every reason to feel positive about this, honey."

"I'm not worried about his leg," Alexa said, hugging her arms. "The doctor keeps saying how well the surgery turned out."

"Here," Lauren pulled off her sweater and made Alexa put it on. "I have a jacket in my gym bag. Your sweater is history. Blood doesn't come out of cashmere. You need to just throw it away."

Alexa squeezed her eyes closed. "I used it to try to stop the bleeding."

Regina walked to the bloody sweater still resting beside Alexa's leg, picked it up and crammed it into the giant purse bag she nearly always carried. "Lauren's right. It's history. I'll take care of it for you."

"You don't have to worry about my sanity," Alexa said sharply, seeing in both their faces how much they were worried about her.

"It's not your sanity that concerns us, Alexa. We're just

trying to keep you looking presentable for when the press figures out you're now dating a wounded hero," Regina said, not for a moment doubting the situation would be exploited by the media.

"I don't care about the publicity this time," Alexa said. "Casey is a hero. He deserves to be recognized for it. A little girl is alive because of what he did."

Alexa put her face in her hands again as she relived the car hitting Casey for the millionth time. "Oh God, I may never be the same, but the little girl is okay."

Lauren knelt and put her arms around Alexa in a tight hug.

"When Casey wakes up and you see he's okay, the scariness will start to fade," she assured Alexa, stroking her hair.

Regina came over and sat beside them. "Casey loves you, Alexa."

Alexa pulled out of Lauren's arms and leaned back in the chair. "I know. He told me," she said sadly.

"Why on earth would that make you sad?" Regina asked. "Casey's sexy as hell, thinks you walk on water, and doesn't let you have the upper hand all the time. He's practically perfect."

"Yes. He is practically perfect. It makes me sad because I didn't say it back when he told me," Alexa confessed, trying to swallow past the knot of anxiety in her throat. "I didn't know what to say to Casey when he said he loved me. So I said nothing. Somehow that seems worse."

Regina studied Alexa for a moment. "You're just on the verge, honey. You're at the edge of the love epiphany. Casey's just a little ahead of you in understanding, that's all."

Regina reached over to hold Alexa's hand. "The man knows you love him. And if he suspected otherwise, he'd probably just set about working to change your mind. Casey told me he loved you the day I met him at your house."

Alexa looked at Regina in shock. Regina just shrugged.

"He's so full of himself," Alexa said, almost laughing. "I don't know if I can love someone like that or not."

Lauren reached out a hand and pinched Alexa.

"Ouch! What was that for? You're as bad as Casey," Alexa protested, laughing completely now, shocked because Lauren had actually pinched her.

"Wake up, Alexa," Lauren demanded. "You're sitting here worried about the man so badly you won't leave his side. You're even willing to deal with the press for him. This is love, and you're living it."

Alexa sniffed and felt her eyes filling again. "Yes. I guess it is."

"Excuse me, Ms. Ranger?" a nurse broke into their conversation.

"Yes," Alexa answered, sniffling.

"Mr. Carter woke up briefly a couple minutes ago. He was asking for someone named Alexa," she said.

"That's me," Alexa said, standing. "Can I see him now?"

The nurse looked at her kindly. "We can let you in for a few moments. He's drifting in and out, but at least he's beginning to wake up. It's a good sign, and we hope he recognizes you," she said, pointing to the doors with her hand.

"Go. We'll be here when you come back," Regina said lightly. Lauren nodded as well.

Alexa followed the nurse through the double doors.

Alexa thought Casey looked worse in the hospital bed than he had lying in the street. His entire left side was in traction, probably because of the surgery. There was a series of bandages on his head as well. Stitches peeked out of the largest one.

Alexa fell into the chair by his bed with relief. Her famous legs were barely supporting her.

She reached out and touched Casey's hand, then lifted it gently, holding it in hers. The pulse in his wrist was more reassuring to her than anything the doctor had said.

Sitting there holding Casey's hand, Alexa had another vision of him sitting by his wife's bed when she was ill. Her heart hurt for him, and once again she thought how unfair it was that Casey was injured once more.

Feeling more helpless than she'd ever felt in her life, Alexa could only hold his hand and pray he would make it through this, too. She leaned over the bed and kissed his hand, laying her cheek against it while the tears flowed. She felt the same need to protect Casey, to care for him, that she'd only previously felt for a handful of people in her life, most of whom had rushed to her side today.

"Well, looks like you won another one, Marine. I guess I love you after all," Alexa announced to Casey's unconscious form. "I'd like to think I'd have come to the same conclusion without watching you get hit by a car, damn you."

"Alexa," Casey moaned, trying to turn his head.

"Ssssh. . .sleep honey," Alexa said, stroking his face the way he often did for her. "I'm here. I'll be here when you wake up. Rest now."

When the nurse showed up, Alexa knew her time was up for now.

Alexa released Casey's hand and leaned over to kiss his cheek. "I love you, Casey," she whispered, feeling the words vibrate through her with a truth that surprised her.

She walked from the room feeling hopeful for the first time in hours.

Chapter 22

They never knew who finally leaked the story to the press, but the next day there was a horde of reporters swarming the hospital.

Despite rare moments of lucidity, Casey remained mostly unconscious, so he was still in ICU being monitored for the head injury.

The hospital, now fully aware of the identities of the patient and the woman in his life, allowed Alexa to put extra guards on their newly discovered local "hero" during his stay. They also gladly helped arrange a press conference on another floor of the hospital.

While Seth sat with Casey in the ICU, Alexa went to deal with the press. Jenna had brought clothes to her mother, who was offered the doctor's lounge to clean up and prepare. To say the hospital staff was shocked by the beautiful woman who walked out of the lounge was an understatement. No one could stop staring at the transformation.

Jenna walked beside her glamorous parent, prouder of her than she had ever been. She knew how hard it was for her mother to leave Casey, even for a short time.

"You look beautiful, Mama," Jenna said when they were standing outside the conference room, knowing her mother needed reassurance.

Alexa put her arms around her daughter and kissed her

cheek.

"Thank you for being with me," Alexa said, wiping the lipstick kiss away with a thumb. "Sorry. I forgot I put on the red lipstick today."

Jenna laughed. "Now remember. Stick to the hero story. Don't go announcing your engagement," she teased. "Casey hasn't discussed his intentions with me yet."

Alexa gave her daughter a grin, appreciating the teasing. "It would serve Casey Carter right if I did announce our engagement. Lord knows I owe him some embarrassment."

Alexa took a couple deep breaths. "Okay. Let's get this over with," she said, pushing open the conference room door.

As Alexa walked to the front of the room, she noticed the mother and little girl Casey had rescued sitting near the podium. Ignoring the press for a few moments, Alexa walked over to them. She'd discovered it had been the mother who had called Sydney.

"Thank you for calling my office and sending my family to me. I wasn't thinking clearly that day," Alexa said, reaching out a hand to stroke the child's hair, shocked when the child reached out her arms to her.

Alexa took the child and held her live, warm body to her chest, keeping her back to the press while the cameras flashed.

"Is he—is Mr. Carter going to be okay?" the mother asked, her voice breaking. "Alicia got away. She's—she's so active—I . . ."

Alexa watched the woman's lips tremble and felt her own throat tighten with emotion. She looked at Jenna, who walked to the mother and put an arm around her.

"Mama knows all about the challenges of raising a lively child with a mind of her own," Jenna said with an easy laugh, making the woman laugh.

"Mr. Carter—Casey's going to be fine," Alexa said with confidence. "And he's going to be very happy to know Alicia is fine, too."

Alexa kissed the top of Alicia's head before handing the child back to her mother. "I guess it's show time," Alexa said, raising her chin.

She shook hands with the hospital staff who had arranged the press conference, and then she stepped to the podium while the cameras clicked and flashed without stopping.

Alexa looked at Jenna, who handed her a pair of reading glasses she'd been holding and some note cards that had been stashed in her pocket. She put on the pair of very attractive readers and peered at the note cards.

"I thought I would just tell the story, and then afterward answer any questions you have. First, let me thank the hospital and staff for the wonderful care they have shown us."

An hour and a half later, the press was escorted out of the hospital by security guards.

Alexa and Jenna walked back to the ICU. Sitting just outside the door in the hallway was Allen Stedman, dressed all in black with arms crossed. A pair of dark sunglasses was clipped to the front collar of a tee shirt stretched almost beyond endurance across Allen's massive chest.

"Ms. Ranger," Allen said, smiling into his boss's face, working hard to keep his eyes from straying to her incredible legs. He had never seen her dressed up before. More than simply gorgeous, Alexa Ranger wore her sexuality like other women wore jewelry.

"Allen? Are you guarding—" Alexa began, then stopped as she realized what he'd called her. "For heaven's sakes, will you please call me Alexa? I'm not your mother."

"No, ma'am," Allen said respectfully. "You are definitely not my mother. I would appreciate it though if you would not tell Gunny Carter I admitted that."

Alexa couldn't stifle the laugh.

"Well, she's my mother, so stop hitting on her," Jenna told him resentfully, hands going naturally to her hips as she had to admit once again her mother had completely charmed the hottest man around.

"Jenna, you are insulting the man. Allen is teasing. He works for me," Alexa said to her daughter.

"Allen, this is my daughter, Jenna Ranger. Jenna, this is Allen Stedman—Sydney's potential replacement. You need to apologize."

Alexa watched Jenna, relieved to see the frown lines start to disappear, but almost laughed again to see disappointment lines take their place. She'd have fun later telling Jenna that Allen was extremely straight, as well as hot.

"Oh," said Jenna, deflated that the man was gay. She sighed heavily. It was a shame she thought, eyeing Allen's muscles with regret. Jenna also wondered why she'd missed the signs. Her radar was usually flawless and it seemed to her the man reeked heterosexual.

Then there was also the way he'd teased her mother, she thought, getting angry again at the man's comments.

Allen smiled at Jenna's study, easily reading her wrong assumptions about his sexual preference, but not minding one bit. If Jenna Ranger hadn't been Alexa's daughter, it would have been a hell of a lot of fun to show her differently. She looked just like her mother, only—well, repressed—Allen thought sadly. It was practically a crime to waste such fine womanhood on a bad attitude.

Allen smiled at Jenna. "It's a pleasure to meet you, Jenna Ranger," he said, liking the blush that stole up the younger woman's face when he said her full name.

"Rough day. Sorry for my rudeness," Jenna said to him, "it's a pleasure to meet you, Allen."

Allen reached out a hand to Jenna to shake, pleased when she flushed even more as she shook it. Yep, sure was a shame she was Alexa's daughter. It might have been a lot of fun loosening her up.

"Did Sydney send you?" Alexa asked, trying not to smile at her daughter's obvious interest in her new office assistant.

"Something like that," Allen said easily, not willing to admit yet he'd volunteered to guard the Gunny, as had several of Allen's military friends.

The original notification of the situation had technically come through Sydney, so he wasn't exactly lying. Gunny Carter was the reason Allen had looked up some old friends and talked to them about some side work guarding people. When Gunny was ready to open his security business, Allen planned to have a staff of guard dogs waiting for orders.

"There's a lot of press wanting to get an exclusive story," Alexa told him. "They can be pretty clever."

"Can't be any more clever than Gunny Carter getting past me," Allen said to her.

Alexa laughed. "Good point," she said, sighing.

Allen grinned as the Ranger women moved passed him into the ICU area. He couldn't stop himself from admiring the enticing view from the back as both walked away from him.

One was as exciting as the other, Allen thought, not the least bit shocked to find himself admiring both mother and daughter. He'd just have to remember never to look too long at Alexa when Gunny Carter was around, he thought with a laugh, turning his attention back to the numerous smiling nurses who spoke to him as they walked by.

Seth lowered his phone in shock when Alexa walked into Casey's room.

"Well, I'll be damned, Casey," he said quietly, unashamedly looking Alexa over from head to toe as understanding came at last. This is what Jenna looked like in the blue dress, but what Alexa looked like whenever she wanted. "Full model mode—I get it now."

Of course, he'd need to tell Casey again when he was actually awake and could hear him.

"Has he woken up again?" Alexa asked, coming over to lightly kiss Seth's cheek in hello. Seth got a whiff of perfume and sighed. Yeah, he got it all right. And learning it made him wonder just how dumb he had been about a lot of things.

"No," Seth said, "but he has been trying to move more. I think he's coming out of it and feeling restricted. He'll probably wake up mad as hell about the leg. Casey's not a good patient."

Seth stood and let Alexa take the chair. He smiled when she reached over and linked her hand with Casey's.

"He's going to hate that he missed seeing you dressed up," Seth told Alexa, his eyes twinkling. "You look amazing."

"Thanks," Alexa said, a tear seeping out of one eye despite her best efforts. "I hope there will be plenty of other times for him to see me."

Seth put a hand on her shoulder and reached down to kiss her cheek. "There will be," he said firmly, believing it beyond doubt. "Is Jenna still in the waiting area?"

Alexa nodded, not trusting herself to speak.

"I think we'll grab some lunch and bring you something back," he told her.

She nodded again, touched by Seth's continued thoughtfulness.

In the waiting area, Jenna watched Seth emerge from the ICU and walk straight toward her. Her heartbeat picked up pace, and she almost rose to go to him. He walked to her like he didn't even see the other ten people sitting there as well.

Jenna looked away, but it didn't stop her from liking how right it felt.

"Hey," Seth said, stopping in front of Jenna. "Let's get something to eat. I told your mother we'd bring her back food. I don't think she's eaten much since yesterday."

Jenna nodded, relieved Seth seemed oblivious to her reaction.

Seth reached out and took Jenna's hand in his, holding on to it despite the little tug of resistance he felt from her. His phone buzzed in his pocket as they walked. Seth ignored it, which had Jenna lifting an eyebrow.

"Too much interference in the hospital," Seth said to explain. That wasn't the whole reason, but it was the one he knew Jenna would most easily accept.

"Cafeteria?" Jenna asked.

"Sure," Seth said easily.

When they walked by Allen's chair, Allen smiled and Jenna smiled back.

"Hey, Allen," Jenna said, dropping Seth's hand.

"Hey, Jenna," Allen said in return, grinning at both Jenna and Gunny Carter's kid, or whatever he was. Allen hadn't gotten the story quite straight, but it didn't take much to interpret the look in the man's eyes about Jenna. He looked a lot like Gunny, Allen thought.

Seth frowned at Jenna as they continued down the corridor. "You know that guy?"

"Allen is taking Sydney's place when he retires," Jenna said with a shrug. "I just met him today when he was flirting with my mother."

"He's not interested in your mother," Seth said bitterly, having caught the man's assessment of Jenna's rear.

"Yeah, I know. He's a friend of Sydney's so I guess he's probably gay," Jenna said in a whisper.

"Yeah. Just keep thinking that," Seth ordered, making Jenna laugh.

"You don't think Allen's gay?" Jenna asked, finding it funny that Seth would take an instant dislike to a man he didn't know.

"Why would I care?" Seth asked in return, picking up Jenna's hand again, only to be more annoyed when she instantly pulled it away.

"Right," Jenna said, biting the inside of her lip. "I was just curious. He seems like a nice guy. I guess I'll be seeing more of him if he replaces Sydney. Eventually, I'm sure I'll find out."

"No doubt," Seth said, irritated with the thought of the muscle guy eyeing Jenna every time he saw her at the office. He looked at Jenna and wondered if she was really naïve enough to not know the man was interested in her.

"Why are you looking at me that way? You can't honestly be jealous of a gay guy?" Jenna asked. "I thought we'd called a truce of sorts because of Casey."

She did think it. Jenna honestly thought the muscle guy could be gay, Seth thought. He closed his eyes and willed the jealousy to not eat him alive.

"I'm not jealous," Seth denied, lying outright. "I'm just stressed over Casey. Sorry if I'm coming across badly. If you want me to bring you back lunch, I will. You don't have to go with me."

The elevator arrived and they rode to the basement

cafeteria as the only occupants.

"Don't be silly," Jenna said easily, leaning back against the elevator wall. "There's no reason we can't be friends."

Seth sighed. He debated blasting Jenna with the hundred-reason argument running through his head, or plastering her against the elevator wall and kissing her until she admitted to wanting him.

"I appreciate your support," he told her instead doing either. "It helps me to have you here right now. I'm sure it helps your mother too."

Seth let out a little sigh when Jenna picked up his hand and held it willingly. For now, he would take what she offered, he decided.

"That's what friends are for," Jenna said, squeezing Seth's hand in friendly support.

It was all Seth could do to keep from punching a fist into the elevator wall.

Chapter 23

The first thing Casey saw when he awoke was Seth sitting in a chair texting on his phone. He opened his mouth to speak to Seth, but what he said was "Alexa."

"Jenna took her home to get some rest and a change of clothes. She's been here the whole time," Seth said, reaching to push the call button for the nurse.

"Where's Susan?" Casey said, turning his head and seeing his leg in traction.

Seth froze. Was Casey reliving the past? Not good, he thought, reaching out to take Casey's hand in his.

"How are you feeling?" Seth asked Casey softly.

"There was a bomb," Casey said, gripping Seth's hand.

"Not this time," Seth said softly, putting his other hand on Casey's arm. "You ran into the street to save a little girl. Do you remember doing that? A car hit you and you broke your hip again."

Casey closed his eyes, trying to figure it out. "No."

Then Casey groaned as the memories swirled, truth slicing through him. "Susan—Susan is gone?"

"Yes, that's right," Seth confirmed gently, watching the emotional pain race across Casey's face as the past met the future. Seth hurt knowing that for Casey it was probably like losing Susan again.

"You're in the hospital in Falls Church, Virginia, where

you've been living with me," Seth told him. "You've been—you've been unconscious for several days. They had to fix your hip again, and you've had a concussion."

Casey closed his eyes. "Head hurts."

"Yeah, I bet it does," Seth said. "Let me call the nurse and we maybe can fix the headache."

Seth pressed the alarm and called the nurse.

Casey suddenly gripped his arm tensely as pieces of the present started to return. "Alexa?"

"Thank god," Seth said at last, letting out the breath he'd been holding. "Yes. Alexa is fine. She'll be back in a little while. I'll call her and tell her you're awake."

"No," Casey said, closing his eyes. His vision of the beautiful woman was clear, but so was the one of his wife. It was making him ill. Had he cheated?

"No? What do you mean no?" Seth said, incredulous. "Alexa has been worried sick. I have to tell her you're okay."

"Stay away. Alexa, stay away," Casey said insistently, gripping Seth's arm.

"I can't promise that," Seth told him, "but I'll tell her if you're sure."

"Please," Casey said, drifting back off into the blackness again.

Seth looked at Casey with disbelief, wondering what was going through his cousin's mind. How could Casey not want to see Alexa? He'd said nothing but her name for days, and now he didn't want to see her. The situation was ludicrous to him.

"Fine," Seth said, looking at Casey's unconscious form again. "Make me the bad guy and pass out. Jenna probably will stop speaking to me when I break Alexa's heart. I hope to hell you have a good reason for this."

The nurse ran Seth out of the room just before the doctor came in to examine Casey. In the waiting area, Seth picked up the phone, looked up a number, and dialed.

"Yes. I need to speak with Dr. Logan urgently. Tell her this is Seth Carter and it's an emergency."

Seth left his number, and minutes later Regina called

back. He explained what Casey had insisted he do, and Regina said she'd be there as quickly as she could.

"Shit," Seth said aloud, after hanging up the phone. "I can't believe I have to do this."

All things considered, Seth thought later, Alexa had taken the news as well as anyone could have. She'd simply sat down in a chair in the ICU waiting area and wept like her heart was broken while Seth watched, helpless to change the situation.

"If Casey wasn't already hurt so badly, I'd kill him," Seth said to Jenna, while Regina and Lauren hugged and soothed Alexa.

It barely registered to Seth that Jenna had put an arm around him in support, until her grip tightened.

"I'm sorry," he said to Jenna, peering down into her earnest face. "I don't understand what this is about. Casey has a strange way of looking at things sometimes."

"There's nothing else you could do but what Casey asked," Jenna said reasonably, rubbing Seth's back, "even if he is being a stupid man."

"What does that make me then?" Seth asked sadly, not able to look directly at Jenna any longer.

"A caring person who is caught in the middle," Jenna said sincerely.

Jenna gasped when Seth spun her into his arms so fast there was no time to second guess what he intended. His embrace was so tight, the press of his body to hers so warm and welcoming. Her arms wrapped around him before she remembered she wasn't supposed to want to hold him anymore.

"Thank you, Jenna," Seth said, bending to kiss her mouth with both reverence and lust. "Take care of Alexa. I'll see what I can do with my hard-headed cousin."

Seth turned and walked away, determined to find out what was going on with Casey and fix it. Then he was damn well fixing his relationship with Jenna.

Jenna was glad Seth never looked back to see her

standing there, hand to her still quivering lips. She understood now that Seth hadn't accepted what she'd said about being just friends. Casey wasn't the only hard-headed man in that family.

Seth had to wait two days before Casey was alert and awake long enough to talk with him about Alexa. The nurse had barely closed the door to their new private room when Seth slid the phone closed and put it in his pocket.

"Okay. Enough is enough. What the hell is wrong with you?" Seth demanded.

"I've been told a car hit me," Casey said shortly, looking away.

"Oh, hell no. That's not it. I've seen you get blown up by a bomb, shot at, and several other kinds of hurt without feeling sorry for yourself. That pride of yours did not get dented by a damn car," Seth said, crossing his arms.

Casey rotated his head slowly, doing the stretching exercises the doctor had recommended, stalling—but knew he was going to have to tell Seth the truth.

"I'm the bad guy who had to watch Alexa cry her eyes out over you. You owe me an explanation," Seth demanded.

Casey thought he probably did, but it wasn't flattering to him, Susan, or Alexa.

"When I opened my eyes, I saw my leg in traction and suddenly I was living my life two years ago, still in love with and married to Susan. Yet somehow I knew Alexa was in my life and I felt disloyal. I still half expect Susan to come walking through the hospital room door. How screwed up am I? What does it say about me for my memories to be all mixed up?" Casey said sadly.

Seth said nothing for a few moments. It had not occurred to him Casey might have deeper emotional scars from his multiple traumas than anyone knew. Considering what his cousin had suffered in his life, the confusion Casey was experiencing now was probably understandable.

"I can see how that would be hard to deal with," Seth said quietly. "You seemed to catch up pretty quickly though when we talked. I think you would have done fine with seeing Alexa. You were never unfaithful to Susan."

Casey nodded and looked out the window. "Every day it gets a little better. The past fades a little more," he said, closing his eyes. "When I'm absolutely sure I won't be calling Alexa by Susan's name in bed, I'll send flowers and apologize."

Seth grinned and shook his head.

"That's not going to be enough. The very rich and successful Alexa Ranger spent every night you were unconscious sleeping on a floor cot next to your bed, waiting for you to wake up. Then when you did, you refused to see her. She cried like her heart was broken. I don't think flowers are going to get the job done this time."

It was sick, but Seth actually enjoyed throwing Casey's words back at him—mostly because they were true.

"I'll figure it out," Casey said, frowning at the thought of Alexa crying over him. It was making him as ill as the other things going on.

"Yeah, well," Seth informed him. "Jenna has decided she and I are going to be *just friends*. You better hope like hell Alexa doesn't decide the same thing about the two of you. It's not fun sleeping alone all the time."

Casey laughed and grabbed his head. "Hurts to laugh," he said. "Alexa would never do that to me."

Memories of being with Alexa were easier to recall for him now—and very intense.

"You didn't see how hard she cried when I told her you didn't want to see her," Seth told him. "I wanted to kill you myself."

"Thanks," Casey said with a disparaging laugh.

"Get well fast and fix this," Seth demanded. "She's obviously good for you. Just an FYI to motivate you, if that titanium hip replacement works, you might even walk without the cane."

"Titanium? Sounds expensive," Casey said with a sigh. "Looks like you might have a roommate for a while longer until I pay for it."

Seth pulled his lip between his teeth. "Well, I wouldn't worry too much about the bill. I think it's mostly paid for already."

"You've obviously never paid medical bills," Casey said. "They can be endless. Military insurance is not so great."

"I think the bill for the replacement was settled by the time they installed it in you," Seth said easily. "Just focus on using the damn thing and walking. That was the point of it."

"Look," Casey said, "you don't have to pay my bills, Seth. It's enough you're letting me live with you. I'll take care of my own bills."

"As far as I know, there is no bill, Casey. Now just drop it, okay?" Seth got up, pulled his phone out, and walked to the door. "I need to go make a call, and you need to rest. I heard they were planning to get you on your feet today."

"Seth," Casey called out but got nothing but the door closing in reply.

Casey sighed, wishing Seth didn't feel the urge to take care of him. It was supposed to be the other way around.

Casey's first attempt at walking went better than he hoped. He had to use the parallel bars for support, but the more steps he took, the better his hip moved. At times, it was like the normal leg and hip could barely keep up with the repaired one.

The therapist praised his walking. "I heard the titanium models were exceptional, but I never worked with a patient who actually got one. You're very lucky, Mr. Carter."

"Yes," Casey agreed, taking a few more slow steps. "This one feels very different."

"Well, look at you," the doctor said, stepping into the therapy room. "Not exactly bionic, but pretty damn good if I say so myself. That's quite a bit of movement."

"Bionic?" Casey asked with a laugh. "I wish."

"Ms. Ranger asked for bionic, but this was the best we could do," the doctor said easily with a laugh. "I think she'll be pleased with your progress. And over time, I think you'll be amazed at how much better you'll get around."

"Alexa," Casey said, his throat suddenly dry. "Alexa asked you to make me bionic?"

"Oh, she didn't tell you?" the doctor asked, laughing himself. "Yes. Ms. Ranger told us money was no object and you were to have the best. So that's what you got. Then just yesterday, I heard she made a healthy donation to the hospital. You're a very lucky man, Mr. Carter. Not only is she beautiful, she's also a good woman with a very generous heart."

Casey walked slowly to the wheelchair waiting for him, easing himself down into it. The magnitude of his mistake was just starting to dawn on him. His body hurt around the incision, but the hip replacement didn't bother him nearly as much as the first one he'd received. Even his other injuries were all steadily improving.

His heart on the other hand might never fully mend. Casey had no idea how to make things right with Alexa. In trying not to hurt her with his memories of Susan, he'd actually hurt Alexa more by rejecting her love when she was finally offering it to him.

"Can I ask you a personal question, Agnes?" Casey looked at his physical therapist, a married woman close to Alexa's age.

When she gave him an arch look, he just smiled. "It's not *that* personal. I just wanted to ask, when your husband screws up, does he send you flowers?"

The woman threw back her head laughing. She handed Casey's chart to him to hold. Releasing the handbrake on the wheelchair, she started out of the room with him.

"Frank knows better than to send me flowers with some lame apology note," Agnes said to Casey. "He knows he better tell me to my face he's sorry. And I want to hear he's thought through what we fought about and come to his senses. I pretty much stay mad until that happens."

Casey sighed. "That's what I was afraid of," he said, frowning.

The woman huffed. "Weren't you in the military? And didn't you run out in front of a car to save a kid, Mr. Hero?

Sharing the truth of your feelings ought to be the least of things scares someone like you," she told him, grinning behind his head as she pushed.

"Marine training didn't cover groveling," Casey said, making her laugh.

"I saw your woman talking to a whole room full of press about you," Agnes told Casey, noting with pleasure the shock on his face. "Yeah, she even put guards near the ICU to keep the reporters away while you healed. I don't blame you for being worried. She looks like she's pretty used to dealing with things by herself and not concerned about having a man around."

"Alexa talked to the press about me?" Casey asked, swallowing the lump in his throat.

"Yeah. Your picture and the story ran two days in the paper. She stood in the conference looking like a queen, answering what she wanted to answer, deflecting what she didn't. That sweet baby you saved was in her arms part of the time with her mama looking on the whole thing. That woman of yours has more poise than the hospital lawyers," the therapist told him, helping Casey from the chair and back to the bed.

"Alexa was a model," Casey said proudly. "She also has her own business. She's incredible."

"Well, I don't doubt that," the therapist answered easily. "Let me tell you, she flicked off the doctors chasing after her like she was shooing away flies."

She poked Casey in the chest with her finger. "That woman is totally in love with you, in case you didn't know. Whatever you did, you better apologize fast."

Casey laughed. "Yes, ma'am. If she ever talks to me again, I will certainly apologize."

That night Casey dreamed of Susan. They were at a picnic and she was flicking flies off herself, getting more and more irritated with them. It made him laugh. She looked at him laughing at her discomfort and told him he would never change. Then she blew him a kiss and disappeared.

The second dream was him dragging Alexa to the floor in

her office, ripping the clothes from her body, but undressing her was as far as he got in the dream. He woke up panting with a throbbing erection, no relief in sight. Casey figured such a punishment was well deserved.

Not dragging Alexa to the floor was the only regret he had with her, until three days ago when he had refused to see her.

There was no sleeping after the dreams faded.

Casey lay awake in the dark, wondering how to explain to Alexa about his memories of Susan. In the end, he had been as disloyal as he had feared, but it had been to the wrong woman.

"I'm sorry, honey," he whispered. "Please don't give up on me."

Chapter 24

"Mama, this is an intervention," Jenna yelled as she came through the front door and walked in the direction of the bedroom. "No more sulking. Regina and Lauren will be here shortly."

She'd visited her mother and found her in tears three days in a row. Today Jenna had decided to change the situation.

"Jenna, what are you yelling about?" Alexa asked, walking out of the bedroom in a new blue dress the color of her eyes, long silver and blue sapphire earrings hanging from both ears. "I have a date, and I want to make sure I get there on time."

"You have a date? But I thought—" Jenna looked at her mother, blinking at how incredible she looked. "Wow. Nice blue dress. I bet you can sit in that one."

"Yes, I can. And you may borrow it sometime. I keep telling you dresses don't have to fit like a second skin to be sexy," Alexa said, smoothing a hand down the front of the dress. She liked the feel of the woven textures banding the waist.

"Sydney made this for me. It feels amazing," she said.

"Looks amazing too," Jenna said. "Uh, who's your date?"

Alexa looked at her daughter. "Seth," she said.

Jenna looked like she'd been slapped.

Alexa put her hands on her hips, wondering how long it would be before Jenna stopped passing such harsh judgment on her.

"Really, Jenna? I know Seth brings out your inner drama queen, but can't you at least give me a little credit?" Alexa frowned at her daughter in open disgust. "For pity's sake, I'm not dating your old boyfriend. I've been meeting Seth every day to get updates on Casey. The dress is because I intend to see Casey Carter today whether he wants to see me or not. And when I do, I damn well intend him to suffer."

Jenna shook her head to clear away the awful thoughts and make room for some clear thinking. Maturity flittered and fluttered around like a butterfly, never landing on her for long.

"So Seth gives you updates?" Jenna asked, her voice a squeak.

Alexa nodded. "Yes. I think if it wasn't for Seth, I wouldn't be functional. He makes me meet him in person and starts every meeting with an apology for both him and Casey."

"Sounds like Seth," Jenna said as she sat. "What about—do you still cry every day?"

Alexa took a seat across from Jenna. "Yes, I do. I cry for Casey and what he's going through. Then I cry for myself because—well, just because I miss him. Seth told me why Casey refused to see me. I cried about that too, and then I got over it."

Alexa rose and went to get her purse. "Casey may still long for the wife he lost, but I'm the woman he's got now. I've decided to let the present be enough for me since it's a waste of energy to be jealous of a dead woman or his memories of her."

"But aren't you still hurting?" Jenna asked, seeing the pain move through her mother's expression in answer.

"Of course I am," Alexa answered honestly. "My relationship to Casey is turning out to be as tough as the one I had with your father. Since Casey is the first man I've loved since Paul, I guess it sort of makes a weird kind of sense."

"But what if Casey hurts you again?" Jenna asked.

Alexa sighed. "I suppose it could happen, but Casey's more likely to make me angry a dozen times a day than he is to seriously break my heart. Loving someone isn't all wonderful, honey. The bottom line is I want what I can have of love with Casey. I'm willing to take the risk of being hurt."

Jenna just continued to look at her mother in amazement. "I don't know how you dig down inside yourself after all you've been through this week and somehow find the will to put on a blue dress and go confront him. I think I only had one of those brave moments in me. After failing, I just can't imagine doing it again."

"When you find a man who's worth the effort, you'll risk anything as many times as necessary, even when you know it might not work out. I'm sure Regina would tell you it's extremely unhealthy. Sometimes though, it's just what you have to do, especially with stubborn men," Alexa said, hugging her daughter and kissing her cheek. "Thank you for the intervention. I am blessed you love me enough to care."

"Mama," Jenna said, running a hand through her hair. "I'm sorry about the Seth thing. I'm just—just messed up where he's concerned. Take the Ferrari today. It goes with the dress. The BMW is too conservative."

Alexa jingled the Ferrari keys already in her hand. "You are so right, sweetie," she said, making Jenna laugh.

As her mother drove down the driveway, Jenna made calls to back off the crowd she had arranged to descend.

Seth felt Alexa enter the cafeteria before he ever saw her. Of course, the whispers, banging trays, and other chaos that ensued would have dragged his attention to her anyway. Today, Alexa was wearing a dress the color of her eyes and looking like she was done being patient. It made him smile. Seth wished he could be a bug on the wall when she confronted Casey.

Though he was still adjusting to seeing Alexa dressed up, it was a pleasure to look at the woman in full model mode again. Seth couldn't help being a little jealous of his cousin. Not because Seth wanted Alexa, but because he wondered how much of her mother's femininity Jenna had inherited, and if he would ever get a chance to find out.

He wondered if he was the reason Jenna didn't dress up more often and frowned at the thought.

Alexa bent to kiss his cheek, then rubbed the lipstick stain with her thumb.

"Sorry," she said. "I have a tendency to forget I'm wearing makeup. I went a long time without doing so."

"You look really good today," Seth said, enjoying the envious glances of tables and tables of doctors.

"Thank you," Alexa said, taking the seat across from him. "How is our patient doing?"

"Casey had a bad night," Seth said. "He woke up dreaming and couldn't go back to sleep."

Alexa nodded, not trusting herself to speak. Lately, she was torn between wanting Casey to be miserable and wanting him to get well.

"I intend to see him today," she told Seth, saying it firmly to convince herself as well.

Seth nodded with a laugh. "Yeah, I kind of figured that out from the dress."

"This old thing," Alexa said, attempting to joke, but not able to laugh it off as easily she'd hoped. She had needed to be at her best, more shaken about competing with Casey's memories of his wife than she'd wanted anyone to know.

Seth reached across the table. "Remember the day you showed up at my condo wearing your ex-husband's sweats."

Alexa snorted. "Quite well. Thanks for reminding me of my humiliation."

"Let me just apologize for all the thoughts I had about your lack of attractiveness and say I stand completely corrected," Seth said. "The only woman who comes close to being as beautiful as you is your daughter."

"Well, aren't you being sweet today?" Alexa said with a genuine smile.

"No," Seth replied. "I'm being honest. Casey told me back then, but I didn't get it. Now I do and I'm happy as hell for him. I also want you to know I'm still in love with Jenna. I plan to get her back, and I don't care how crazy that will make our family."

"One more exciting thing in my life to look forward to," Alexa said laughing, squeezing his hand back.

Seth looked at his watch. "I think you need to head on up to the physical therapy treatment room. Casey should be about half through by now. You really need to see what you paid for in action. He's slow as Christmas still but walking without a cane, crutches, or any support at times."

Alexa closed her eyes and said a quick prayer of thanks. "That's wonderful, Seth."

"Yes. It is. Now go. Make him work for it. Don't give in too easy. He's too used to getting his way with upset women," Seth joked. "I don't know why he should have it any easier than the rest of us poor saps."

The phone rang and Seth gladly took the call.

"Agnes, I hear this is the last day you get to torture me," Casey said to his therapist, strapping the ankle weights on by himself. He stood, glad that the effort was easier than it was yesterday, and braced his weight on the parallel bars to begin his walking treks.

"Good. I'm ready for a break," Agnes said. "I think I'm going to turn over my job to the woman in the blue dress. She looks like she can handle you just fine."

Casey looked up to see Alexa walk into the treatment room. He was as speechless and overwhelmed as he had been the first time he saw Alexa dressed up. His eyes dropped to her legs for a long time before he could drag them back up to her face. By that time he managed it, Alexa's arms were crossed, but she was at least smiling. He decided to take it as a good sign.

"If I start by saying how damn sorry I am for not explaining, will you walk down here and hug me?" Casey asked. "I've missed you like hell, lady."

"You wish it could be that easy," Alexa said, narrowing her eyes and tossing her hair over one shoulder. She had to steal herself not to run to him.

"Maybe you should have sent the flowers after all," Agnes said in a whisper.

"Now you tell me," Casey said, taking a slow step forward.

"Seth explained two days ago. I've been ignoring you on purpose," Alexa told him.

Casey took another couple of steps. The weights really added to the workout. Or it might be the pain in his chest.

"So why did you come today?" Casey asked, panting as he worked his way down the bars.

"I lost the stubborn contest," Alexa told him. "I missed you, too."

"No, you didn't lose," Casey told her. "They wouldn't let me out and Seth refused to help me. I'd have come the day after to take it all back. I was—I was just scared when I woke up. I didn't know where I was or who I was or—"

"—or which woman you were with?" Alexa finished for him, hoping her tone said volumes about how much she didn't give a damn.

"It's not as bad as it sounds," Casey said, stopping. "Though I can see how you might not feel the same way about it."

"Lucky for you, my ego doesn't fit in any of my cars," Alexa told him, eyeing his walk with as much interest as she had in their conversation. "Since the entire hospital heard you calling my name over and over while you were drifting in and out of consciousness, I think that trumps your dream about still being married to Susan."

"I just didn't want to get you confused with her," Casey said sadly.

Alexa slid her purse from her shoulder and hung it on the bar. She stepped into the walkway to be there when Casey got to the end of it.

"Yet another insensitive statement that does not help your cause with me," Alexa said, planting her feet firmly to keep from walking into his arms. "If you ever get down here, I'll see if I can clear up any remaining confusion about which woman I am."

"I told Agnes you were hard and unforgiving," Casey said,

almost within reach at last.

"If I am, it's your fault," Alexa agreed. "You bring out the worst in me, but I'm in love with you anyway."

"Thank god for that," Casey said, putting his arms around her. "I love you, Alexa. Don't stay away so long next time. Just come back and kick my ass."

"Deal," Alexa said, wrapping her arms around him and hanging on, leaning back against the bar and taking his weight on her.

Casey put his hands in her hair and kissed her like his life depended on it, because it did.

Alexa laughed against his mouth and kissed him back as she held him to her body.

"Lord, you two," Agnes said, fanning herself. "You could start a fire with all that heat. Good thing they're springing you tomorrow, Carter."

"Is there anything special I need to know about taking care of this stubborn man?" Alexa asked Agnes, as Casey turned around and headed back down the bars.

"It's too late," Agnes told her. "You gave in too easy, girl. He'll think he can get anything over on you now because you let him off the hook so fast. You should have seen how sorry he was two days ago."

Alexa laughed. "What can I say? I guess I'm just easy."

"That's not what those doctors you refused to date are saying about you," Agnes told her around a smirk.

Alexa shrugged one elegant shoulder. "I got a thing for Marines," she said with a sigh. "It hit me after I turned fifty."

"Takes all kinds," Agnes said with a laugh, looking her over. "You sure don't look fifty. Maybe you could do better than him."

Agnes nodded her head in Casey's direction, making Alexa laugh again.

Casey got to the end of the bars where Agnes and his chair waited. "You know, I am still in the room and not deaf."

"Turn your butt around and walk back down those bars again. Put some real weights on those ankles first," Agnes demanded. "No, wait—don't sit. I'll do it for you. That way I know you aren't cheating. I'm not as nice as your lady. I know better than to trust you military guys. Frank was in the Navy."

"Figures," Casey said, wincing as Agnes tightened the extra ankle weights.

"Walk," Agnes ordered. "Two more times, and then we're done. I'm sending you to the clinic after this. Let someone else work on keeping you honest."

Alexa watched Casey struggle with walking with the extra weights, working hard to keep the tears from flowing.

Agnes elbowed her. "He's fine. This is necessary. Both of you will be glad for it a month from now when he doesn't need a cane to get around. The titanium replacement is the best thing to happen to him. It was the silver lining in the cloud."

Alexa nodded. "Thank you. I needed to hear that."

Agnes patted her shoulder. "Get into his face more often girl. Don't let him boss you around. You give those military men too much control and they think they can run everything."

"I heard that," Casey called from the end of the bars.

"Good," Agnes yelled. "Cause it's true and you know it."

Alexa laughed. "I may bring Casey back here just to listen to you yell at him. It gives me a break."

Agnes laughed so loudly several orderlies came to see if everything was okay.

Seth was waiting in the room when Alexa pushed Casey's wheelchair inside. He rose to help Casey get back into the bed only to receive a frown.

"I was hoping Alexa would help. I was going to talk her into getting in bed with me," Casey told Seth.

Seth laughed. "Sorry to mess up your plans."

"It wouldn't have worked," Alexa said with a smile, "but we'd both have had fun while he tried."

Seth laughed again. "So I guess you two made up again?"

"No, not really," Alexa said. "I don't think Casey and I will ever settle anything. We just sort of move on anyway. I guess it helps that both of us don't hold grudges."

Casey held out a hand to Alexa, who walked over to take it. "Look, I'm genuinely sorry about the flirting argument. I see now I was probably a little bit wrong about that."

"*Probably a little bit wrong,*" Seth repeated. "Just like you *maybe should have listened more* or *maybe should have explained.* You can't be that good in bed, Casey. Can't you just straight up apologize for crying out loud?"

Alexa laughed while Casey grinned.

"Well, actually—" she began, winking at Casey. "He is pretty damn good in bed."

"Stop," Seth said, holding his hands over his ears. "I definitely do not want to know this."

Then he changed his mind. "Wait—" Seth pulled down his hands, thinking of Jenna. "Maybe I do want to know. Okay. What's Casey's secret, Alexa?"

"Casey holds nothing back—physically or emotionally," Alexa told Seth. "I've never known a man like him before."

"He doesn't hold back? Well, what does that mean?" Seth asked, irritated.

Casey laughed and closed his eyes, needing to rest. "I'll blog about it and you can read it on your phone," he said sarcastically, starting to drift off to a restful sleep at last.

"Fine," Seth said, pocketing his cell and patting it. "Make sure you don't use euphemisms for sex, especially military ones. Otherwise, I'll never understand what the hell you're talking about. Are you staying, Alexa?"

"Yes. Casey hasn't finished apologizing yet. Looks like he may need a nap first," Alexa said.

"I'm heading home then," Seth told her, kissing her on the cheek. "Take care of each other."

"We will, honey. Thank you for everything." Alexa stood and hugged him.

Seth left smiling and smelling like Alexa's perfume.

Chapter 25

Casey walked out of the bathroom wearing briefs and a US Marines tee shirt, just as Alexa was heading into the bedroom to check on his progress in getting dressed.

"Love the look," she said, smiling and walking over to him. "But Lauren is here. It's been at least six years since she's seen a naked man. I don't think she could handle seeing you in your underwear."

Casey laughed, looking down. "If you keep smiling at me that way, I'm not going to fit in my jeans, and then we'll have an even bigger problem."

Alexa snorted. "The only thing making your jeans tight is weight-lifting. Your thighs are getting bigger every day."

Casey reached out and grabbed the front of Alexa's shirt, pressing her breasts together as she laughed. "Are you telling me my thighs are getting fat?" he challenged.

"Let go. You just want feel me up," Alexa said. "I'm on to you and your dares."

"Fine," Casey said, turning loose of her shirt and sitting on the bed. "If you want me in jeans, you have to help me get into them."

Alexa sighed and retrieved them from a nearby chair. "Here, lift your feet."

Casey complied, lifting each leg in turn and sliding the jeans over his ankles.

"Now stand up," Alexa ordered. She reached a hand out to help Casey stand, and then squealed when Casey leaned back and dragged her across his body, sliding her intentionally over the bulge that truly was not going to fit well in his jeans.

Alexa swore, laughed, and kissed him until they were both reeling. "We do not have time for this. People are already here."

"I thought this was supposed to be my party," Casey said, letting her loose and pushing her back down over his bulge again.

"It is your party, moron. That doesn't mean you get to hide out in the bedroom and have sex. You have to go be social with the people who care about you."

Alexa groaned as Casey stopped her downward slide just a little too long in just the right spot, before he finally let her off him.

"Damn it, Casey. No fair. I'll be thinking of this all night now." Standing was a challenge since she was weaving on unsteady legs weakened with lust.

"Good," he said, reaching out a hand for her to pull him upright again. "Me too."

Casey stood slowly, and Alexa slid the jeans up around his hips. She adjusted him front and center before zipping the jeans along the ridge. "See. They fit just fine. I wouldn't sit though until your interest dies down a little."

Casey dipped his mouth to hers for a probing kiss that made Alexa dizzy. "It never goes away when you're around. Maybe in a decade or so I might actually get my fill of you."

Alexa slapped him on the chest. "I've lost five pounds since you moved in here, and I hardly exercise anymore. You've kept me so busy in bed I've not needed another kind of workout. I don't want to hear about how deprived you are."

"I didn't say I was deprived," Casey told her, laughing. "I said I can't get enough of you. That's entirely different."

"I'm sure whatever problem you have will fix itself over time," Alexa told him, patting his cheek. "You'll get tired of me and prefer watching football instead."

Casey laughed. "Do I look stupid? Who does that anyway?"

"Lots of men, I hear," Alexa said wisely.

"Lots of stupid men maybe," Casey said, following her out of the bedroom slowly but steadily.

Much to Casey's surprise, the living room was filled with people, including Paul, Sydney, Allen, Regina, Lauren, Seth, Jenna and some strange guy who seemed to be with Jenna.

"Look who finally decided to attend his own party," Sydney said. "Alexa turn you down for a quickie? You're losing your touch, Carter."

Seeing no one in attendance under the age of twenty-one, Casey held up his middle finger to Sydney.

"No thanks," Sydney said, grinning. "I brought my own date. I appreciate the offer though."

Casey shook his head in defeat and started looking for a place to sit. Verbally sparring with Sydney was more deflating than arguing with Alexa. Both of them were too good at getting in the last word.

"No sitting. Walk around first," Alexa yelled to him from the kitchen. "You haven't exercised enough today."

"I would have if you hadn't been so intent on me getting dressed," Casey yelled back, hearing Alexa's answering giggle.

When his attention came back to the rest of the people in the room, he noticed Regina was laughing and Lauren was blushing. Casey shook his head over the two women and how different they were. He headed to sit with them but got stopped.

Jenna put her arm around Casey's waist. "Come on, handsome, let's take a walk. We'll head to the kitchen if you'll let me watch you torture Mama."

"Deal," Casey said, taking Jenna's hand for support. "She swings a mean spatula, but I've learned how to duck."

"Since you seem to make Alexa mad every couple of minutes, a ducking skill is probably a good thing," Paul said grinning. "Don't get me wrong. I'm grateful the pressure is off me at last. I owe you. If you ever need to invest any money, I'm your man."

Sydney patted Paul's knee and rolled his eyes. "You're a prince," he said, making a tipsy motion to Casey. "We stopped at Lucinda's for drinks with friends on the way over. Paul's tongue is a little loose. He'll be better after Alexa feeds us."

Once in the kitchen, Alexa shoved trays into Jenna's hands. "Here. Take these out. The pizzas are on the way, but we've got another twenty minutes to wait. Feed your father first or he'll start singing."

Casey leaned against the counter and laughed. "Paul sings when he's drunk?"

"Badly," Alexa said, hearing the laughter from the other room. "Come on, I'm your ticket back. I've got to balance the tray with the other hand."

When they walked back to the room, Allen plucked the tray from Alexa's hands and started walking around with it. He lingered a long time in front of Jenna, talking and smiling.

Alexa and Casey both sighed and looked at each other. They had both been hoping things would swing in a different direction.

Seth rose from where he'd been sitting and walked to them. "I need to run," he said. "Good to see you getting around better, Casey. Don't be a stranger. Just because you're staying with Alexa doesn't mean you can't come by and visit. You still have a key."

Seth hugged Casey tightly, profoundly glad his cousin's life had been spared.

"I'll walk you out," Alexa said, gently taking Seth's hand in hers as they walked to the door.

She stepped outside with him as Seth started to walk away. "Seth," she called, watching him turn back to her. "Jenna's date is a gay friend of hers."

Seth nodded. "But Allen Stedman isn't gay, is he?" Seth asked.

Alexa sadly shook her head no.

Seth walked back and kissed her cheek. "Thanks for telling me," he said before turning toward his car.

Alexa went back inside. Jenna was talking animatedly to Allen, who was hanging on her every word while her 'date' was trying unsuccessfully to flirt with Sydney. Alexa didn't know whether to be glad her daughter seemed interested in Allen or scold her for giving up on Seth. She was now torn. Her ideas about Seth had changed a lot in the last few weeks.

Casey was seated between Regina and Lauren with an arm around each of them when Alexa brought her attention to the group again.

"I swear," Alexa said to him. "I'm not going to invite Regina and Lauren anymore when you're around. You're turning into a big flirt."

Casey smiled at her with love in his eyes as she turned to answer the door and collect the pizzas. "You know you're the only woman I love," he called as she walked away.

"Sitting with us will not stop Alexa from flirting, you know," Regina said to him. "Give up trying to change her nature and enjoy the ride."

Casey smiled and patted Regina's arm, making her snicker.

"I think Alexa is just really good at friendly conversation," Lauren said, feeling a need to defend her friend, even to the man who loved her.

Alexa made the pizza guy bring the pizzas into the living room and set them down. She gathered the cash she'd prepared from the bar and hooked her arm in his to walk him back out.

Casey snickered. "Help me up, ladies. I have to go act jealous now or I'll never get the woman into bed tonight."

Regina looked at him, pity in her gaze. "You dug this hole yourself," she said with a laugh.

Casey looked at Lauren, knowing she would be a softer and faster sell. "Please, Lauren. Help me stand up."

"Give me one good reason why I should help you," Lauren demanded.

"I love her madly," Casey said sincerely.

Lauren looked him over thoroughly with only a little doubt in her gaze. "I guess I believe you," she said finally. She stood and pulled Casey to his feet without even straining.

"Wow. You are impressively strong," he told her. "Thanks for the lift."

Casey walked slowly to the door and found Alexa standing in the hall giggling, obviously waiting for him.

"I thought you needed more exercise," she said, watching Casey's eyes darken as he got closer to her.

"You mean you thought I'd come chasing after you," Casey corrected.

"That too." Alexa admitted, hooking her arms behind his neck when he pressed his body to hers.

"Well, you were right," Casey said, planting a knee between her legs and bracing his hands on either side of her.

Alexa's hands curled into his tee shirt and her breathing grew ragged waiting to see what he would do.

Casey couldn't do what he wanted with a living room full of friends waiting, so he leaned into Alexa to brush his lips over her neck, smelling the ginger and peaches on her skin. He groaned against her and felt her shiver in response. Well at least they were both suffering, he thought.

"You're right. I need a lot more exercise," he said on a sigh, moving back and walking to the living room slowly. "Be prepared to help me with that later."

"Casey," Alexa whispered. "I love you."

"I love you too, honey," Casey said.

Alexa laughed and took his hand as they walked back to the living room together.

# # #

Note From the Author

If you enjoyed this book, please consider leaving a positive review or rating on the site where you purchased it. Reader reviews help my books continue to be valued by distributors/resellers and help new readers make decisions about reading them. I value each and every reader who takes the time to do this and invite you all to join me on my Website, Blog, Facebook, Twitter, or Goodreads.com for more discussions and fun.

You are the reason I write these stories and I sincerely appreciate you!

Many thanks for your support,
~ Donna McDonald

Excerpt from *Dating Dr. Notorious*

After a day made more grueling due to several nights of interrupted sleep, Regina tiredly locked her office door and happily dropped the keys into her portfolio bag.

She still wasn't sure how her friend Lauren McCarthy had coerced her into being the entertainment for her latest fundraiser, but that's where she was headed now instead of home to a hot bath and a glass of cognac. She was running on empty and her sneaky, manipulative friend would just have to forgive her for running a little late.

It had taken a while to come up with a talk tame enough for the country club crowd Lauren typically drew. Regina knew how to practice restraint in her subject matter when necessary, but she was more used to saying things others barely dared to think about.

In the parking lot, Regina pulled her attention away from her surly thoughts to the present and smiled. The day got measurably better when she saw her favorite male waiting for her in the parking lot.

"Hello, Harry," she purred in her best sexy voice, "you're looking very handsome today. Want to go for a ride?"

Regina walked the short distance to her car, an excited hand reaching for the sleek door handle of her metallic baby blue Porsche. Delighted to be comforted at last, she let herself sink into the plush leather driver's seat. It rumbled beneath her rear as she started the car and she sighed in pleasure, laughing softly at her intense response.

Ironically, it had been 'Saint McCarthy' who had pointed out to Regina her relationship to her car was the most sexual one in her life. While Regina had laughed hard at Lauren's unusually blunt teasing, she would readily admit to anyone that a growling car sure as hell beat a vibrator for her any day.

Driving Harry made the craziness of her life seem at least a little more worth it. So Regina worked hard on letting Harry and the good she did for others be enough to keep her content.

Tonight she stroked the leather shifter firmly, groaning in happiness as she pushed in the most responsive clutch she had ever known. She touched a button on the dash and the Stones soulful music filled the small car. It was reassuring somehow to hear the sexy lead singer complaining about the same problem of finding satisfaction that Regina had.

"Come on, Harry. Let's go talk to some stuffy rich people about sex," Regina said to the car, peeling out of the parking spot.

Ben Kaiser walked the long hallway to the country club offices, trying to remember the last time he had been to a function like this. It probably had been before Catherine had even gotten sick, which was three years ago at least.

He hadn't really been very social since she'd died, though not from grief exactly. His grieving had taken place over the entire two years of her illness as he lost her a little at a time. By the time Catherine had finally died from her illness, sheer relief she was finally out of pain was stronger than what he felt over the final loss. The six months since her death had been about figuring out next steps for him.

His family was encouraging him to start dating, and Ben wasn't opposed to it. He just wasn't thinking about it much or taking any action yet. Getting out again was one of the reasons he had decided to come tonight and deliver the bid himself. It had crossed Ben's mind several times lately to ask Lauren McCarthy out to dinner. She was divorced, had been for years. A tall, sleek blond who dressed meticulously, Lauren was as polished as Catherine had been, though she didn't seem to have the same warmth.

Not that he was looking for another Catherine exactly.

Actually, Ben didn't really know what he wanted next time around. After being married for twenty-five years, he didn't know how dating worked anymore or what it was like to look for someone new. His not knowing was one of the reasons Lauren seemed like a safe first date. It was a well-known fact Lauren McCarthy wasn't looking for anything more than a pleasant dinner companion.

Though fifty felt too him a bit late in life to be starting so completely over, Ben prided himself on having an open mind. He knew he wasn't meant to be alone. He liked sex too much for one thing, or least he used to. He hadn't been able to express those needs in a long time, and was looking forward to doing so again soon. Being a man who trusted his instincts, Ben was willing to wait a bit longer and let them lead him in the right direction. If they didn't, then he'd probably ask Lauren out to jumpstart his dating.

In his mind, instincts were Plan A. Dating a safe woman was Plan B. There was nothing wrong with planning, was there?

Besides, Ben had always enjoyed the hunt, even though he did tend to settle into a monogamous relationship more quickly than most men. Maybe he was just an all or nothing kind of guy. He had only ever chased women that he thought would be potential wife material. Since he'd found Catherine with that attitude, Ben figured the same method should work well for him this time around too.

Finding the office locked, Ben slid the manila envelope containing his company's estimates for renovating the McIntyre Retirement Community under the door. The deep discount for the work was his business's contribution to the fund, and Ben was glad his company was wealthy enough to do it.

Heading into the ballroom of the club, Ben saw the tables were filling and the music had begun. Lights had been lowered to an intimate level to entice dancers to the floor. Lauren was talking to a group of people off to one side of the room.

Along the other side, there was a table overflowing with food. Standing at the food table was a smiling redhead with a trim, but generous figure. She was wearing a fitted black dress that seemed to Ben to be working pretty hard to restrain the curvy woman inside it. The fact he noticed her body made Ben smile.

He watched as the woman spoke to someone else getting food, casually popping a grape into her mouth as she talked, all the while nodding at something said. Ben tried to tear his gaze away from watching her, but he couldn't.

Then realization hit him.

I'm attracted to her, Ben thought, his blood pumping a bit harder and faster as he adjusted to the unfamiliar feeling.

Well, he reasoned, rubbing the tightness in his chest with one hand, at least this was how the game was supposed to work. You saw someone interesting, and then just took a chance.

And why not, he asked himself? But his feet were already moving him toward her before he could ponder the answer to his own rhetorical question.

Ben walked up to the woman just as she was tossing her now empty plate into the trash.

"Hello," he said. "Would you like to dance? It's for a good cause I hear."

The polite refusal Regina had been about to make died on her tongue when she raised her eyes to the man's smiling face. It was a rare occurrence for her to be rendered speechless, but she was as she met his direct, obviously interested gaze.

Damn erotic dreams, Regina fumed, fighting a sudden urge to wipe damp palms on the sides of her dress. Her dream man would undoubtedly have this man's face tonight. Somewhere between the ages of forty and fifty, the incredible specimen standing in front of her was both handsome and masculine in spades. Only a little taller than her five-foot-eight height, there appeared to be a lot of solid male packed into the space he occupied.

His mostly jet-black hair was streaked with silver on each side of his head. Like a magazine model, his skin was tanned and clear, and his very nice clothes were perfectly suited to him.

But it was the man's rakish smile—as he openly appraised her—that was severely testing her composure. He hadn't said more than a few words to her, hadn't even touched her yet, but she was already turned on just looking at him.

Confusion over her sudden, intense attraction rose inside Regina. It threatened to overrun her normal sense of self-protection like a rising tidal wave preparing to conquer a shore. Fortunately, before she could do something totally stupid, like giggle or reach out to touch him, her normal self-protection urge finally overrode her hormonal reaction.

"Thanks, but I shouldn't dance—really, I have—well *things* I have to do shortly," she stammered. If she had heard anyone else say something so lame, she'd have rolled her eyes. Her tongue, which habitually said things that shocked everyone—sometimes even her—seemed unwilling to just say a simple no to a man who looked as good as he did.

Regina watched the man's eyes crinkle in amusement as he smiled at her attempt to politely refuse. Rows of perfectly straight, perfectly even white teeth sent unexpected butterflies fluttering around in her stomach. His knowing, disbelieving look was much more alluring to her than his polite words.

Not to mention, his smile was lethal.

And as he simply smiled at her knowingly, Regina realized he wasn't going to take no for an answer. Her reaction to his persistence landed somewhere between *here-I-go-again* and *holy-hell-he's-hot.*

Regina sighed, unable to remember the last time a man had pursued her so blatantly and openly. *Down, girl*, she ordered herself as the butterflies took flight again, but it was too late.

His smiled widened as his gaze swept over her, his knowing look challenging her to say yes simply because he could tell she wanted to.

For the first time in her life, Regina literally felt her willpower being sucked away as she all but drowned in the man's emerald gaze.

Ben looked the woman over thoroughly, feeling genuine relief when he saw no ring on her left hand. She was older than he had guessed from across the room, with faint but definite smile lines softening her eyes. Ben liked the lines. They were marks of a real woman, someone with character, he thought happily, thanking the instinct that had sent him across the floor to her.

"Just a dance—I promise I won't keep you long," Ben said sincerely, holding out his hand.

Sighing reluctantly, and looking more resigned than pleased, the woman put her hand in Ben's and walked out to the dance floor with him. Her obvious reluctance made him smile even more.

Sure, Ben could tell he made her a little nervous, but her gaze returned his interest, which he found intriguing. Her color was high and her breathing erratic as she stepped into his arms. It was exciting as hell to coax her, Ben realized, and equally exciting to think the woman wanted to be coaxed. It also didn't take long for him to notice how thrilled he was to get his hands on her at last. If she hadn't felt so good, Ben would have laughed at his reaction.

Too delighted with his own spontaneity to be shocked with the speed and direction of his thoughts, Ben simply wrapped the woman in his arms and spun her off to the music. In her low heels, she was the perfect match to his five-ten height. They moved around the floor slowly while she worked out her comfort level with dancing with him.

Ben sighed in relief when she finally relaxed, and used the opportunity to move in to her a little more. His face brushed her hair when they had to dodge the other dancers, and Ben noticed she smelled like a rich dessert, something with vanilla ice cream and warm cherries. His body tightened, reminding him it had been a very long time since he had even thought about dessert, much less wanted something so specific.

Like an impatient kid, Ben found himself testing the attraction between them by pulling her even closer, inappropriately close for strangers no doubt, but the fleeting concern over proprieties didn't stop him.

Ben found he was suddenly beyond polite as her scent filled him and he felt himself connect to a woman for the first time in years.

She drew in a sharp breath as their fronts brushed. Since he pretty much had the same reaction, Ben ran a hand across her back to let her know. To his amazement, she leaned more into him then, bringing her breasts against his chest until he could actually feel her heart beating rapidly against his. Ben took another deep breath, pulling her scent further inside him.

When he felt her sigh and sag against him in surrender to what was happening between them, Ben swallowed hard. The urge to kiss her came swift and strong—too strong not to act on it. Dipping his head, intending to follow the urge, Ben felt her ease their bodies apart.

Then he noticed her flushed, almost embarrassed face. Instead of feeling guilty, it only confirmed for Ben that she felt exactly as he did. That was why when she started to draw away, Ben immediately tightened his hold to stop her full escape. When their fronts brushed again during the silent struggle, they finally just stopped moving altogether.

Then they were just standing still in the middle of the crowded dance floor, staring at each other in shock, arms still linked in the dance form. It was a toss-up though which one of them was breathing harder.

When Ben checked in with himself about what to do, his instincts laughed at his hesitation.

"We need to take a walk," he said decisively, pulling the woman along with him, not really giving her time to formulate a reasonable answer—or to refuse.

"No, really—I can't, I—I really don't have time to take a walk," she protested finally, trying to clear her throat to speak more clearly even as she reluctantly let him lead her outside.

Ben slowed a little as they followed the brick path through elaborate English gardens. They passed by red roses draped and flowing over trellises. A large fountain spilled water over several layers of concrete and rock. Finally, he stopped near a very old magnolia tree already half in bloom. Ben walked them over to it, his urge to connect to her overcoming his usually impeccable manners.

Using the full length of his body, Ben pressed her into the tree, not the least bit surprised when she let him. He'd never been so in sync with a woman.

"I know this is crazy, but I really need to kiss you," he told her at last, hoping the explanation was enough to justify his boldness.

The woman looked at him with confusion again, but also with the most honest desire Ben had ever seen in a woman's eyes. His heart beat hard in anticipation, knowing she wasn't going to stop him from kissing her, and even harder thinking she might want what was happening as badly as he did.

"Okay," she conceded softly, her sexy voice a tiny whisper across the distance between their mouths.

Ben kissed her lightly at first, testing the strangeness of her lips against his, but found only a sense of absolute rightness. He tasted the sweetness of the grape he'd watched her eat earlier. Then he kissed her a little harder, letting his tongue ride the seam of her lips, asking to be let inside. When she finally opened her mouth to him on a moan, his tongue dove in, delighted to tangle with hers at last.

And as he kissed her, Ben explored her, letting his hands travel boldly over her body. When his hands eventually found her hips, he held her tightly to him, rocking rhythmically against her as his tongue made love to her mouth.

The sweet pleasure of what they were doing gave Ben the most astounding sense of hope. Need deepened and Ben eagerly ground his still growing erection against her, pushing her back into the tree with little thought of her comfort or his.

On some level Ben knew it was crazy to be making out with a woman he didn't know, but he still didn't want to stop. Like some randy teenager, the question of who she was became a secondary consideration to the one about how long he would have to wait before he could be inside her.

Regina ignored the alarms sounding in her brain about

kissing a stranger. Delighted with the erotic madness the man was creating with his mouth and hands, she chose to forget the fact she didn't even know his name. She didn't even want to acknowledge the tree scraping her back through her dress. Instead, she willingly let him rock his impressive hardness against her, the pleasure of each press sending her spiraling a little higher.

Surrounded by the wonderful smell of magnolia blossoms, what they were doing was a fantasy come to life for her. The man's mouth on hers was its own kind of heaven, better than any erotic dream, better than any man she had ever known.

Where had he been all this time, she wondered?

Then an awful thought intruded. What if she hadn't come tonight? What if she hadn't agreed to help Lauren? *No—no*, Regina denied in a panic, pulling the man with the talented mouth tighter to her and straining against him more, thrilled every time she felt him pulling her hips up against his in time with what his mouth was doing.

From far away, she heard Lauren calling her name. The man pulled away a little, ceasing to rock against her.

"No—please, don't stop kissing me," Regina begged, groaning into his mouth, kissing him again, wanting his hips against hers.

He laughed roughly, hiding his face against her throat. "I don't want to stop either, but someone is coming," he told her sadly, his voice husky and low in her ear.

Yes, and I so wish like hell it was us, Regina thought sadly, her true self surfacing at last from the haze of lust the man's kisses had generated. It was all she could do not to speak the complaint aloud.

Regina closed her eyes, trying to reign in her libido before she exploded. As Lauren's voice got closer, the man stepped away from her body, pulling her away from the tree in the process. His eyes were still dazed, still dark with passion. Regina imagined hers looked pretty much the same. She sighed hard in resignation.

"Lauren," she called, having to clear her throat before

continuing. "Stop yelling. I'm over here."

Regina reached behind her and dusted her rear to make sure no tree bark had stuck there.

"It's time for your speech," Lauren said, amused, taking in Regina's mussed hair and missing lipstick, as well as Ben's stunned expression and rumpled clothes. She couldn't help smiling at their guilty expressions.

"Get your Dr. Logan butt back inside and dazzle some money out of these people for me," Lauren teased. "Hi, Ben. I see you met my friend Regina."

Ben looked at the woman he'd been kissing in absolute shock.

"Regina? Regina Logan? You're—*Dr. Regina Logan?*" he exclaimed. He ran a hand through his hair as he glared at her. "Shit—I don't believe this. Why didn't you tell me who you were?"

Over the years, many men had rejected her just for who she was or what she did for a living, and Regina had survived those rejections. Eventually, she'd survive this too, but at the moment she could still taste him, still feel his hands exploring her, still feel him rocking against her in passionate possibility. The loss of what could have been between them broke what was left of her forty-seven-year-old romantic heart.

Okay breathe, she ordered herself. *Screaming will not help. Do not scream. Do not let him know how destroyed you are.*

Regina glared at the man's embarrassed face, derision curling her mouth into a regretful grimace. In a matter of moments, the amount of anger rolling through her equaled the amount of attraction she had originally felt for him. She welcomed the anger because it was better than the pain.

"Well, excuse the hell out of me," she said sarcastically, stepping an arm's length away so she wouldn't be tempted to punch the gutless man in the nose. "It was impossible to talk with your tongue in my mouth."

Regina lifted her chin and moved past both the man and a shocked Lauren.

"Give me five minutes and I'll be ready," she said as she walked away, not glancing back.

After Regina was out of sight, Lauren gave Ben a sheepish look and shrugged.

"Sorry about the interruption," she said to him in apology.

Horrified, Ben stood there staring, watching the passionate woman he had kissed striding angrily away from him. He could tell he had embarrassed her, but Ben was too stunned by what he had learned to be able to feel bad about it yet.

Everyone in the club had seen him all but drag the woman—*Dr. Regina Logan*— out the door. His predominant concern at the moment was that he had to go back inside the country club now as if he had done nothing out of the ordinary. The gossip about his behavior would be worse if he ran away as he wanted to do. God only knew what kind of hassle he would get when Alfred and Daniel heard about it.

"I just saw her across the room," Ben declared in his defense, as if it somehow explained the insanity of it all. "I had no idea who she was."

Lauren smiled wistfully, wishing something as romantic could happen to her sometime. She took Ben's arm to guide him back.

"How utterly wonderful for both of you," she told Ben in reply, squeezing his arm in approval.

Ben couldn't tell if Lauren was being serious or sarcastic, but she dropped him just inside the door of the club, and walked up to the podium to introduce Regina.

Then Dr. Regina Logan, the woman who had only moments ago begged him not to stop kissing her, stepped up to speak. When a spotlight hit her full on, the applause in the room was deafening, complete with catcalls and whistles.

Ben looked around at the smiling, laughing faces in stunned disbelief. Then he looked back at the now smiling woman who was commanding the attention of the entire crowd. How could he have not known? How could he have been attracted to the one woman here that was her?

"I see we have a lively crowd tonight," she began, raising her voice above the whistles. "Okay people, let's talk about sex."

The crowd roared and clapped. Ben heard Regina Logan laugh huskily into the microphone. He felt himself getting aroused again as she began to talk, her teasing tone punctuated by her laughter. When she saw him, Ben could have sworn she winked in his direction. No one seemed to notice, but he blushed anyway, glaring back at her in response.

It wasn't fair. He could still taste her, still feel the uninhibited response of her hips meeting his. Her uninhibited reaction, he supposed, could now be explained by what she did for a living, by what she understood about the physical side of things.

Ben ran a frustrated hand through his hair before putting both hands in his pockets to restrain them. He wanted to hit something or someone. He wanted the violence almost as badly as he wanted to drag the woman behind the podium back to the garden and kiss her again to see if it was her or him or them.

Damn it, he thought. Why in the hell did that woman have to be Dr. Regina Logan?

Regina's legs were shaking the whole time she talked, but she glared back at the man glaring at her from the back of the room.

Let him be shocked. She didn't care. She had learned years ago to handle the pressure of intense disapproval. By the time the evening was over, the man would officially be on the long list of just-didn't-work-out relationships in her life.

Still, her emotions had tired her, and Regina was immensely grateful when Lauren rushed to rescue her after the speech, pulling her away from the lingering crowd and down the hall.

Since there were only a few stragglers left milling around, Lauren closed and locked them in her office.

"Great speech, Regina! People were laughing the whole time. You should see the donation baskets. People were putting triple digit bills and big checks in them all evening," Lauren beamed, hugging her. "Thank you. Thank you. Thank you."

"Who was he, Lauren?" Regina demanded, rubbing her forehead and fighting not to cry.

"Who was who?" Lauren asked, her mind still floating on her success cloud.

"Who was the man that kissed me before he found out who I was?" Regina asked savagely. "The man who pulled me to the damn dance floor when I tried not to go, turned me into a melting puddle at his feet, tongue fuc—" Regina bit off the words and swore more softly, struggling to constrain both her temper and tears.

She rubbed her eyes and groaned.

"I'm *sorry*. I know you hate crude language," Regina said more quietly, pacing in front of Lauren's desk with hands fisted.

Being this close to Regina Logan in a full mad was downright scary, Lauren decided. How Regina had gotten through her speech with so much angry emotion toward Ben trapped inside, Lauren didn't know. How a nice man like Ben Kaiser had so completely destroyed Regina's virtually unshakeable composure was even more of a mystery. Regina didn't let men disappoint her to such a degree. But it was the hurt she could see in Regina's gaze that worried Lauren the most and had her answering carefully.

"Well, okay. Let me think. The guy in the garden with you was Benjamin Kaiser. Ben just turned fifty and has been widowed about six months. He has a killer smile and always dresses like a male model. Oh, and he's the CEO of Winslow-Kaiser Builders. He continues to run the business and work with his dead wife's family, which could be a little weird if you two hook up. Ben's a really nice guy—well, usually," Lauren said, fading off at Regina's renewed swearing.

Regina wiped her eyes with her hands. She would not cry just because another nice guy had rejected her.

"Ben Kaiser wanted me when he didn't know who I was, Lauren. He was the one that walked across the room. *He* dragged *me* out to the garden to make out."

The admission choked her. The memory of his passionate lovemaking lingered and made her want to weep. The sheer enormity of her loss had Regina genuinely screaming in frustration, making Lauren jump.

"Shit. Sorry—really, I'm—sorry," Regina apologized, mortified at her complete loss of self-control. She stopped pacing, took a few deep breaths, and then slowly gathered up her things.

Venting her temper wasn't going to help and now she'd frightened Lauren half to death. There was nothing left to do but go home, have a drink, and cry it out.

But damn the man—damn Benjamin Kaiser—she wasn't going to be able to sleep tonight without reliving those moments with him over and over again.

She had to dig deep for it, but Regina finally collected the shreds of her pride and pulled her composure back together.

"Just more water under the same old bridge, right?" Regina said as calmly as she could manage. She located her car keys before swinging the portfolio bag over her shoulder. "I'm glad tonight worked out well for you, Lauren."

"Regina, are you going to be okay?" Lauren asked softly, glad to see her friend mostly calm again.

"Sure. It's just been a while since I got this churned up," Regina said sadly. "Sorry you had to witness my meltdown. I shouldn't have let myself get so emotional over a few kisses."

"Oh, honey, one day the right guy is going to stand his ground and realize what a great catch you are," Lauren told Regina, sincerely hoping it could be true.

Regina laughed, but there was little humor in it.

"I'm forty-seven, Lauren. The *right guy* better hurry before I'm too old to care anymore," she said sadly, closing the office door behind her as she left.

Regina walked outside, noticing darkness had already fallen. There was barely any moonlight to guide her way to the parking lot. She had her hand on Harry's door before she noticed Ben Kaiser leaning against the black beamer parked next to her car. Her heart pounded fiercely as she glared at him in the dark.

Damn the man for looking so good, Regina thought resentfully. Her first impression had been that Ben was absolutely the most attractive man she had ever come across. It only made Regina madder to reconfirm it.

She stared back at him, waiting for him to say why he was obviously waiting on her. A lame apology was coming, no doubt, but she was ready to blast him if he said anything further to hurt her. She was too tired to be polite, and there was no one listening this time.

Available for sale at your favorite book retailer

More from Donna McDonald

WEBSITE

www.donnamcdonaldauthor.com

EMAIL

email@donnamcdonaldauthor.com

TWITTER

@donnamcdonald13 and @scifiwoman13

FACEBOOK

Donna McDonald Contemporary Romances
Donna McDonald SciFi Romances
Donna McDonald Recommends
Donna Jane McDonald

CONTEMPORARY BOOKS BLOG

www.donnamcdonald.blogspot.com

PARANORMAL/FANTASY/SCIFI BLOG

www.donnamcdonaldparanormal.blogspot.com

Contemporary books

NEVER TOO LATE SERIES

Dating A Cougar (Book One)
Dating Dr. Notorious (Book Two)
Dating A Saint (Book Three)
Dating A Metro Man (Book Four)
Dating A Silver Fox (Book Five)
Dating A Cougar II (Coming 2013)

ART OF LOVE SERIES

Carved In Stone (Book One)
Created In Fire (Book Two)
Captured In Ink (Book Three)
Commissioned In White (Book Four)
Covered In Paint (Coming 2013)

NEXT TIME AROUND SERIES

Next Song I Sing (Book One)
Next Game I Play (Coming 2013)
Next Move I Make (Coming 2013)

SINGLE TITLE (NON-SERIES BOOKS)

The Right Thing
Quickies Volume 1 (Coming 2012)

Paranormal/SciFi/Fantasy books

FORCED TO SERVE SERIES

The Demon of Synar (Book One)
The Demon Master's Wife (Book Two)
The Siren's Call (Book Three)
The Healer's Kiss (Coming 2012)
The Demon's Change (Coming 2013)

SINGLE TITLE (NON-SERIES BOOKS)

The Shaman's Mate

About the Author

Donna McDonald is a best selling author in Contemporary Romance and Humor, and lately has been climbing the Science Fiction list.

Science Fiction reviewers are calling McDonald "a literary alchemist effortlessly blending science fiction and romance". Contemporary and humor reviewers often write to tell her that the books keep them up reading and laughing all night. She likes both compliments and hopes they are true.

McDonald's idea of highest success is to be sitting next to someone on a plane and find out they are laughing at something in her books. This would of course be while she was heading off to some new place on her next adventure to feed her creative soul.